Readers love
ARIEL TACHNA

Château d'Eternité

"…this is a very romantic, passionate story… Thanks, Ariel, for the stimulating visit to the past."

—Rainbow Book Reviews

"I found this to be a very engaging story of self-discovery and love."

—Live Your Life, Buy the Book

Testament to Love

"I can count on Ariel to give me a fantastic story; she does wonderful things with big intense novels, and sweet little ones like this."

—Love Bytes

The Path

"…never have I felt so connected, so involved in the past and present as I did here in *The Path*… I read this book twice, and each time its magic grew as did its hold on my imagination and heart."

—Scattered Thoughts and Rogue Words

"This story is one of growth, of passion, and of two men who are so right for each other that words cannot do it justice. *The Path* is just a really excellent read."

—Joyfully Jay

Readers love
NESSA L. WARIN

Syrah

"I would happily read more books from this author, this was my first experience with Nessa Warin's books and I hope to have many more."

—The Novel Approach

"This is a good contemporary love story that will pull at your heart strings and shows you how loving someone isn't always so easy when you have responsibilities to yourself and your own dreams."

—Top 2 Bottom Reviews

"I thought it was well written and good for a night by the fire with a warming glass of wine."

—Fresh Fiction

Storm Season

"I'd recommend this for anybody looking for a long leadup to a sweet m/m romance, and a leisurely-paced mystery set inside a really interesting SF/F scenario that's close enough to home to give you a bit of a shiver."

—GLBT Bookshelf

"I enjoyed this book… It has adventure, romance, evil forces, and a strong fantasy element. The story builds, as does the tension, and by the end, you'll be a little nervous for our heroes."

—Gay List Book Reviews

By ARIEL TACHNA

Best Ideas
Château d'Eternité
With Nessa L. Warin: Dance Off
Fallout
Her Two Dads
Highland Lover
Home for Chirappu
In Search of Fireworks
The Inventor's Companion
The Matelot
Music of the Heart
Once in a Lifetime
Out of the Fire
Overdrive
The Path
Rediscovery
Revelations in the Dark
Rose Among the Ruins
Seducing C.C.
Stolen Moments
A Summer Place
With Madeline Urban: Sutcliffe Cove
Testament to Love
Why Nileas Loved the Sea

GAMES LOVERS PLAY
Amorous Liaison • Best Behavior • Ride 'em Cowboy

HOT CARGO
Healing in His Wings
With Nicki Bennett: Hot Cargo • Something About Harry

LANG DOWNS
Inherit the Sky • Chase the Stars • Outlast the Night • Conquer the Flames

PARTNERSHIP IN BLOOD
Crossroads in Blood • Alliance in Blood • Covenant in Blood
Conflict in Blood • Reparation in Blood
Perilous Partnership • Reluctant Partnerships • Lycan Partnership • Partnership Reborn

With Nicki Bennett
All For One • Checkmate • Under the Skin

THE EXPLORING LIMITS SERIES
Exploring Limits • Stretching Limits • Refining Limits
Breaking Limits • Transcending Limits • No Limits

Published by DREAMSPINNER PRESS
http://www.dreamspinnerpress.com

By NESSA L. WARIN

With Ariel Tachna: Dance Off
Mergers and Acquisitions
Sauntering Vaguely Downward
Stamp of Fate
The Stars are Brightly Shining
Storm Season
Syrah
To Dream, Perchance to Live

Published by DREAMSPINNER PRESS
http://www.dreamspinnerpress.com

DANCE OFF

ARIEL TACHNA & NESSA L. WARIN

Published by
DREAMSPINNER PRESS

5032 Capital Circle SW, Suite 2, PMB# 279, Tallahassee, FL 32305-7886 USA
http://www.dreamspinnerpress.com/

Dance Off
© 2015 Ariel Tachna & Nessa L. Warin.

Cover Art
© 2015 Bree Archer.
http://www.breearcher.com
Cover content is for illustrative purposes only and any person depicted on the cover is a model.

ISBN: 978-1-63216-895-5
Digital ISBN: 978-1-63216-896-2
Library of Congress Control Number: 2014920686
First Edition March 2015

Printed in the United States of America
♾
This paper meets the requirements of
ANSI/NISO Z39.48-1992 (Permanence of Paper).

To Nicki, for believing in this story even when we didn't.

Chapter 1

"Oh, I'm excited to be chosen for this season of Dance Off, *and I couldn't be happier with my partner, Joel. He's definitely the best-looking of all the pros, and, well, really, can you imagine me with someone... ugly?"*

"*Dios mío*! That girl should be ashamed of herself!" Abuela tsked at the television, rolling her eyes as the talk-show host coughed politely into her hand. Abuela didn't watch talk shows as a rule, but she made a point to tune in every time the show hosted the new contestants for *Dance Off*. "I can't believe Javi has to be on the show with her. She's not a real celebrity."

"They had Paris Hilton on the show a few seasons ago, and you didn't complain then. Maybe Makayla isn't as bad as we think," Mama said, continuing the conversation in Spanish. "We don't know her."

"I don't need to." Abuela stuck her nose up in the air. "I see what she does on television. She's a poor excuse for a Hispanic girl."

"So tell me, Makayla, what charity will you and Joel be dancing to support this season?" the host of the talk show asked when she had recovered her composure.

"Reach Out and Read," Makayla said. *"They're a charity that promotes literacy in preschool children."*

"See?" Mama gestured toward the television, pointing at the screen as though Makayla's last statement backed her up. "She's dancing to help kids in poor neighborhoods learn how to read!"

"They're all dancing for something," Abuela protested with a snort. "When do you think she was last in a poor neighborhood?"

"Fine." Mama knew better than to argue with her mother when she used that tone. "Just give her a chance. Maybe she'll surprise you."

"She'd better not beat Javi." Abuela crossed her arms and glared at Makayla as she and Joel talked a little more about being on *Dance Off*. "Or come on to him. I know about all her boyfriends." She narrowed her eyes farther as though her glare alone could convince Makayla to stay away from Javier.

"And now our next celebrity dancer, a NASCAR driver with five championships under his belt, Troy Phelps and his partner, Ella Peters." The couple appeared from backstage and joined Makayla Chavez and Joel Somerset on the set, the pro dancer moving with her typical grace while her partner clomped next to her. *"Welcome to* Dance Off, *Troy. Are you excited to be here?"*

"It's an honor to be chosen," Troy said. *"I've been a fan of the show since it first started, and to be partnered with Ella is a dream come true. I just hope my fans will help me support St. Jude Children's Hospital and all the wonderful research they do for children with terrible diseases."*

"Well, that's nice." Abuela smiled as the camera focused on Troy. "He knows about his charity."

"And he looks nice," Mama added, taking in Troy's clean-cut appearance. "Though I'm not sure he'll be much competition for Javi. He stomps."

"Next on our roster, Rini Cho, host of Out in the Wild, *and her partner, Luis Reyes,"* the host said. The applause from the on-set audience was louder than it had been for the two previous contestants. *"Welcome, Rini."*

"Thank you," Rini said, shaking hands with the host. *"I'm used to being on TV, but this won't be like hosting* Out in the Wild. *I'm looking forward to the challenge."*

"And your charity?"

"Luis and I will be dancing to support the World Wildlife Fund," Rini said. *"Appropriate, wouldn't you say?"*

The host laughed in agreement.

"Oh, now she's cute," Mama commented, grinning as Rini continued to answer the host's questions. "Do you think Javi will like her?"

"Maybe." Abuela took in the slender girl, her lips pursed as she looked her up and down on the television screen. "She is pretty."

"And smart." Mama smiled as she watched Rini laugh with Luis. "She could be good."

"And now, our biggest steal of the season! Put your hands together for US Olympic gold, silver, and bronze medalist JC Webster and his partner, Chelsea Burton."

"Look!" Mama leaned forward as though it would give her a better view of the flat-screen television. "There's Javi! He looks so handsome!"

"He's the best-looking man out there," Abuela agreed, leaning forward as well. "And his partner, she's pretty."

"You've had a lot of experience with training as you prepared for the Olympic swim meets last summer. Do you think that gives you an edge?"

"I learned at an early age never to assume anything gives me an edge," JC replied modestly. *"If anything gives me an edge, though, it's Chelsea. My mother and grandmother are fans of the show, and I've seen enough episodes with them to know I have a fabulous partner."*

"And what charity are you supporting?"

"The Trevor Project," JC said. *"Because no one should have to live with being bullied for being gay or bi."*

"He mentioned us!" Mama clapped her hands together, grinning as she leaned in closer to the television.

"Hush, María." Abuela cast a stern look at her daughter before returning her gaze to the television, where her eldest grandchild was talking with the host and Chelsea. "He's telling us about his charity!"

"That's a very worthy cause as well," Elizabeth said. *"We have a lot of those this season. That sounded a bit like experience talking there."*

JC shrugged. *"I may not wave a rainbow or bi-pride flag everywhere I go, but it's no secret I'm bi, either. Unless maybe you missed the Olympics entirely last year. And yes, I took flak for it in high school and from teammates at various levels of competition."*

Mama scowled at the mention of the bullying JC had experienced in high school. "I hope those kids see him now," she muttered. "I bet none of them have won Olympic medals."

"Our next celebrity dancer is former Republican congresswoman from Iowa, Christine Thompson, and her partner, Michael Einarsson! Welcome, Congresswoman."

"Please," the woman on screen said, *"call me Christine. Hopefully I'll be spending a number of weeks on* Dance Off, *and I'm not here on the campaign trail. I'm here to support the National Breast Cancer Foundation and their fight against breast cancer."*

Abuela frowned at the screen, uncertain how to feel about the woman on the television. She settled on, "She's supporting a good cause. I hope she doesn't make trouble for Javi, though."

"I don't think she will." Mama frowned as well, tilting her head as though she could look around the television and see Javi where he was hovering just off camera. "I think she's one of the Republicans more concerned about money than other issues."

"She'd better not." Abuela scowled at the screen again as though her glare could keep Christine from being rude to JC.

"And now, straight from New Orleans and the French Quarter jazz clubs, Feisty Freddy FitzPatrick. He's been a guest on the show before with his jazz ensemble. This season he comes back to join us as a dancer alongside defending champion Sharon Nichols. Welcome back, Freddy."

The large black man leaned in and kissed Elizabeth's cheek. *"The pleasure is all mine, darlin',"* he said, the sultry slur of the South rampant in his voice. *"I've wanted to do the show since the first time I played for them, and this season it worked out."*

"And we're so glad it did," the host said. *"What cause will you and Sharon be supporting this season?"*

"D'ya need to even ask?" Freddy said. *"Save the Music, of course. That is, the VH1 Save the Music Foundation. I always forget to say the whole name."*

The host laughed. *"I should have known."*

"I remember him!" Abuela grinned as she thought back to the night Feisty Freddy had performed during the results show. "He was fun!"

"He was." Mama remembered the night as well, particularly how her then seven-year-old daughter had danced to Freddy's song, and she was glad to see him back. "I'm not sure he'll be good at dancing, though."

"He could be one of those people who loses weight on the show," Abuela said with a shrug. "I hope he does. I think he'll be fun to watch."

"Yes. Solita will be thrilled. She made me buy some of his music after he performed, and she still listens to it." Mama smiled at the memory. "I hope she's not too disappointed that he's dancing instead of playing."

"She'll like him whatever he's doing." Abuela shook her head. Solita was a handful, passionate about things she liked, and she would be excited just to see Freddy on her television screen. "He could sit on a chair and do nothing and she'd watch."

Mama laughed. "True."

"And now, another former Olympian—from the Winter Olympics this time—ice-skating champion and businesswoman Deborah McMillan, and her partner, Brody Flanagan," Elizabeth announced.

The woman who appeared on screen had retained some of the athleticism that had taken her to the heights of figure skating, but her conservative suit proclaimed her current profession as clearly as the announcer's introduction. "Thank you. I'm looking forward to the season and to getting back in shape. I had to take some ballet when I was still skating, but this should be a different kind of challenge. Brody assures me he's up for it."

"And what charity will you be dancing to support?"

"Count Me In, a charity that helps women start their own businesses," Deborah replied.

Mama smiled in delight as Deborah introduced herself. She remembered her from the Winter Olympics when she was a teenager, and it was good to see her doing well. "Oh! I didn't know she went into business!"

"Yes. She owns Arabesque."

"Really?" It was one of the most exclusive restaurants in Los Angeles, a place nearly impossible to get into without celebrity status above that usually found on *Dance Off.* "I didn't know that."

"She owns a restaurant group." Abuela had also been a fan of Deborah the year she skated in the Winter Olympics, and she'd followed the news when Deborah had purchased her first restaurant, Salchow. It had seemed almost magical at the time, when women weren't encouraged to aspire to be more than secretaries. "There's a few others too. I think that one Solita and Roberto like is one of them."

"Oh." Mama made a note to look it up—or ask JC to look it up for her—later and returned her gaze to the television. She'd have to tell Solita and Roberto later. "Good for her."

"And now our youngest star of the season, rapper Kevan, and his partner, Lisa Murray," the host announced.

The young man came out onto the stage conservatively attired in a sports coat and light-colored slacks. "Thank you. It's a real trip to have been asked to do this show. I've been, like, a fan for seasons. My homeboy Little Z was on the show a couple of seasons ago and said it was da bomb, so when the chance to do it came up, I jumped at it."

"And what charity have you chosen to represent?"

"The Boys & Girls Club of America," Kevan said. "They work with at-risk kids to try to keep them out of gangs and off the streets."

"Oh, Roberto and Manuel are going to love him." Mama grinned as she watched the young rapper on stage. His conservative dress contrasted with the usual baggy pants, T-shirts, and jewelry he wore in the posters on her sons' walls.

"If they recognize him," Abuela commented dryly. She'd seen the posters too, and barely recognized the young man on-screen.

"They will." The rest of Mama's children were in Texas with their father, unable to leave school and work to come to Los Angeles like Mama had, but she knew they'd be watching because JC was on, and her two youngest sons would be thrilled.

"Our next celebrity dancer is Dawn Woodhouse, best known for her beloved performances as Trixie in the Trixie Belden *mysteries miniseries, and her partner, Preston Ross. Welcome, Dawn."*

"You would bring up Trixie, wouldn't you?" the actress, well into her forties now, commented with a laugh. "I'm not quite as boyish as I was then."

"I remember her!" Mama grinned at the memory of her childhood favorite. "I haven't seen her in anything for a while."

Abuela nodded. "You watched that show so much I had to buy the tapes for you." She shook her head, lamenting that of all the shows her daughter had fallen in love with, it had been those instead of some good Spanish television. "I never could get you to watch *El Chavo del Ocho*."

"Trixie was so pretty! I wanted to be her." Mama looked closer at the television, taking in Dawn's elegant look. "She's still gorgeous."

"You wanted to get into trouble," Abuela corrected, though she too had to admit that Dawn had aged well.

"And what charity are you supporting this season?" the host asked the former child star.

"The March of Dimes," Dawn said. "I lost a sister at an early age because she was born too early to live. The work the March of Dimes does has helped fund research that saves babies born her age and even earlier now. They deserve all the support I can give them."

"Good for her." Abuela's sister had lost a child born prematurely as well, and she'd seen how it had affected her. "I'm glad she picked them."

"Yes." It wasn't a charity as close to Mama's heart as to her mother's, but she still supported the idea behind it. "It's a good reason to support it too. We know it means something to her."

"And now, an extra special guest, talk-show host Eugene Carruthers, host of The Right Way, *and his partner, Carmen Ibañez." The reaction of the crowd betrayed more than a little surprise. Carruthers got polite applause but none of the wild cheering like some of the earlier stars. "What charity are you supporting, Eugene?"*

"The Multiple Sclerosis Society," Eugene said without ever looking at the partner on his arm.

Mama rolled her eyes and made a disgusted noise. "I hate that man." He was known for his socially conservative values, in particular his strong stance on immigration, and tended to assume all Hispanics were in the United States illegally. "I hope he's the first one voted off."

"I hope he doesn't cause problems for Javi," Abuela murmured, her mouth turned down as she stared at the television. JC was visible in the back corner—the only thing that kept her from looking away completely—and she tried to focus on him despite the camera's focus on Eugene.

"Or Carmen," Mama agreed with a frown. "I like her."

"And now the question that has been on the minds of America for over a year. She was named the most beautiful woman in the country as the winner of the Miss America pageant in 2010, but can Amber Moore dance? She's here this season to find out along with her partner, Tyler Harrell."

"I doubt it." Mama snorted. She didn't have a high opinion of Amber. Every time she was on television, which was a lot since she'd won the pageant, she was either standing around looking vapid or partying. "I'll be surprised if she makes it past the first elimination."

"I hope she does. That way Eugene can go." Abuela sighed, not happy with either of the last two contestants. "All the men watching will probably vote for her so they can stare at her more."

"I'm absolutely thrilled to be here supporting Amnesty International," Amber said, beaming at the talk show host.

"Thank you, Amber. And now our final star this season, a relative newcomer to the United States, rugby star Olivier Gautier and his partner, Tricia Kettner. Olivier, what convinced you to give Dance Off *a try?"*

"We have a similar show in France," Olivier said. "I watch it sometimes with my family, and so when the chance came to dance here, I said, why not?"

"And your charity?"

"Médecins Sans Frontières," Olivier said. "Doctors Without Borders. The work they do around the world deserves every recognition we can give them."

"Oh, he's cute." Abuela grinned and nudged Mama with her elbow. "Do you think Javi will like him?"

Mama tilted her head to the side as she studied Olivier. "Maybe. He's going to focus on dancing, though, and you know how he gets when he's focused." There had been many times when they'd despaired of getting JC out of the pool when he was practicing because he'd been so focused on his laps.

"True, but how could you not notice that?" Abuela leered at the screen, waggling her eyebrows up and down. "I want him to stay on until the end."

"Mama!" Mama cast an appalled look toward her mother. "We're rooting for Javi!"

"Well, yes, but that doesn't mean I can't want him to make the finals." Abuela grinned. "He can come in second, maybe. Then we get to watch him all season."

Chapter 2

OLIVIER GAUTIER looked around the staging area of the American talk show where the names of this season's competitors were first announced and sized up his competition. Most of the names and faces were unfamiliar to him, the disadvantage of not being American or living here long enough to be steeped in the culture. Two years spent playing rugby almost constantly had not given him a lot of leisure time. The musician, Freddy, was older and overweight. Olivier had heard tales of people losing twenty or thirty pounds while on the show, but at least at first, Freddy would be at a disadvantage. He dismissed Eugene out of hand. He might be clueless about American culture, but he recognized a bigot when he saw one. Eugene was entitled to his opinions, but Olivier was equally entitled to avoid him. He suspected he'd take enough flak from Eugene for being French. If Eugene knew the rest of his secrets, he'd never hear the end of it. Troy was a competitor but not an athlete. He spent all of his time in his car. His mental toughness couldn't be discounted, but he didn't have the body of an athlete. The two other male stars, though, would bear watching. Kevan was a singer, not an athlete, but even looking at him in a conservative shirt and pants, Olivier could see the muscle beneath. The man worked out and kept himself in shape. And then there was JC. An Olympic swimmer with four medals to his name. If anyone in the competition had the physical stamina to compete with Olivier, it would be JC.

JC Webster was about to lean in and say something to Chelsea to break the ice when he saw the rugby player watching him and decided to go say hello. He touched Chelsea lightly on the arm, not wanting to leave her behind, and crossed the stage, taking the long way to get to Olivier so he could avoid walking too close to Eugene. He'd almost missed both Amber and Olivier being introduced, he'd been so busy glaring daggers at Eugene's back, and he didn't intend to spend even a second more than he absolutely had to in the man's presence. Olivier, on the other hand, looked exactly like the kind of person he'd like to know better, and he put on his brightest smile—the one he used at PR events—as he sauntered up, Chelsea right behind him. "Hey. I'm JC."

"'Ello," Olivier said. "Olivier Gautier." He offered his hand. "I watched you swim last year. You are fast." He winced at the inanity of his comment, but he hated small talk, and living in the US for two years hadn't made doing it in English any easier.

JC laughed, ducking his head at the compliment even as he took Olivier's offered hand. He knew he was fast—he wouldn't have made the US Olympic Team if he wasn't—but it never stopped embarrassing him to have it so casually mentioned. "Thanks. I've never seen you play. Sorry." He hated that he had to say that, especially since he'd seen all the other contestants in *something,* but the little time he spent sitting around watching sports was dedicated to American football with his father or cheering the Olympic teammates he'd befriended during the 2012 London Games.

"Rugby is not a well-known sport here," Olivier said with a shrug. "I knew that when I came to play, but it has been worth it. I don't know these people, even by name. Only what the host says in the introduction. Who will be competition for us?"

"Deborah, probably. She used to be a gymnast and figure skater, so she's got some talent in the right area. It looks like she's stayed in shape too. Other than her...." JC shrugged, mentally sizing up the rest of the stars. "Rini, maybe, or Kevan. They're not athletes, but they're in shape, and they're young enough that the hours won't be too hard on them."

"I'd guess either Amber or Makayla too," Chelsea said, nodding a greeting at Tricia and Olivier. "They're young and in shape."

"And a little more interested in how they look than how they dance." JC knew what his mother and grandmother thought of both women and shared their views.

Chelsea grinned, looking around the stage at the other stars and their partners. "You might be surprised."

"And Tyler and Joel are fierce competitors," Tricia, Olivier's partner, added. "They aren't afraid to push the boundaries. Not that any of us got here by being lazy or conservative in our dancing, but those two are always the ones to beat, even with partners you wouldn't expect to do well."

"And my partner?" Olivier asked with a flirtatious smile. He might prefer to sleep with men, but that didn't keep him from appreciating a beautiful woman when he saw one. "Is she one to beat as well?"

"With a man like you to lead me around the floor? Hell, yeah."

JC laughed at the flirting and let his gaze roam over both Olivier and Tricia, hoping Eugene wasn't watching. He wasn't ashamed of being bisexual, but he really didn't want to deal with comments from Eugene tonight. That would be two strikes against him. "I don't know," he said, winking at Tricia and slinging his arm around Chelsea's shoulders. "I think Chelsea got the better end of the deal." Chelsea laughed and patted his chest. "Of course I did. But I wouldn't mind trading for Olivier, if you get bored with him, Tricia."

Olivier would trade with Chelsea too, especially since he knew JC was bisexual. That didn't mean he was automatically interested in Olivier, but it meant he might be open to persuasion. He'd wait until he knew his partner a little better before saying that where she could hear him, though. They had to work as a team, and if she distanced herself from him because he was gay, they would start the season with a handicap.

"Maybe we'll get lucky and end up on one of the team dances together," Tricia said. "If we get that far, of course."

Olivier looked around the room at the other celebrities again. "We will get that far."

"Absolutely." JC flashed a grin, glad he'd found a kindred competitive spirit in Olivier. "Even if we're all right and everyone we mentioned is competition, that's still seven, including us. Isn't that when they start the team dances?"

"Usually. But they like to mix it up sometimes too." Chelsea glanced over to where Elizabeth, the *Dance Off* host, was talking to Christine. "Elizabeth might know, but sometimes the producers don't even tell her until a few weeks ahead of time."

"It is not worth asking now," Olivier said. "We have other dances to learn first. Do we have our first assignment?"

"We have a cha-cha," Tricia said. "What did you get, Chelsea?"

"Fox-trot." Chelsea rubbed her hand over JC's chest. "I get to have this one all dressed up in a nice suit."

JC laughed. "I'm not sure I clean up all that well." Mostly he felt like a little kid wearing his grandfather's clothes when he wore a suit, his long limbs always making it hard to find shirts and jackets that fit both in the arms and the torso, and he'd yet to wear one that didn't feel awkward from the moment he put it on. "I guess we'll see, though. Do we get to watch the other dancers this year?" He was looking forward to seeing Olivier and Tricia in the revealing outfits that usually accompanied the Latin dances.

"I'm sure you do," Tricia said, saving Olivier from trying to find a way to say the same thing. "In the meantime, I get to take off Olivier's shirt." She ran her fingers down the line of buttons holding Olivier's dress shirt closed.

"Open, maybe," Olivier said. "Not off." He had recovered physically from the car accident that had benched him for a season, but he still bore the scars on his back and left shoulder. He had no plans to go on national TV without them covered.

"Start with open," JC suggested, his eyes twinkling. "Then if you make it far enough in the season, you can take it off. You don't want to give the viewers everything the first week." He'd regret saying that if the first week was Olivier's only week and he never got the opportunity to see Olivier shirtless, but he'd take open for now.

"You can use it to convince them to vote for you," Chelsea said with a grin. "Just so long as you don't take *our* votes."

Olivier laughed as he knew they expected him to, but he also knew where his comfort level lay. "We will see, but you will have votes to spare. Everyone knows JC Webster after the Olympics. Me, I'm just an unknown rugby player from France. The judges will have to save me, not the voters."

"Oh, I think you'll get plenty of votes on your own, especially if you show your chest." JC laughed, letting his gaze roam over Olivier again. "Look at the competition." Troy wasn't bad-looking—a little scruffy and rugged, perhaps, but not ugly. Kevan and Freddy had a certain appeal in their own way, Kevan with his very boyish looks and Freddy with the kind of face that made people want to like him, but their appeal was limited. Eugene might appeal to the older crowd, though JC thought his personality nullified his classic looks, but none of them could match Olivier for sheer mass appeal. Even JC, with his classic Hispanic looks, couldn't quite match him, though he wasn't being arrogant when he thought that he was probably second in line as far as mass appeal went.

Olivier studied the men. "Perhaps, but the men will all vote for Amber or Makayla, and many women may as well because they wish to be like them."

"That's probably true," Tricia agreed, "but there's nothing like the appeal of a good-looking man, and most of our viewers are female. We'll look at what our options are and what you're comfortable with, but don't discount plain old sex appeal when it comes to winning votes."

"Just don't count on it to replace dancing, either," Chelsea added. "It might get you through a week or two if your dancing isn't what it should be, but eventually people will vote for the person who can dance over the eye candy." She glanced up at JC. "That goes for you too."

JC held up his hands and took a step back. "I'm planning to work hard!" The idea of doing anything less would never occur to him. He was here because it was good publicity now that the Olympics were more than a year in the past and because his mama loved the show and had been thrilled at the idea, but he wasn't the kind of person who did anything halfway. He'd committed, and he was going to do everything he could to win. Besides, the Trevor Project needed all the funding it could get, and it was something he really did believe in. If he could get that top prize, it would help so many kids.

And probably piss Eugene and his cronies off a lot too.

That was just a bonus, though, not the goal. As his gaze drifted over to Eugene, drawn by the thought, he noticed Carmen, Eugene's partner, standing off to the side, and he rolled his eyes. "I'll work *with* you too," he added, glaring at Eugene for a moment before turning back to his partner. "I can't promise I'll get all the dances, but I'll do my best to learn."

That was the attitude that had made JC a champion. Olivier turned to Tricia and asked, "How soon do they let us start?"

"Tomorrow morning at eight o'clock," Tricia said. "We can hang out and talk all we want tonight when we get to the house you'll all be staying in, but we can't start actually training until tomorrow morning. Now, if you decided you wanted to go study videos of previous seasons' cha-chas, that wouldn't technically be considered training."

Olivier laughed. "But perhaps it would still be considered starting too soon. We will start in the morning like everyone else. I am not afraid of long hours of rehearsal. It cannot be harder than long hours of running drills on the rugby pitch."

"Or long hours in the pool," JC added with a grin. It would use different muscles, he knew, and he was sure he'd be sore by the end of the day, but the hours wouldn't be a problem. "If we can't start until eight, it'll feel like I get to sleep in."

Chelsea smirked. "It won't for long. I promise, you'll hate mornings within a week."

JC slung his arm over her shoulders. "Impossible."

"Tomorrow is the only day with a start time," Tricia explained. "After tomorrow, you can start as early and work as long as you and your partner can stand each other, but remember that you have fourteen weeks of rehearsal if you make it to the finals. You don't want to wear yourself out too soon."

"Part of being an athlete is knowing how to pace yourself so you peak at the right time," Olivier said. "JC knows this too."

"Exactly. I know my body, and I'm sure Olivier does too. Just like you do," he added, squeezing Chelsea's shoulder.

"Hey, now!" Joel came up on Chelsea's other side and slipped an arm around her waist. "Are you hitting on my girl?"

"Your girl?" JC raised an eyebrow and took a step back, pulling his arm free of Chelsea's shoulder.

"Just because she's your dance partner doesn't mean she has to give up the rest of her life," Joel said.

"Joel," Chelsea scolded. "Quit acting like a jealous boyfriend. We've been over this. We hug and kiss and flirt with our partners for the cameras and go home to each other when it's over."

"Doesn't mean I can't give him a hard time." Joel stepped free of Chelsea and held his hand out to JC, then Olivier. "It's nice to meet you both. Just ignore me. I say all sorts of stuff I don't mean. I have to psych you two out so Makayla can win."

He pulled his partner close, slipping his arm around her waist.

Makayla giggled as she wrapped her arm around Joel, leaning in possessively. Chelsea might get to go home with Joel for now, but it looked like Makayla was going to take advantage of every minute she got to be the one wrapped around him. "That's right. We're going to kick your asses. Joel here is the best."

"It is hard to argue with a record like his," Olivier agreed before turning to Tricia. "And should I be worried about a jealous lover appearing to steal you away as well?"

"Only a feline one," Tricia said with a laugh. "She gets pissy if I don't come home and feed her in the evenings, but she's the only demand on my time."

Olivier grinned at her before turning to the other two couples. "And this is why we will win this season. No distractions."

JC gave Olivier a once-over and curled his lips into a smirk. "Oh, I don't know. I bet we could come up with one for you."

Chelsea smacked him lightly on the arm. "Focus! Joel and I are pros at this. Our relationship won't interfere with us winning."

"You mean *us* winning," Joel corrected.

Olivier left them to their bickering, far more intrigued by JC's unabashed perusal. Some of the swimmer's other comments and glances could have been open to interpretation, but there was no missing the frank appraisal in that one. Perhaps this method of filling the off-season would be less tedious than he had imagined.

He smiled slowly, leaving it up to JC to decide how to interpret his reaction. "We will see who the winner is," he agreed. *In more ways than one.*

CHAPTER 3

JC FOUGHT back a yawn as he walked up the sidewalk to the converted hotel serving as a dance studio as well as a residence for those stars who didn't have a place in Los Angeles. It wasn't early for him, per se, but the official introductions on the talk show and talking about them with his mama and abuela when he'd gotten back to his cousin's house had kept him up past his usual bedtime, and the commute across town required he get up earlier than he would have liked.

The front door was unlocked, and JC slipped inside, taking a moment to gape at the opulent lobby before heading down the hall on the right toward the studios. He was early, but not by much, and when he opened the door to Studio 8—once the Magnolia meeting room, he noticed with amusement—he could hear Chelsea moving inside. "Hello?"

"Hi, JC!" Chelsea said with what JC thought was far too much energy for that hour of the morning. "Ready to start work? I've got the basic choreography all planned, but I've also got a few extras I want to see if we can work in. It never hurts to set the bar high the first week. Then the judges look favorably on you later."

JC laughed as he set his bag down and pulled Chelsea into a hug. "I'm always ready to work." He'd have to drink an extra cup of coffee tomorrow, though, if he was going to have to learn choreography in the morning.

"Fantastic!" Chelsea said, hugging him back. She led him over to two chairs sitting against a mirrored wall. "So before we get started, do you have any dancing experience? Ballroom dancing classes in seventh grade? A girlfriend who made you learn to waltz for the prom? Anything like that?"

"I've, uh, had to dance at a few quinceañeras, so I can sort of waltz?" JC shrugged. He doubted vague memories of dancing at a few parties when girls he knew turned fifteen really counted, but Chelsea had asked about any experience at all. "Nothing other than that, though. I'm much more graceful in the water than out of it."

"Then we'll start at the beginning," Chelsea said. "At least you're graceful somewhere. Some of the people I've gotten partnered with in the past wouldn't know grace if it hit them with a ten-foot pole." She stood up and gestured for him to do the same. "So dances are divided into ballroom and Latin, and in ballroom dances, some parts are in hold and some are out of hold. The fox-trot can have a mixture of in hold and out of hold, but if you can't manage the hold, the rest doesn't matter."

"All right." JC stood where Chelsea had indicated. "How do I do the hold?" He let Chelsea manipulate his arms into position, his right hand on her waist and his left hand holding her right at shoulder level. It felt strange, the long arms that gave him an advantage in the pool making the hold awkward, but he did his best to stand exactly how Chelsea wanted him. "Like this?"

"It's a good start," Chelsea said. "Think of yourself as the frame. If you're in this position, I can move around and look pretty and win points, but if your posture slips, then we both end up looking bad. Now, the basic steps of the fox-trot are like this: slow-slow-quick-quick. Try it with me."

Slow-slow-quick-quick sounded simple, but between thinking about his feet, trying not to step on Chelsea's feet, and keeping his body in the frame, it was a lot harder than it sounded. It took several tries for him to get through the sequence once, and by the time he'd managed it multiple times in a row, he was more frustrated than he could ever remember getting while swimming.

"Okay, deep breath," Chelsea said when JC had almost reached his breaking point. "You're training your body to do something new. You can't expect that to happen the first time you try it. You weren't winning gold medals the first time you got in the pool, were you?"

"No." JC took the deep breath as commanded. "Apparently, I almost drowned. My parents didn't want me to go near a pool again, but I insisted. They finally got me lessons, and the rest is history."

"We're still at the almost drowning stage," Chelsea said, "but we won't be that way for long. I know you're frustrated because you're used to your body doing what you tell it to effortlessly, but you're doing a lot better than my partner last season. Believe me, you'll get this."

JC laughed. "If this is a lot better than last season, I'm not sure I want to know how badly that first day went." He shook his arms, rolled his head, and stepped back into hold. He did feel a little better. "All right, let's try this again."

"Show me your frame," Chelsea directed.

"WE ARE doing the cha-cha?" Olivier asked when he came into the studio for the first morning of training. He knew the names of most of the ballroom dances, even in English, but that was about the extent of his knowledge.

"We are." Tricia pulled Olivier into a hug and kissed his cheek before she pulled back. "The other teams have either the fox-trot or the cha-cha. Have you ever danced it before?"

Olivier chucked. "Tricia, *chérie*, I have danced *le rock*, which we dance at parties and weddings in France, and I have danced in clubs when I was interested in… what is the expression? Getting laid? That is all the dancing I know."

Tricia laughed. "All right, we're starting from scratch, then." She pulled Olivier into the center of the room. "The basic step of the cha-cha is two, three, cha-cha-cha." She demonstrated the steps as she said them, starting with her left foot so Olivier could see the steps he would be dancing.

Olivier figured he'd have a lot to learn about dancing, but if there was one thing rugby had taught him, it was how to move his feet. He mimicked Tricia's footwork with relative ease. "If that's as difficult as it gets, we may be able to do this after all."

"Very good." Tricia was genuinely impressed with Olivier's footwork. It was still rough, but not many people were able to get even the basics of the steps right on the first try. "There's a little more to it than that, but it's a good start."

"So what is next?" Olivier asked. "Or should we keep practicing this first?" He bit back his instinctive impatience, the other virtue rugby had taught him, knowing how important it was to master one aspect of a skill before moving on to the next.

"Let's get this right before we move on to something else. Don't shift your weight all the way on the first step. And keep your right leg completely straight. Like this." Tricia demonstrated the step again, slower this time. "Two, three, cha-cha-cha. See?"

Olivier imitated her again. His feet went where he told them to, but his hips were less cooperative. "I feel like I am shaking my ass for the whole world to see."

"You are." Tricia smirked. "Remember what we talked about yesterday with JC and Chelsea? This is that sex appeal that will win you votes."

"Yes, but I have to look sexy doing it," Olivier reminded her. "There is nothing sexy about the way I am moving right now." He repeated the steps, trying to smooth the movement and add a little vavoom to the flow, but that messed up his feet. "See?"

"Don't worry too much about your hips. You'll throw yourself off if you try too hard. Focus on your feet. If you get your legs right, your hips fall into place." Tricia did the steps again. "See? My hips move because I shift my weight."

Olivier tried again, focusing on his feet and legs instead of his hips. It still felt awkward, but in the mirror, it looked more like what Tricia was showing him. He tried it a few more times. "Is it getting any better?"

"Yes." Tricia moved behind Olivier and put her hands on his shoulders. "Now keep your shoulders still. We want your hips to move, not your whole upper body. Try again."

Olivier did it again, losing the position of his legs somewhat as he tried to keep his upper body still. "*Merde*," he muttered. "This is harder than it looks."

"You're doing great," Tricia assured him. "You've picked up the basics quickly. Practice it a little more, and then we'll move on to the next part."

Olivier ran through the basic step a few more times until he didn't feel like he had to concentrate on every aspect of every movement. He knew it wouldn't stay this simple, but at least he felt like he was doing something right. "What now?"

"Now you do the same thing, only start with your right foot. Your weight should already be on your left foot when you finish, so you move straight into the next set. Like this." Tricia demonstrated, starting with her left foot and moving straight through to the second set of steps. This time she counted solely using the beats. "Two, three, four-and-one, two, three, four-and-one."

"Slowly," Olivier said, shaking his head. He understood what Tricia wanted, but his eyes could only process so much at first. She repeated the steps, and he moved with her, trying to match her steps and alternate from leading foot to leading foot. "You are going to be sorry you ended up paired with me."

"No I won't. You're doing really well. You know the steps. Now try to do them without thinking so hard. Focus on your shoulders." Tricia stood behind Olivier and put her hands on his shoulders, holding them as still as she could. "Try again."

Olivier did as Tricia said, focusing on keeping his shoulders as still as possible beneath her hands while still moving his feet as she'd taught him. It took a few tries, but with a little more work and a lot of concentration, he managed to do what she wanted.

"Excellent." Tricia grabbed two bottles of water from the corner and handed one to Olivier. "Here. Rest for a minute. We'll start on choreography in a few minutes."

JC STRETCHED up on his toes in the doorway to the old restaurant that had been converted to a dining room for the cast, hooked his fingers over the molding at the top, and leaned forward a little to stretch his chest muscles. It hurt with the good kind of pain, and he stayed on his toes until Chelsea came up behind him.

"Move," she said, smacking him lightly on the ass and knocking him off balance. "Some of us want to eat."

"Some of us don't want cramps later," JC countered as he stumbled forward. "I forgot to stretch my arms before coming up."

"Well, you've stretched. Now let's eat. We need to get back downstairs." Chelsea grinned and started making a sandwich from the deli meat platter on the island. "The more we practice, the better you'll be."

"Not if I'm so stiff I can't move."

The sight of JC's strong, compact body in a full stretch was, as far as Olivier was concerned, the perfect anodyne for four hours of dancing in shoes that felt like they were solid steel. He figured whatever Chelsea had spent the morning doing to her partner, she needed to keep doing for another several hours so Olivier could get another such view at the end of the day. "What's this about being stiff?" he asked as he took a plate for himself and prepared a sandwich.

"Chelsea seems to think I should scarf down lunch and head straight back to work." JC took four bottles of water out of the refrigerator and handed them around to Chelsea, Olivier, and Tricia. "I think I should take time to stretch so I can move in the morning."

"Worry about tomorrow in the morning," Tricia said. "You've still got four hours of rehearsal this afternoon. Everyone will be exhausted by the end of the first week. It's just the way it goes."

"It can't possibly be worse than the start of off-season training after we've had a break post championships," Olivier said. "Yes, it's eight-hour days, but we aren't lifting weights or running drills."

"I'm just worried about using muscles I'm not used to using. Swimming is very repetitive once you learn the right way to move. This is different." JC pulled his arms across his chest one at a time, stretching them. The pull of muscle felt good and let him relax a little as he took a long swallow of water and picked up his sandwich.

"You'll be fine," Chelsea said with a wink. "Though I would like it if you could move in the morning."

Olivier took another moment to appreciate the play of JC's muscles beneath his T-shirt and then forced himself to concentrate on lunch. He still didn't think it would be worse than the start of off-season training, but that didn't mean he intended to let anyone get the best of him. "You didn't stay here at the house last night," he said to JC after a few minutes. "Do you live nearby?"

JC swallowed the last of his sandwich and grinned. "No. I live in Texas when I'm not training. My aunt has a house here in LA, though, so Mama and I are staying with her." He ducked his head as he realized he'd just admitted he'd brought his *mother* with him, and he tried not to think about whether he was more embarrassed because it was Olivier or not. "She's a huge fan of the show and insisted. My aunt said she could stay too, and, well...." He shrugged, trying to play it off.

"And well, you love your mama, and that's as it should be," Olivier replied. "Don't disappear every night, though. We had a good time sitting around playing cards last night. Tyler says tonight he will teach me to play rummy."

"Tonight is family dinner. Mama, my aunt, all my cousins…." JC chuckled ruefully. "There's no way I can stay around tonight. If I miss it, I'll never live it down. You, uh—" He bit back the urge to invite Olivier over, though he knew his mama would love it. "Let me know how the rummy goes. Maybe I'll stick around later in the week, and we can play."

"Yes, another night," Olivier said. This way he could learn the game without JC present to see him embarrass himself. "You should bring your mama to watch a rehearsal. I'm sure other couples would let her watch as well."

"Maybe once we've had a few more days to practice. I don't think Chelsea would appreciate Mama trying to give advice when I'm just learning the moves."

"I would be happy to meet your mother, but maybe not just yet," Chelsea said. "I'd hate for you to be embarrassed."

"She's more likely to embarrass you. I'm used to her." JC grinned. "She loves dancing, and she's watched every episode of *Dance Off*. She'll probably try to give you advice about what the judges like and what gets audience votes. I wouldn't *dare* let her watch other couples yet."

"Maybe we should get her to come give us advice too," Olivier said with a wink for Tricia. "I could use all the help I can get."

"Don't you worry about that," Tricia said. "We'll make sure to give the audience what they want. I already have an idea for your costume."

"Nothing too over-the-top," Olivier insisted.

JC smirked. "Oh please, Tricia, over-the-top. I want to see Olivier shirtless. It'll make all the girls swoon."

No one would be swooning if they saw the burn scars on his back, but he'd worry about convincing Tricia of that if it actually came up with the costume department.

"Careful or I'll get you shirtless too, JC," Chelsea warned as she bumped her shoulder against his. "I'm sure all the girls would love to see your abs as well."

"I've competed in a Speedo," JC pointed out, trying to hide his amusement and failing. *Dance Off* was different from swimming, but shirtless was shirtless, and on the ballroom floor, he'd still have on pants and shoes. "*Dripping wet* in a Speedo, mind you. No outfit you put me in could possibly be more revealing than that."

"Don't tempt her," Tricia said. "I saw some of the outfits her partners wore in previous seasons."

Don't tempt me, Olivier thought, but he wasn't quite ready to share with everyone else just yet. He didn't know Tricia and Chelsea that well, and while he knew JC was bi, he didn't know how JC would react to anything more than the light flirting they had done so far. Olivier was willing to find out, but not when they had an audience.

"I thought this was a family show," Olivier said instead. "Doesn't everything have to be appropriate for children?"

"Swim meets are generally considered family friendly." JC had definitely gotten some well-concealed enjoyment out of watching some of his teammates climb out of the pool at the end of practice or after swimming in a meet, but there was no doubt that families of all sorts had watched them in competition. "No one objected to the Speedo when I won races."

"Swimming pools and dance floors are a little different," Chelsea said. "People expect you to be mostly naked and soaking wet at a pool. Not while you're dancing."

"The costume designers know the guidelines," Tricia added. "They'll keep everything in line. They do a fabulous job with fitting everything. We'll probably have the first meetings with them tomorrow so they can take measurements."

"It will be interesting to see what they come up with," Olivier said. He finished his sandwich and his bottle of water. "But now it is time for more practice, yes?"

"Yes." Chelsea finished her water and tossed the bottle in the recycling bin under the counter. "Come on, JC. Time's a-wastin'."

"Slave driver," JC muttered fondly, but he tossed his water bottle in the bin and followed Chelsea out of the dining room, pausing to touch the top of the doorframe as he passed through. "Don't work too hard, Olivier."

Olivier narrowed his eyes as JC disappeared down the hallway. If they had known each other better, Olivier would have sworn that last little stretch was for his benefit. As it was, he was left hot and bothered thinking about it without any way to do anything about it.

"Don't work too hard, *mon œil,*" Olivier muttered. "We will show them how to do the cha-cha, *n'est-ce pas,* Tricia?"

She smiled at him. "Believe me—you have advantages in this he doesn't. Come on. Let's get back to work."

CHAPTER 4

JC SQUARED his shoulders as he pushed the door open, trying to shrug off the unease he felt at coming back to the house two hours after practice was over. He'd been invited to join the others for dinner several times over the week since rehearsals started, first by Olivier and then by Kevan and Rini, but this was the first night he'd been able to get away from Mama and Abuela. It felt weird to be walking in dressed in jeans and a T-shirt instead of workout clothing. He was still feeling self-conscious when he got to the dining room, and the feeling increased when he saw everyone else was already sitting at the table. It was strange not to see the ubiquitous cameras everywhere, but the crew all went home after rehearsals ended unless they were filming a special spot for the show. "Hope I'm not too late."

"Hi, JC," Rini piped up. "Glad you could make it back."

"You could have just used one of our showers, you know," Kevan added. "You didn't really have to drag your skinny ass all the way out to the 'burbs and back just to get clean."

"Yeah, well, it would have been weird," JC admitted. "I don't know you guys very well. Besides, I didn't have any other clothes."

"I could've lent you some," Kevan said as he carried some rolls to the table. "I'm sure I have something that would fit you."

"Maybe next time," JC said as he walked to the stove in the industrial-size kitchen and peered into the pot Olivier was minding. "What are you cooking?"

"*Haricots verts*," Olivier said, the words coming out in French before he could stop and think to say them in English. "Green beans, but not the kind you Americans usually eat. The small ones like we have in France. And toasted almonds. It's my night to cook. The chicken is warming back up in the oven."

"He's been regaling us all evening with stories about how this would be so much better if we could have chicken like they do it in

France," Makayla said, sidling up to Olivier and putting her hand on his arm. "He's almost convinced me to buy a plane ticket."

Olivier shrugged. "In France, you go to a charcuterie, and they give you a rotisserie chicken that is cooked to perfection—moist and tender and ready to serve. Here it is overdone, too dry and tasteless most times, but I don't have time to roast it myself, so hopefully this market will be better than the ones I usually find."

JC ruthlessly suppressed the urge to glare at Makayla. "I'm sure it will be delicious, even if it's not up to French standards."

Olivier switched off the gas on the stove. "Find a plate and you can decide for yourself."

The plates were stacked on the counter next to the stove. JC grabbed one, handed it to Makayla, and took another for himself. It was awkward watching her flirt so blatantly as she dished up her dinner, but she was gone soon enough, and JC winked conspiratorially as Olivier spooned beans onto his plate. "You want me to get you a drink?"

Olivier shot JC a look of pure gratitude. "Would it be too French to want a glass of red wine instead of a beer?"

"Does it matter? I'm sticking with beer, though. If someone can tell me where it is." JC put his plate on the table in front of one of the empty chairs and looked around questioningly.

"Beer is in the refrigerator," Rini said, waiting as Olivier dished up her beans. "Grab one for me too, if you don't mind. Wine glasses are in the cabinet over the sink. Wine is over there."

"Sure." JC pulled out two beers, set one at Rini's place, and looked at the wine. There were several bottles of red, and he spent a moment reading labels, half hoping one of them would say it went well with chicken and green beans. He had no such luck and turned back to Olivier, hoping he didn't sound like too much of an idiot. "Which red wine?"

"The Beaujolais," Olivier said, indicating a bottle with the wave of his spatula. "A rosé would work as well, but I didn't see one of those. Not a good one, anyway. The Beaujolais isn't too heavy, though, so it will go with dinner."

JC found the bottle indicated and pulled it out. He read the label as he carried it over to the counter, wondering how Olivier knew all that without looking at it, and rummaged in the drawer next to the sink for the corkscrew. This, at least, he was familiar with, though his experience with wine was mostly limited to whatever his grandmother got out at family dinners and a few $6.00 bottles he and his friends had bought at the grocery store. He opened the wine with ease, poured some into a glass for Olivier, and held it up to the rest of the room. "Anyone else?"

"I'll have a glass," Tricia said, "since the bottle is open. I figure this is as good a chance as any to learn something about wine. You are going to teach me this since I'm teaching you to dance, right, Olivier?"

"Of course," Olivier said with a smile and a tip of his glass in her direction. "And anyone else who might want to learn." If he couldn't stop a glance in JC's direction as he said it, he hoped the fact that JC was holding the bottle would cover his slip.

"Not tonight," JC said as he poured a glass for Tricia. He'd listen if Olivier started giving lessons at the table, but what he really wanted was a private lesson. "I have to drive home. But sure. It could be fun."

Olivier toasted JC with his glass as he took another sip and hoped the interest in wine could lead to an interest in other things as well. Not tonight, though. Not with the other competitors and pros all sitting around the table. Not with Eugene's disapproving stare hard on his back at the wine and the beer—or maybe at the flirting, although Olivier didn't think they had said anything to ruffle the man's delicate sensibilities. For that matter, he only *thought* he and JC were flirting. It was hard sometimes to tell for sure. He took a bite of the beans. They had turned out as well as he hoped, and if the chicken was not as good as it would have been at home, it was still better than any he'd found since moving to the US.

JC tore his gaze away from Olivier. The way Olivier's throat stretched as he sipped from his wineglass was distracting, and he had to look down at his plate before he said something embarrassing. "This is good," he said after a few bites. It wasn't anything like what he would have had at his aunt's and it was a nice change. He loved the traditional dishes his family made, but he'd gotten used to a wider variety between his father's love for American dishes and traveling with the Olympic swim team.

"I'm glad you like it," Olivier said with a smile. "It's nothing fancy, but it's hard to make fancy for more than twenty. If I stay long enough, I will cook something for a smaller group, something really worth enjoying."

"Well, now I'm torn!" Amber exclaimed, laughing as she put her hand over her heart. "If this is nothing fancy, I want you to stick around long enough for me to see what you think something really worth enjoying is. I still don't want you to win, though."

JC laughed as well. "You want him to get second? Then he can stay and cook for you the whole time?" He liked that idea a lot too, though with him as the winner and Olivier in second place. It would be a fun contest right up to the end if they both lasted that long.

"Exactly!" Amber beamed as she scooped up another bite of chicken. "I need to keep him around to feed me."

"He might sabotage you with food," Rini pointed out dryly, though it looked like she also hoped she would have the opportunity to experience one of Olivier's special meals.

"My mother raised me to be a gentleman," Olivier insisted, grinning at the joking around the table. "No sabotage—just honest competition and friendly rivalries on the rugby field. Or now on the dance floor."

"Just the way it should be," Chelsea agreed. "We do what we have to for the cameras, but we do get some time without them." She leaned over and kissed Joel quickly. "You'll learn to take advantage of those times before the season's over."

JC looked down at his plate again, hiding his smile at Makayla's scowl. She got so upset over every bit of attention directed away from her that it was hard to take her seriously sometimes. Personally, JC thought Joel and Chelsea were cute together. If they could manage a relationship when the cameras weren't around, maybe it wasn't a complete waste of time to flirt with Olivier, at least not from a competition perspective. He still had to feel Olivier out on the rest of it.

This wasn't the time for that, though, not with Makayla and Eugene both scowling and threatening to ruin the pleasant atmosphere. "I'll have to use some of that downtime to work out," he said, changing the subject. "Chelsea has me doing a lot of cardio, but I'm used to weight training too. I need to keep these muscles if I'm going to lift her later in the season."

"I will join you if you don't mind the company," Olivier said. "Tricia looks like a stiff wind would knock her over, but I saw the moves she had her partner do last season. And when this is over, my team expects me back and still in shape."

"Not at all. My cousins said they'd take me to a gym on Saturday. I'd be happy to have you join us. Any of you," he added after a moment when he realized it was rude to extend the invitation to Olivier and not to anyone else sitting at the table.

"I've been doing sit-ups and using a pull-up bar in my room, but maybe if I stick around long enough," Kevan said, patting his stomach. "I got to keep my fantastic physique, you know."

"Obviously," JC said with a smile, relieved that no one else seemed to want to take him up on the offer right away. It would give him at least one session with just Olivier. If they were lucky, he'd be able to get them away from his cousins too, and maybe he'd get a chance to feel Olivier out.

"What time on Saturday?" Olivier asked. "Tricia has promised I don't have to be in the studio until noon."

"Eight?" JC shrugged. He wasn't sure he could get his cousins out of bed that early, but he could always get directions from them on Friday. "That way we'll have a couple hours to work out before we have to come here."

"It is a plan," Olivier agreed.

OLIVIER WAS not so sure it was a good plan when he dragged himself out of bed on Saturday morning. He was used to getting up early, often earlier than he had since he started training with *Dance Off*, and he worked hard with his training, but it was not usually quite this intense. His brain hurt with all the new moves Tricia had been teaching him. Ronde kicks and his hips… he didn't think men's hips were supposed to move that way, certainly not outside the bedroom.

He pushed that thought aside. JC would be here in a few minutes, and thinking of bedrooms and bedroom activities while wearing thin workout shorts and meeting the man who had featured in sweaty dreams the past few nights was a recipe for embarrassment. Hopefully once they got to the gym, he'd be too caught up in the workout to think about it.

JC wasn't doing much better by the time he pulled up in front of the converted hotel his cast mates called home for the duration of the show.

His sleep had been restless last night, filled with dreams of Olivier and worries about what would happen when they were alone. He was both dreading and anticipating today, excited about the possibilities and afraid time alone would show Olivier didn't live up to his fantasies.

Olivier came out of the house as soon as he saw JC drive up. He didn't see any reason to make the other man come inside when they would just turn around and leave again. "Your cousins didn't want to join us?" he asked when he saw JC was alone in the car.

"My cousins informed me 8:00 a.m. on a Saturday is an indecent time to do anything but sleep," JC said with a laugh. He pulled the car away from the curb, grabbed one of the cups from the center console, and took a sip. "I don't know if you drink coffee, but I brought you a cup just in case."

Olivier laughed. "I am French. I can't live without my coffee. Although I am not sure much of what you Americans call coffee deserves the name." He took a sip from the extra cup. "This one, though... it is good."

"This isn't the standard Colombian coffee most Americans drink." JC took another sip of his before returning it to the cup holder. "My abuela is very picky about her coffee. She has my father import it specially for her." He pulled out onto the main road, heading for the gym. "I don't drink it often, but I needed some this morning. Dancing is more exhausting than I thought it would be."

"Your abuela has wonderful taste in coffee," Olivier said, "and you're right about the dancing. I haven't been this tired since my first season of professional rugby. I had a lot of respect for the pro dancers before we ever began, but now I am in awe of them."

"Me too. I thought I'd be able to keep up because of all the exercise I get swimming, but this is exhausting in a completely different way." He cast a quick glance at Olivier before taking a left turn. "Then again, can you imagine any of the pros in a pool or on a rugby field? They'd probably be just as exhausted as we are."

"I'm sure they would be," Olivier agreed. "I'm not sure I could make it from one end of a pool to another, it's been so long since I've gone swimming. Is your family from LA originally?"

"No. My mother's family is from Mexico. They moved to Texas when she was a teenager, and my aunt moved out here after college."

JC chuckled. "Mama stayed in Texas for school and met my father. What about you? I know your family isn't from here, obviously, but where are you from?"

"I grew up in Carcassonne, in southern France, not far from the Spanish border. The south of France is rugby mad. There are more teams in my region than in the rest of France combined," Olivier said, "but as much as I always dreamed of playing for Carcassonne, I ended up in Grenoble instead. It means I could go skiing in the winter when we were not playing, so I can't complain too much. You probably do not ski in Texas."

"No." JC laughed. "Well, some water skiing, but not snow skiing. I've never been. I don't handle cold weather well." He shuddered dramatically as he pulled the car into the parking lot at the gym. "I picked a summer sport for a reason."

The thought of JC's sport—and the tight uniforms that accompanied it—left Olivier with an embarrassing problem, but he hoped JC wouldn't notice as he jumped from the car and kept its bulk between them while he willed down his erection. "If you ever change your mind, I could teach you."

He regretted saying it the moment the words left his mouth. Not because he didn't want to teach JC to ski, but because the offer was not really justifiable based on the length of time or the depth of their acquaintance. Of Olivier's desired acquaintance, perhaps, but he didn't know if JC was interested in that just yet.

JC bit back a smile. If anything could get him to brave the cold and the snow, it was the prospect of Olivier teaching him, but he wasn't going to let his cards show until he had a better idea of Olivier's hand. He was picturing intimate lessons that probably wouldn't result in him learning much about skiing, but it could be that Olivier just meant a friendly lesson like one JC could get from any instructor. "Maybe. You're going to have to convince me it's worth braving the cold."

"Ah, but it is coming in from the cold that makes it all worthwhile," Olivier said with a wink.

CHAPTER 5

JC HURRIED through the backstage area, tugging at the bottom of his coat. It had seemed to fit perfectly when the tailor had given it to him, but it had pulled in dress rehearsal, and he hadn't been able to get his arm out far enough to twirl Chelsea. They'd managed to get through their performance, but as soon as they'd stepped off the stage, she'd told him to have the shoulders adjusted.

The area was crowded—it took a lot more people and things to produce shows than most viewers ever saw, a fact JC was intimately familiar with from his Olympic performances—but he slipped through the crew with ease and stopped in a well-lit area where a few costumers were making last-minute adjustments to other costumes. "Excuse me?"

One of the women looked up from the fabric she was pinning and smiled. "Can I help you?"

"My jacket is pulling in the shoulders." JC raised his arms forward as far as they would go. "I can't stretch as far as I need to."

"Oh!" The woman—Sylvia, if he remembered correctly—put down her scissors and motioned for JC to come over. "I should be able to fix that."

She fussed around JC's shoulders for a few minutes before asking him to take his jacket off.

"I thought we saved the stripping for the after-party," Luis, one of the pro dancers, said with a wolf whistle as he walked by. "Looking good there, JC. I do love a man in a well-fitting suit."

JC looked Luis up and down, taking in his tight-fitting pants and open-front shirt. "And I do love a man out of one."

Luis laughed. "There's plenty of that going around tonight. I love the nights when we have Latin dances. The eye candy is always worth the price of admission."

Olivier frowned at the overheard comment as he came up to where the costume designer stood with JC and Luis. He had suspected Luis was gay from the looks he'd caught the man giving the other pros and male stars, but this was the first time the dancer had been so direct about it.

"*Pardon*, Sylvia," Olivier said, choosing to ignore the comment and the tension in the air for the moment. "There is a problem with my shirt. It keeps falling open."

"It's designed that way," she replied with a smile.

"Yes, but perhaps we could do something to make it less obvious? I am not used to being on TV with so much skin showing."

"Didn't you do the *Dieux du Stade* calendar a couple of years ago?" Luis interrupted. "That's a whole lot more skin than what you're showing tonight."

Olivier flushed. He had indeed participated in the French rugby league's charity calendar that featured nude or nearly nude photos of rugby stars and other athletes, but that had been a one-time thing. It was also before his accident. "It was for charity."

"So is this," Luis reminded him. "You'll get more votes with more skin showing."

JC looked over when he heard Olivier's voice and took a moment to appreciate the way he looked in his open shirt and tight pants. The outfit was remarkably similar to the one Luis was wearing, but as nice as Luis looked in it, JC thought Olivier looked better. Something about the curve of Olivier's muscles made it hard for JC to tear his gaze away. "I'd vote for you in that outfit," he said, adding a wink so Olivier could take it as a joke if he wanted.

Olivier flushed at the compliment and at the pleasure it gave him, but he brushed it off as a casual joke and focused on Sylvia instead. "Are you sure we could not put a stitch or two here to keep it closed?" he said.

She fussed with the fabric of his shirt for a moment. "Yes, but not there," she said finally, pulling the shirt so the two halves met just above Olivier's navel. "With the way the shirt is cut, anything higher than this could interfere with your movement, and you don't want that while you're dancing."

"Thank you," Olivier said. "When I'm on the rugby field, it's my skills that are on display, not my body."

"The voting public will want your body *and* your skills on display," Luis pointed out. "The more skin you show, the more votes you get." He smirked at Olivier. "At least, if you have the body for it, and believe me, you do."

"I thought this was a dancing competition, not a beauty pageant." JC frowned down at his outfit. He was dressed in a pinstripe suit with a white shirt and tie. He felt handsome in it and knew his mother would approve when she saw him, but he wasn't going to win any beauty competitions when put up against someone dressed like Luis or Olivier.

"It *is* a dance competition," Luis said, "but the costumes are part of that. For the fox-trot or the quickstep or the waltz, suave sophistication is the name of the game. For the Latin dances, like the cha-cha or the salsa, sex appeal is half the battle. The judges' scores make up half your final score, so never underestimate the value of giving them what they're looking for, but the viewing public makes up the other half, and they don't all know how to look for the elements of dancing. That's where entertainment value and crowd appeal come in. Watch some of the previous seasons. We've had some mediocre dancers who had crowd appeal because of their showmanship who lasted longer than they should have. We've had strong dancers with bad attitudes get voted off earlier than their dancing would merit because viewers didn't like them. It's a delicate balance. That's why you have a partner to help you make choices about costumes and choreography as well as to teach you the steps."

"Oh." At least the outfit JC was wearing was appropriate for his dance, though if what Luis said was true, it was unfair to have some of the contestants in classic outfits while others were dressed for Latin dances. If he wanted to make it through this round, he would have to out-dance sexier competitors dressed in more revealing outfits and somehow find enough charisma to get the votes to make it through.

"You'll do great," Luis said. "I watched your dress rehearsal. Even with your jacket too tight, you looked good for a first week of competition. Relax, enjoy it, and remember to smile."

"THIS IS unreal," Olivier said, leaning over to speak to Tricia as they gathered in the skybox after they had all been introduced. "I know we practiced it all in rehearsal, but…."

"But there's nothing like showtime," Tricia agreed. "Nothing like having an audience cheer when you walk into the ballroom with the

33

lights and the costumes and the music. I know. Believe me, as long as I've been dancing, I still remember what that first time felt like."

Olivier looked up as JC and Chelsea joined them along the edge of the skybox, followed closely by Joel and Makayla.

Down on the floor, Elizabeth, the host of the show, was explaining to the audience, both in the studio and at home, how the course of the evening would run. Corey Rogers, the cohost, who Olivier was about 90 percent convinced was gay, joined them in the box as well, waiting for his chance to talk up the stars and their partners after each dance. Olivier knew how this would work. He had watched enough seasons to know the rhythm of the show, but now he was the one in the spotlight.

"Ready for this?" Chelsea asked as she and JC joined him and Tricia.

"Um, no?" Olivier said.

"Yes, you are," Tricia corrected him with a gentle bump to his shoulder. "Stop worrying. You'll be great."

"That's easy for you to say," JC commented as he slung his arm over Chelsea's shoulder. "You've done this before. We've only practiced."

"And you've performed in front of crowds before." Chelsea playfully poked JC in the side and held a hand out toward Joel. "You can't expect me to believe this is scarier than swimming in the *Olympics*."

"Or playing in a rugby championship," Joel added, squeezing Chelsea's hand discreetly before stepping closer to Makayla for the cameras. "And Makayla is on TV all the time. You should all be fine."

"I'm *good* at swimming," JC said, looking down to try to hide his nerves. He'd done fairly well in the dress rehearsal, but he knew from experience that anything could happen in the actual event. It would only take one thing going wrong to send him home this week and ruin any chance he had to see what, if anything, could happen between him and Olivier. "I'm not so great at dancing."

"I think tonight isn't for worrying," Olivier said after a minute. "Tonight is for cheering for each other and having fun. Freddy is getting ready to dance. We should watch him, *non*?"

The others agreed, and they all turned their attention to the ballroom floor, where one of the world's greatest jazz musicians prepared to take the stage for the cha-cha. He was a large man, but the thing that struck Olivier most as Freddy and Sharon began their dance was how well he moved despite his size. Even more than that, he was so clearly *connected* to the music that everything else faded away. The grin on his round face as he moved, the way his hips caught the rhythm of the music, the way he spun Sharon around and caught her back in his arms—maybe not quite leading (something Tricia had tried for three weeks to pound into Olivier's head) but definitely doing more than just following—the collection of moves made for a surprisingly enjoyable first dance.

The audience clearly agreed as it roared approval at the end of the dance. Freddy and Sharon moved to stand in front of the judges' table, and Olivier braced himself. He had watched these judges praise and castigate prospective dancers for the past eight seasons. Now it was for real.

"Fantastic job," Elizabeth said, smiling at Freddy and Sharon. "How did it feel?"

"I'm so glad to be done!" Freddy leaned over and put his hand on his knees, panting. "I didn't think I was gonna make it through the last minute there!"

"He did great, though." Sharon patted him on the shoulder. "The stamina will come."

"I thought I had good lung capacity from playing, but, man!" Freddy straightened and made a show of wiping his brow. "This dancing is a lot of work!"

Elizabeth laughed and turned to the judges. "Well, let's see what the judges say. We'll start with our head judge, Henrietta."

"The cha-cha is all about rhythm and sensuality, and your jazz background showed in this dance. You're not afraid of the music, and you're not afraid of your body. That's something not all of our stars can say. You have what it takes to be a great dancer. It's just a question of increasing your stamina and your control. Well done." Her clipped British accent reminded Olivier of his English teachers, but their voices had never been so warm with praise.

"Thank you." Freddy put a hand on his chest, still gasping for breath, but he grinned.

"Edoardo?"

"You, my friend, know how to move." Edoardo leaned forward and pointed at Freddy from across the judges' table. "I could not take my eyes off your hips. You *get* the music, and that really shows. And don't take this the wrong way, but you're a bigger guy, and yet you still managed to bring a *lot* of energy to this dance. That's not something many men your size can pull off. You do need to work on your frame a little, but other than that, awesome job."

"And finally, Emma Leigh."

"It was an admirable first dance," Emma Leigh said at Elizabeth's prompting. "It's never easy to be the first dance of the season, but you delivered. You moved your hips, you connected to the music, and I even saw you leading a couple of times. I want you to work on your shoulders. Don't push them up. And like Edoardo said, hold your frame. But, really, great job."

"Positive comments from all our judges," Elizabeth said with a smile for the two stars. "Head up to the skybox with Corey to get your scores."

Freddy and Sharon hurried across the floor to another round of audience applause. Corey, the cohost, met them at the top of the stairs. "What *delicious* dancing!" he said, tucking an arm through Freddy's as he drew the man to the cameras' focal point. "How did it feel to open the show?"

"Nerve-racking!" Freddy laughed, accepting Corey's affection with grace. "Fun, though," he added, shaking his hips and bumping them between Corey's and Sharon's. "I got to *move*."

"And, *boy,* can you move!" Corey shimmied, completely out of time with Freddy's swaying. "It was *marvelous* to watch. I couldn't take my eyes off you. This is going to be a *fun* season."

"It is." Sharon leaned around Freddy to speak into the microphone. "Freddy's a great partner. I have a lot of fun things planned for this season."

"Oh? Do tell."

"It's a secret. You'll find out if we stick around." Sharon looked directly into the camera. "So vote for us, if you want to know."

"*Please*," Freddy added, looking into the camera as well. "She won't tell me either, so please, please, please vote for me so I can find out what she's got up her sleeve."

Olivier hooted and hollered with everyone else at the comment, patting Freddy on the back.

"And now the judges have their scores," Corey interrupted, drawing everyone's attention back to the ballroom.

"Emma Leigh Cox."

"Seven."

"Henrietta Wright."

"Six."

"Edoardo Bassanelli."

"Six."

"That gives you a score of nineteen," Corey announced. "A strong showing for week one. How do you feel?"

"At this point," Freddy said with a laugh, "I'll take anything the judges give me."

Corey patted Freddy on the back again as they moved off to the side, and attention turned back to the dance floor, where Deborah and Brody were preparing for their first dance. The lights went down as Elizabeth began the introduction, showing footage from training over the past three weeks, and then the music started, and Deborah and Brody glided onto the floor in an elegant fox-trot.

JC leaned over the railing of the stars' box and watched as Brody guided Deborah around the floor. Personally, he thought the female stars had a slight advantage in the early weeks, as they didn't have to try to lead as well as remember the dance, but watching Deborah, he had to admit she played her part with grace, and she seemed to be keeping up with Brody. It was probably her gymnastics background coming into play, as she managed the tricks with ease and was barely panting by the time she and Brody stopped next to Elizabeth.

The next few minutes followed what had happened with Freddy—a short conversation with Elizabeth, mostly positive comments from the judges, and outrageous flirting from Corey while they waited for Deborah's scores. "Behave," she said with a fond smile as Corey stepped a little too close, though it was clear she didn't really mind his attention.

"Sorry." He stepped back a little, looking chastised, but kept his arm around her waist. "The judges have their scores."

Deborah seemed pleased when the scores were announced—a six and two sevens for a total of twenty—and JC kissed her on the cheek when she stepped over to the rest of the stars. "Congratulations. You're going to make me look bad."

Deborah laughed and started to say something in response, but her words were drowned by the introduction for Rini and Luis.

JC leaned over the railing to watch Luis lead Rini out to the dance floor. She moved hesitantly at first, her hips stiffer than Sharon's had been—not surprising since Sharon was a pro—but as the dance went on and Luis encouraged her, she loosened up. By the end of the dance, her hips were shaking right along with Luis's, and she even smiled cheekily as she pushed up one breast to strike the ending pose.

"If she can learn to let go of her nervousness before she steps out on the floor, she'll be someone to watch," Chelsea commented from her place at JC's side. "She'll probably get, I don't know, sixes, maybe a seven, but it would be all sevens if she'd moved like that the whole time."

"I don't think the cha-cha is her strength," JC said, watching as Rini and Luis walked over to the judges' table. "If she'd been dancing the fox-trot, she would have done better."

"If she'd been dancing the fox-trot, you might be in trouble." Chelsea took JC's hand and tugged him away from the railing. "Come on, it's time to head down. We're up after Kevan."

"And that's such a great way to boost my confidence," JC muttered as butterflies flipped in his stomach. If Rini lasted long enough to get a ballroom dance, he had no doubt she'd look elegant and graceful even next to Amber and Makayla, thanks to her natural grace, but that didn't make him feel any better heading into his own dance.

"I said *if* she'd been dancing the fox-trot. She didn't, so you're fine. Besides, I think you can hold your own against her." Chelsea winked and tugged again. "Now come on, we can't be late."

Olivier didn't let himself do more than glance at JC as he disappeared down the stairs to the dance floor, making himself concentrate on Rini and Luis as they came back into the skybox to chat with Corey while the judges debated. Rini blushed and fluttered as both Corey and Luis flirted with her, making Olivier wonder if Luis was gay after all, and then the judges had their scores: straight sixes.

Kevan and Lisa had a fox-trot as well, and Olivier immediately saw the advantage of a male pro over a female pro in a dance like this one. Kevan did his best to look suave and in control, but everything about his posture proclaimed how awkward he found the suit, the formality, the frame necessary for one of the ballroom dances. He kept it together and didn't miss any steps as far as Olivier could tell, but even with his untrained eye, Olivier could see the difference between this dance and the one before it.

When it came time for the judges to share their commentary, Olivier could hear the difference in that as well. While they still did their best to phrase their comments constructively, the criticism outweighed the praise.

The audience cheered for them, though, as they climbed up to the skybox.

"Rough comments," Corey sympathized, "but if it's any consolation, you look fantastic."

"I'm a rapper," Kevan said. "Smooth ain't my thing, but that's okay. Lisa's determined to teach me, and as long as she'll put up with me and the viewers will support me, I'm gonna keep learning what she got to say."

"Let's see what the judges have to say."

The scores came back straight fives, making Olivier wince in sympathy. Yes, it was just the first week, but they all had their pride, and a five was hardly a good score.

"Fifteen. Not a bad score for week one," Corey said, although Olivier thought he was trying too hard to be sympathetic. "Now it's up to the viewers to do their part. If you want to see Kevan and Lisa back for another week, cast your votes now."

Olivier applauded with everyone else and then turned to watch Elizabeth introduce JC. He chose to pretend he wasn't watching this next dance with any more interest than the others.

CHAPTER 6

JC STOOD on the dance floor as his introduction played on the large screens behind him and wished he could have been waiting in the wings like some of the other contestants had. It was awkward hearing the way they'd cut down the interviews he'd done over the past three weeks, and really, the last thing he needed right now was to be reminded of all the trouble he'd had managing the holds and sweeping gestures and all the trouble he'd had mastering the carefree appearance the fox-trot required while worrying so hard about the steps.

At least he didn't have to worry about the crowd. It was large—he'd seen that from the skybox—but the lights kept him from being able to see it, and the music drowned out most of the noise. JC was aware the people were there, but this, at least, was a lot like swimming. He could push the crowd to the back of his mind and pretend it wasn't there while he focused on what he was doing.

When the introduction video wound down, JC took a deep breath, looked across the floor at Chelsea, and centered himself. He pushed everything else out of his mind when the music started, just like he did when he stepped onto the block before a race, and focused only on counting the beats.

When the music hit the right count, JC crossed the floor, his eyes on Chelsea and his mind on the dance. There was so much to think about: his feet, and his hands, and his shoulders, and his head, and where he was supposed to go next, and what Chelsea was supposed to do, and—

For a second, he was overwhelmed by all the individual components of the dance, but then he reached Chelsea. As their hands touched, he remembered the way she'd compared it to swimming: if he focused on the whole stroke, he didn't have to think about each little thing his body needed to do. It wasn't kicking and pulling and breathing and floating, it was swimming. He knew this dance the same way he knew the breaststroke. Not as well, perhaps, but the concept was the same. If he focused on the fox-trot and not what each part of his body needed to do, he'd get through the dance.

And, miraculously perhaps, it worked! His body did what it was supposed to do, frolicking across the floor in the unique combination of control and flirtatiousness that was the fox-trot. Chelsea laughed and grinned and encouraged as they moved, playing out their little story of true love's first kiss. Her grin was as infectious as always, and he found himself smiling back, playing to her and to the crowd, trying to make the story come alive. Wasn't that what Luis had told him? Showmanship carried the day with the audience.

It was a strange concept for JC, but fun. In the pool, races were won with speed, and speed came from strength and technical perfection. There was no room for goofing off or playing up to the audience when he swam, so he relished the chance to do it now. As the dance went on, he got more flirtatious and even found the courage to try one move they had practiced but he had told Chelsea he wasn't comfortable doing. She laughed as he pulled her in close after it, and her delight buoyed him through the rest of the number.

By the time the music came to an end and they finished the dance with a flourish, his heart was pounding in his chest, and his lungs were tight, but the flush on his face was from delight, not exhaustion, a considerable improvement over the first few days of training. They bowed and blew kisses to the audience, and then Chelsea grabbed his hand and pulled him over to where Elizabeth waited at the judges' podium. Now came the hard part: hearing what the judges thought.

Olivier let out the breath he hadn't realized he'd been holding as JC and Chelsea finished their dance. "They did well?" he asked Tricia.

"Very well," she said. "Let's see what the judges have to say, but I'd say that was as good as Freddy or Deborah."

Olivier turned his attention back to the judges to see what kinds of comments they would give JC. Olivier wasn't dancing a fox-trot tonight, but eventually he would have to. He could learn from what the judges said to everyone.

Edoardo leaned across the table and pointed at JC. "You are delightful to watch. That was suave and graceful and *fun*. I loved every second of it. There was a tiny bit of hesitation toward the beginning, but once you got into it... mmm. It was *wonderful*. I will say you need to work on your form a little bit—you move your arms just a touch too much—but overall a fantastic first dance."

Olivier smiled in relief at the positive comment. Watching JC dance had been fun, and Olivier figured they all still needed to learn control. He certainly felt like it when he swung his hips around for the cha-cha. Tricia said he was doing it right, but Olivier just felt like he was everywhere.

"I agree with Edoardo," Emma Leigh said. "Except for that slight hesitation at the beginning, you nailed the flair, but your control needs work. Your arms are long, and that makes it more noticeable when your elbows flop. You need to focus on that, especially when you're in hold. You did, however, capture the fun of the dance, and you made some very courageous moves for week one and did them well. Good job."

"Henrietta?"

"The fox-trot is a classic dance," Henrietta began. "It requires control and precision without sacrificing flair or, as Edoardo and Emma Leigh said, fun. It's a deceptively simple dance that demands far more underneath than appears on the surface. You still need some work on the control and precision, not unexpected since this is week one, but you turned in a very agreeable first effort."

Olivier relaxed at that. Henrietta could be stuffy at times. Certainly she was the most demanding of the judges on a technical level, and her comments sometimes bordered on scathing. Her words to JC had been on the mild side, definitely encouraging if not effusive, and Olivier figured that was probably all any of them could hope to get the first week out.

The audience applauded again as JC and Chelsea made their way back to the waiting area. Olivier turned to add his applause as they came in, still flushed and grinning.

Corey slung his arms over JC's shoulder as soon as they stopped in the skybox. "Great job! How do you feel?"

"Exhausted!" JC slumped and leaned dramatically on Chelsea and Corey for a moment before straightening with a wink. "That was worse than a 400-meter race."

"Well, I couldn't tell watching you," Corey gushed. "That was quite a show you put on, and I *know* I'm not the only one up here who enjoyed watching it."

Olivier had certainly enjoyed it, but that had as much to do with how he felt about JC as anything else. He knew enough about dancing to know what he liked, but not enough to say more than that.

"Well, I did the best I could. And Chelsea was a big help."

Chelsea leaned toward the microphone. "JC has been fantastic. I couldn't have asked for someone more dedicated. We worked hard and danced hard. I hope it was enough for decent scores."

"I hope so too. I *really* want see what you can do with those arms." Corey patted JC's bicep. "Let's see if the judges agreed with me, shall we?"

"Seven."

"Six."

"Six."

"A total of nineteen," Corey said, "leaving you tied for second place right now. What do you think of the scores?"

"I'm thrilled with them." JC grinned widely, letting his relief at the decent scores show. He'd tried to hide it because he knew a good attitude would go a long way toward getting him more votes, but he'd been worried he'd messed up, despite what the judges had said. "I hope we get the chance to come back next week and improve, of course, but I'll take these for now."

"Yeah, we really want to come back next week. These scores are awesome, but I know JC can do better." Chelsea winked at the camera. "Vote for us, and we'll show you *everything* we can do."

Olivier certainly wanted to know what else JC could do, but he thought the less attention he drew to himself at the moment, the better. Some of the other celebrities had reached out to pat JC on the shoulder or to kiss his cheek, but Olivier held back, feeling like any move on his part would be too blatant. He felt ridiculous even thinking it when no one else seemed so constrained, but he was almost as new to American culture as he was to dancing, and this was one area where he was still less comfortable than his counterparts. He settled for clapping for JC as the camera cut back to Elizabeth and the setup for the next dance.

As Christine and Mike took to the floor, Olivier left the viewing area to go backstage in preparation for his own slot in the lineup. They had a few minutes still, but Olivier had a routine before every match, and he wasn't about to break it now. Before he went out on the field, he always did a series of stretches in the same order and with the same number of repetitions. His teammates teased him about his superstitions, but he felt more centered when he completed them, more able to focus on the task at hand. Tricia had encouraged him to go through the set before each practice, and she followed him into the wings now to keep him company as he prepared.

He could hear the music start, hear the applause, and then the judges' scores of straight sixes for Christine and Mike. Eugene didn't fare as well, tying with Kevan with straight fives. Dawn and Preston got a seven to go with their pair of sixes, and Makayla and Joel got two sixes and a five, and then it was time for Olivier and Tricia to take the stage.

JC spent the next four dances wondering why Olivier had disappeared so early, but he did his best to pay attention and be supportive of his fellow cast mates. They had all cheered for him. He wasn't going to do any less for them. It got much easier to pay attention when Olivier's montage came up on the screen. This was the dance he wanted to see, though he wished he could have told Olivier good luck before he'd gone backstage.

Olivier cringed a bit as the video montage of his interviews and rehearsals aired for the audience. He hated the way his voice sounded, the way his accent got stronger when he was nervous or on the spot, the way the rehearsal footage always seemed to catch him at his worst rather than at his best, but he couldn't do anything about that. He had to focus on Tricia, on the music and the upcoming dance, and on making an impression on the judges and on the audience. He had the disadvantage of being relatively obscure as far as celebrities were concerned, which meant he'd have to work harder to win each and every vote.

The video ended, the music began, and Olivier let the past three weeks of training kick in, moving in time to the beat as Tricia had taught him. "Smile," she whispered as the lights came up, and the dance took over. The next minute and a half was a blur of lights, music, movement, and applause, and then it was over, and he was standing in front of the judges, winded but not panting the way some of the others had been. He figured that had to be a point in his favor.

JC let out a breath as Olivier stopped in front of the judges. The way Olivier's hips had moved had been mesmerizing. JC had barely blinked the whole time he was watching Olivier dance. It was good the dance hadn't gone on any longer. Otherwise JC might not have been able to control his reaction.

He leaned forward as Henrietta pursed her lips and looked Olivier up and down. The stern expression didn't bode well, but it softened just before she spoke. "I liked it. It wasn't phenomenal, but it was good, with fluid hip movements and good footwork. You need to work on your frame, though, and look at Tricia when you're in hold. You're dancing with her, not watching a field."

They were valid comments, Olivier thought. He was so used to having to be conscious of the entire rugby pitch and everyone on it that focusing in on one person was a change from his usual situational awareness, and if Tricia'd told him once, she'd told him a hundred times to watch his frame. It was important enough with the cha-cha. When they got to the more traditional ballroom dances, it would be even more critical.

JC agreed too, though he didn't have much time to reflect on it before Edoardo stood and cocked one hip to the side. "Well, Olivier, I have to say, I *loved* the hip movement. The way you swung them back and forth was just.... Mmm. However." He pointed at Olivier. "Henrietta is right. You didn't look at Tricia enough. The cha-cha is supposed to be sexy, and when you're in hold, you're seducing her. You're not going to get her in bed if you don't look her in the eyes, no matter what kind of hip action you have going on."

The crowd laughed and cheered at Edoardo's metaphor, as they were wont to do when the judge went a little over the top with his innuendo. Tricia bumped Olivier's hip with hers, and he managed to smile through the flush he could feel rising up his neck. He hadn't mentioned to her or anyone else that he was gay. If he'd been interested in women, Tricia would have been perfect, but he was far more interested in the men on the show. If he were dancing with one of them, he'd be hard-pressed to tear his eyes away. He'd just have to get better at pretending.

"If he manages to look Tricia in the eyes, she won't be able to look away," Chelsea murmured in JC's ear. "Not with the way he moves those hips. He's got a bit of a disadvantage now because no one knows him, but if he stays here very long, his popularity will go through the roof."

"Yeah." JC let himself imagine Olivier moving his hips like that against him. "He's going to break all sorts of hearts." He just hoped his wasn't one of them.

Chelsea looked at him speculatively, but before JC could figure out if she knew about his crush or not, Emma Leigh started her comments. "I absolutely agree with everyone else on the hip action," she said, leaning forward. "Fantastic. I could watch you swing that ass all day long. The rest of it, though, I'm not sure I agree. I think your frame is more important than where your eyes are. Tricia might feel better if you were looking at her, and you'll learn to pick up cues that way, but your face was always pointed in the right spot, so I don't so much care that your gaze wandered. Your arms were limp when they shouldn't have been, though, and that bothered me."

Olivier nodded, not sure what he'd done with his arms to qualify as limp. He'd thought they were right where Tricia told him to put them. He'd have to watch the footage of their dance later and see if he could pinpoint what he'd done wrong so he could fix it. He'd spent too many years studying game footage to learn without seeing now.

"Head up to Corey," Elizabeth instructed. "He's waiting to chat with you before you get your scores."

Tricia grabbed Olivier's hand, and they jogged across the dance floor toward the stairs. As with everyone else, Corey met them as soon as they reached the area where the stars watched the show. Corey sidled up to Olivier, giving him an unsurreptitious pat on the ass. "Nice job," he cooed. "We definitely want to see more of what you can bring to the table. How did you feel out there, first time out?"

Olivier tried not to wince at the choice of words. "It was fun," he said, wishing once again that he had a better command of English. He'd like to have something to say besides "fun" occasionally. "Tricia has been very patient with my two left feet."

"Two left feet?" Corey asked. "Really, Tricia?"

"Not at all," Tricia said. "He's a wonderful partner, and I'm looking forward to a long season of dancing with him. Vote for us, number nine!"

"Yes, if you want to see more of Olivier's *delightful* hip movements, and maybe a little skin, vote for them." Corey squeezed Olivier's ass one more time. "Now, let's see what the judges think."

"Six."

"Six."

"Six."

"That's a total of eighteen points. Not bad for a first night. How do you feel about it?"

"Mostly just happy to have survived the dance," Olivier said. "It is a good first score, though, *non*?"

"It's a very acceptable first score," Tricia agreed. "We're very happy with it, and we're looking forward to getting the chance to take the judges' suggestions to heart."

When Corey released them, Olivier turned to accept the congratulations from his fellow competitors before tucking Tricia's hand into his arm and moving back to the edge of the balcony to watch the last three dances. If he picked a spot right next to JC and kept Tricia on his other side so no one was between them, that was between him and his conscience. No one else had to be any the wiser.

JC leaned in as Olivier settled next to him. "I thought you were fantastic. Best cha-cha of the night." That was mostly because it had given him the chance to watch Olivier's hips swing for close to two minutes, but Olivier didn't need to know that. "I'd vote for you if I could." He thought he saw Olivier flush, but whatever his answer was, it was drowned out by Makayla's introduction.

That was all right. He shouldn't have said as much as he did, and the dark and noise meant no one could call him on his own blush.

CHAPTER 7

ABUELA HOOKED her arm around Mama's as they walked into the theater. There were special seats set aside for the family and friends of the contestants as well as other stars from the network and any special guests they wanted to draw attention to on the show. The tickets Javi had given them let them in a special entrance that led straight to the floor seats and let them skip the long lines outside the doors the general public used.

"Oh, María, look at it," she said as they found their seats in the front row. "All the lights and the seats and just think! Our Javi is going to be dancing here!"

"Our Javi has already danced here," Mama replied with a smile. "He had good scores for week one. Better than that awful Eugene man and that poor Troy. I hope he got lots of votes. He should stay another week, and Eugene should go home, even if Troy didn't dance quite as well. Troy at least was nice to his partner and to Javi."

Abuela snorted. "That man should never have been allowed on this show." She'd refused to watch when Eugene danced last night. "And of course our Javi did well. He's a good boy. He knows how to listen to his partner."

"He'd better, after all these years of listening to his coach," Mama said with a laugh. "He will have to worry about Deborah. She has many more years of listening to a coach than he does, and she was always a performer, not just an athlete."

"Javi has more stamina than she does," Abuela insisted. She wasn't going to listen to anything even remotely disparaging about Javi. "But the competition will be good for him. With people like Deborah and Freddy and Dawn, he won't forget he needs to keep working."

"Who needs to keep working?" JC squeezed between his mother and grandmother before they could sit down and slung his arms around their shoulders. "Not me, I hope."

"Of course not, *mi hijo*," Mama said. "You are brilliant already. We were just saying you already know how to listen to your coach, so listening to Chelsea will be easy for you. Are you nervous about tonight?"

"A little. I'm trying not to think about it, though. I remembered a lot of things I wanted to do while I danced, but there's nothing I can do now. The judges' scores are in, and everyone voted, so all I can do is hope we got enough votes." He steered them toward the back. "Come on, I want you to meet Chelsea and Ol—" He stopped himself before he said Olivier's name. "And the others. I've told them all about you."

His mother and grandmother beamed at him. "We'd love to meet everyone. After all the seasons we've watched, I feel like I know most of the pros already, but to meet them in person…."

"Come on. We don't have much time, but they all want to meet you." He led his family past the security guard into the back and over to the makeup station where Chelsea was sitting. "Chelsea, I want you to meet my mama and abuela. Mama and Abuela, this is Chelsea, my partner."

"It's nice to meet you, Mrs. Webster and Mrs….."

"Carillo, but for you, I am Abuela. You teach my grandson to dance. You can call me like he does," Abuela said when Chelsea trailed off. "I have watched you since your first season. When Javi said he would come here to dance, you were the partner I hoped for him."

"Aww. Thank you!" Chelsea blushed and gave Abuela a hug. "Your grandson is a wonderful person."

"Of course he is!" Mama puffed up her chest with pride. "We raised him right! He has good values and knows how to work hard."

"Yes, he does." Chelsea hugged Mama as well. "I've really enjoyed working with him."

"JC, is that lovely lady your sister?" Olivier asked with a wink for Mama and Abuela as he joined them. "You must introduce me."

"This is my mama and my abuela. *Mamá y Abuela*, this is Olivier. He's my competition, but we're keeping it friendly for now."

Olivier kissed each of the women's hands with a courtly bow. It might be over-the-top, but his own grandmother had pounded courtesy into him, and he thought JC's mother and grandmother would appreciate it. "It is a pleasure to meet you, *mesdames*. Your son is a joy to have as a friend and competitor."

Abuela put a hand to her chest and leaned over to Mama. "Oh, *Dios mío*. He is so sweet. Can we keep him?"

"Abuela!" JC blushed as he looked at Olivier. "I'm so sorry. She doesn't mean anything by it."

Olivier winked at JC and turned back to Abuela, taking the hand she had pressed to her bosom. "My family is all still in France. Yes, you can keep me, as long as you teach me Spanish. I studied German in school. Many years ago."

"Oh, *mi hijo*, of course we will." Abuela nudged Mama. "He wants to learn Spanish. Did you hear?"

"Yes, I did." Mama smiled at Olivier. "It is very nice to meet you, Olivier. You will have to come by for dinner some evening. Any friend of Javi's is always welcome at our table."

"It would be a welcome change from some of the dinners in the residence," Olivier said. "Our fellow competitors are warm and generous people, but they are not all good cooks." He shuddered a little remembering the meal Troy had made for them. It was supposed to be chicken and dumplings, but it didn't look or taste like any chicken or any dumplings Olivier had ever seen before.

Tricia joined them before he could say anything else. "Are you trying to steal my partner again?" she teased Chelsea, her Australian accent broader than usual in her amusement. When she caught sight of the two women standing there, she smiled at them. "Is this your family, JC?"

"They're my family now too," Olivier said, putting an arm around Tricia's shoulders. "They've adopted me."

Tricia flashed him a grin before leaning in toward Mama and Abuela. "You need to tell JC to stop stealing my partner. If I turn around for more than a minute, Olivier disappears, and I always find him with JC."

Mama leaned in and nudged JC. "¿Te gustaría, Javi?"

"Sí, Mamá, pero yo no voy a hacer nada al respecto." JC smiled, then switched back to English so people wouldn't feel left out. "We're too busy learning how to dance. Chelsea and Tricia would never let us get away with goofing off too much."

"That's right," Chelsea said, taking JC's arm and smiling at Mama. "JC has to work hard so we can take the trophy and get the big donation for charity. The Trevor Project deserves the big prize."

"*Sí*, it does," Abuela agreed, "and JC is a good boy to support them. And you are a good girl to help him. Even the ones who I think know less about their charities, they are good ones. It is good what everyone here is doing."

"JC, I want to meet Carmen before the show begins. Your Chelsea is sweet, but Carmen has always been my favorite."

"Yes, Mama." JC smiled at Olivier and Tricia. "Good luck tonight." There was nothing they could do to change the results now, but he still meant it.

"You too."

As Olivier and Tricia headed off to start getting ready, JC led his mother and grandmother over to where Carmen and Eugene were getting ready. "Carmen, Eugene, can I introduce you to my mama and abuela?"

Carmen turned from the mirror with her usual brilliant smile. Eugene looked up and nodded but didn't try to move from where the makeup artists were working on him. "Nice to meet you both," Carmen said, ignoring her partner's slight. "It's wonderful that JC has family to come support him."

Mama smiled at Carmen and then glared at the back of Eugene's head. She lowered her voice as she leaned forward. "Don't you let him get you down," she said in Spanish. "You're worth ten of him."

"*Gracias.*" Carmen squeezed Mama's shoulder and nodded at Abuela. "I appreciate it. Best of luck to you as well, JC," she said louder. "You'd better get them back to their seats, though. I can hear Elizabeth and Corey warming up the crowd. They don't want to miss anything."

"No, we don't," Abuela agreed. "Show us the way back, JC."

The crowd in the studio was on their feet and cheering already as Mama and Abuela returned to their seats. Moments later the hosts brought the judges out to the roar of the fans. Mama and Abuela clapped and cheered along with everyone else as Henrietta, Emma Leigh, and Edoardo waltzed, shimmied, and spun across the floor to their seats. The noise rose to a fever pitch as the spotlights flashed to the band and then went dark momentarily. When the lights came back up, the pros and company were on the dance floor, ready for the opening number. Without the benefit of the cameras to focus in on one couple or another, the bodies were a blur of movement, of light and dark hair, jewel-toned dresses against solid black shirts pulled tight over muscular chests. The effect was positively breathtaking.

"Is that Chelsea?" Abuela asked as one of the blonde dancers in a sapphire blue dress whirled by.

"No, she was wearing green. She's over there. I think that was Tricia."

"It's so hard to tell like this. I'm glad we didn't come last night. I wanted to see Javi's dance." Abuela peered out at the floor. "I can hardly tell what most of them do, they move so fast!"

"I think it will be easier to watch when it's only one couple on the floor," Mama said as she applauded along with the crowd. "We'll get a chance to see Javi dance live before he goes home."

"Hopefully he won't go home," Abuela said. The pros cleared the floor, the crowd returned to their seats, and the hosts began their introduction.

"Welcome to the first elimination round of season twelve of *Dance Off!*" Elizabeth said. "Tonight we will be giving $1,000 to one of twelve worthy charities, so let's begin with a reminder of the causes our stars support."

The lights went down, and the video screen lit up with a montage of the twelve sponsored charities, their missions, and a brief clip from the star that supported each. When the video finished and the lights came back up, the twelve competing couples had repartnered on the dance floor.

"It's never easy to say good-bye," Corey said, "but tonight it's inevitable, so let's get the first of our results. The first couple who will continue to dance for their charity is…." Corey paused dramatically to let the audience shout the names of their favorite stars. "Eugene and Carmen! The Multiple Sclerosis Society will receive at least $2,000."

Abuela rolled her eyes as she applauded along with the rest of the audience. "That man should go home," she muttered.

"The Multiple Sclerosis Society does good work," Mama said. "Just remember that."

On the floor, Eugene looked pleased at his accomplishment, though he didn't hug his partner like most of the other contestants had in past seasons. He accepted a congratulatory handshake from Troy but ignored Carmen completely.

"Next up, Troy and Ella." Corey stood next to them and put a hand on Troy's shoulder. "Troy, I'm sorry, but you're in jeopardy. We're going to have to wait until the end of the show to find out if St. Jude's hospital will get more than $1,000."

The crowd booed and hissed at the announcement, as they always did. Nobody liked to see any of the couples in jeopardy. "That's too bad," Mama said to Abuela. "He seems like a nice man."

"Being a nice man doesn't make him a good dancer," Abuela replied. "He was painful to watch last night."

"No more than Eugene was," Mama disagreed. "And Eugene is safe."

"Eugene has a bigger following."

Mama couldn't argue with that.

"We can also now reveal," Elizabeth continued, "that Freddy and Sharon will be back next week to earn more money for school music programs."

The crowd went wild at that.

"And when we come back," Elizabeth continued, "we'll have a special performance by our company of dancers."

The spotlight on Elizabeth faded to black while the viewers at home switched to commercials, but in the studio, two of the pros spun out onto the dance floor as the band struck up a song that was all the rage on the radio.

JC turned back from the curtain as the dancers took the floor and the three couples who'd learned their fate came backstage. "This is more nerve-racking than dancing was. At least then I could control what I did." He didn't like waiting to find out how he fared. When he swam, he knew right away how he placed, at least against other people in his heat, and he never had to wait long to find out if he was advancing. Putting the final result in the hands of viewers was disconcerting.

"It's like a rugby match that drags out over two days," Olivier agreed. "When we are playing, so much is out of our control, but even that is not like giving control to viewers who have nothing invested in our success or failure."

"It definitely brings in a different element," Chelsea agreed. "Winning the viewers' support is crucial. It's one reason to always keep a good attitude while we're training. If you ever get upset, the viewers will see it, and it could count against you."

That hadn't been an issue for JC yet, but he nodded anyway. He remembered some of the training videos he'd seen when his Mama and Abuela had watched past seasons. Some of the stars had thrown temper tantrums when they'd struggled. "Got it. Though you have nothing to worry about. Mama raised me to be a gentleman."

"We'll see if you still feel that way when she's teaching you how to do lifts," Tricia said. "That's always the roughest week."

"Why is that?" Olivier asked.

"Because it is harder and has the potential to be more dangerous than anything else we do," Tricia said. "If you were to drop me, I could be seriously injured."

JC gulped. Olivier could easily lift Tricia, though it might be a challenge to do it gracefully while dancing, but JC wasn't sure he could lift Chelsea. He was wiry, not muscular. "Do we have to do lifts?"

"If we make it that far, yes." Chelsea turned back to the stage as the next set of competitors came out. "Don't worry. There's ways to make it safe."

JC wasn't reassured, but he pushed it out of his mind for the moment and watched as Dawn, Amber, and Kevan took the stage with their partners.

In what seemed like seconds backstage but was surely an eternity for the couples waiting for a decision, Elizabeth and Corey announced that Dawn and Amber were safe, but Kevan was in jeopardy.

They went to another commercial break, and Olivier turned to JC. "We're next. Are you ready?"

"No," JC said, though he straightened his jacket and led Chelsea over to the staging area. The commercial break performance was followed by a performance that would be aired before they had to go out, but he didn't want to be scrambling when it was time to step onstage.

"Breathe," Chelsea said as she hooked her arm through his. "We'll be fine."

Olivier felt about as sure of that as JC looked, but so far the two people in jeopardy had gotten the lowest scores from the judges, even if Eugene had gotten the same score and was now safe. Still, they seemed like reasonable results to date. He'd watched the show enough to know that reasonable didn't always play into it, though, and he wasn't ready to go home.

They lined up along with Deborah and Brody and waited for their cue to walk out onto the stage for the next set of announcements.

Elizabeth smiled at all of them as they took the dance floor, but it didn't make JC feel any better. She'd smiled at everyone who had come out and was far too good a host to reveal anything early. "It's time for our next set of results," she said from her place in front of the judges. "The next couple that is safe is…."

"Brody and Deborah," Corey announced. The crowd cheered. Olivier wasn't surprised at the result. Deborah had the highest scores last night. He was more concerned about his own results and JC's. Top of the board was usually safe and bottom of the board rallied fan support. Middle of the board was just luck of the draw.

"Olivier and Tricia," Elizabeth said, joining them on stage, "you had straight sixes last night. What can we expect from you next week if you make it through tonight?"

"Whatever Tricia tells me to do," Olivier promised.

"A jive to knock your socks off," Tricia replied with a grin.

Elizabeth laughed. "Good thing you're coming back, then."

Butterflies started doing loop-de-loops in JC's stomach as Elizabeth turned to him. So far, there had been one person in jeopardy in each group of people. If the pattern held true, he was in danger.

"Relax," Chelsea whispered, leaning back against his chest. She was standing in front of him in the loop of his arms, and he leaned forward to make it easier to hear her. "There's only one more couple in jeopardy, and there are still three more people left to find out their fate. We're probably safe."

"Right." JC nodded. That made sense, but it did nothing to calm the butterflies in his stomach.

"JC and Chelsea, your fox-trot earned you a solid nineteen. But is it enough to save you?"

"I hope so." JC grinned at the camera. "I've really enjoyed dancing with Chelsea. I'm not ready to go home yet."

"Good, because you're also safe."

Olivier smiled widely as JC hugged his partner. When JC released Chelsea, Olivier and Tricia joined them to congratulate them as well, Deborah and Brody right behind him. "One week down, nine to go," Olivier said to JC with a smile.

The spotlights focused back on the floor and another performance number, so the stars were free to move backstage again as the crowd clapped and cheered for the dancers onstage.

They met the other couples in the waiting area, and everyone patted them on the shoulder enthusiastically or pulled them into hugs.

When they separated, JC found himself again standing next to Olivier. "If we're not careful, we're going to prove Tricia right," he murmured, though he made no move to step away. He was perfectly content to watch the rest of the show from right here.

Olivier could think of worse things than for Tricia to be right about JC gravitating to Olivier's side. "Who do you think will go home tonight?" he asked as the last three couples took the stage to get their results.

"It's hard to tell. Either Kevan or Troy could go." He doubted whoever was in jeopardy from this round was truly in the bottom two—they'd all danced too well for that—but it was possible. He knew the voters could be capricious, and if Rini, Makayla, or Christine went home, it wouldn't be the first time someone without the low judge scores went.

They quickly found out that Rini and Makayla were safe, but Christine was in danger of going home. Rini and Makayla came backstage, and Kevan and Troy joined Christine on stage with their partners. The tension backstage was palpable. Everyone's eyes were glued to the three couples on stage even as they congratulated Rini and Makayla.

"And here we come to the moment of truth," Elizabeth said. "We have three couples in jeopardy, three charities at stake here. Which of these couples will leave us tonight? Kevan and Lisa, the judges want to see your smooth side. Will you get the chance to show us? Christine and Mike, last night the judges praised your first efforts. Did the viewers agree? Troy and Ella, the judges said your fox-trot lacked pizzazz. Will you get another chance to wow them?"

"We can now reveal that one of these three couples is safe. Kevan and Lisa, you are safe!"

"Okay, that's just wrong," Tricia murmured at Olivier's elbow. "Christine outdanced Kevan and Lisa by a mile."

"Does that mean Christine and Troy have the lowest total scores?" Olivier asked.

"Sometimes," Tricia said. "Other times, they don't confirm that. We'll have to see what they say tonight."

"Christine and Mike, Troy and Ella, if you could come down here, please," Elizabeth said. The spotlight highlighted the two couples as they made their way to Elizabeth. "While not necessarily in the last two places of our rankings, one of these couples does have the lowest combined total of judges' scores and votes and will be going home."

JC took Chelsea's hand as Elizabeth moved to stand between the two couples. "I know she's going for the drama, but does she have to drag it out like this?"

"Yes," Chelsea said, although her grip on JC's hand was tight. "They have to fill the time slot and keep viewers around for as long as absolutely possible or they risk losing advertising revenue. It sucks when you're up here. It's a thousand times worse when you're down there."

"The couple going home tonight is...." The ballroom fell silent for the first time all evening. "Troy and Ella. We will donate $1,000 to St. Jude Children's Research Hospital on behalf of Troy and everyone here at *Dance Off*."

JC breathed a sigh of relief. He liked Troy well enough and was sorry to see him go, but he had danced much worse than Christine. If it had to be between the two of them, he'd rather see Troy go. "That was intense."

"Just wait until there are only six couples left. Or less." Chelsea led JC out to the stage with the rest of the couples. "The smaller the group gets, the more competitive it is."

As they were walking out, Amber hurried in front of the group and wrapped Troy in a hug. "I'm so, so sorry you have to go. St. Jude's is a great cause. They deserve more than $1,000."

"That's all right, darlin'," Troy drawled. "It is what it is, you know? It's a thousand bucks they didn't have before."

Olivier shook Troy's hand. "Good luck with next year's races. I will be watching and cheering for you."

"Good luck to you with the rugby league," Troy replied. "I'll be watching that from now on too. Just goes to show what an opportunity like this can do for you, right?"

"Right," Olivier said. "I have new friends I would never have met otherwise." He resisted looking at JC as he spoke. This moment was about Troy, not about Olivier's budding attraction for his costar.

JC stepped in and shook Troy's hand as well, then went over to find Mama and Abuela. He had to get out of his costume before he left, and he needed to take care of a few other things too, but he wanted to say good-bye first. He didn't want them waiting for him. All he was going to do when he got home was crash. Tonight had been almost as exhausting as the competition, and they got to start the crazy routine again tomorrow.

CHAPTER 8

OLIVIER SLUMPED on the floor of the practice studio. "This… jive is light and bouncy." He looked down at his arms and especially his legs, thick trunks of muscle perfect for playing rugby. "I am not light and bouncy."

Tricia sat down cross-legged next to him. "No, but that doesn't mean you can't dance the jive. I know it's hard, but you do move fast on the field, don't you? You just have to use that speed differently."

"Nobody cares how I place my feet on the field as long as I don't fall on my face or drop the ball," Olivier pointed out. "The judges will not be so forgiving on Tuesday."

"They won't, but you have all week to work on moving them the way you need to. You know how to move your feet fast. You just need to learn to move them right." Tricia patted Olivier on the knee. "Come on, let's go over the steps slowly. We can speed up once you get them right."

"*D'acc*," Olivier said. Tricia had been the epitome of patience so far, but they'd gone from having three weeks to prepare a dance to having one. It changed the game immensely. "Very slowly, yes?"

"Yes, we will start very slowly," Tricia said with a laugh. She climbed to her feet and held out a hand to Olivier. "Now come on. Up. You can't learn them sitting on the floor."

Olivier took her hand and levered himself to his feet. As promised, Tricia walked through the steps at a snail's pace. Olivier mimicked her, committing them to memory. "Again," he said, "same speed."

"All right. One more time. Then I'm speeding it up." Tricia smiled at Olivier's worried expression. "Just a little bit. We'll ramp this up gradually, but we *are* ramping it up." She pulled Olivier back to the starting spot. "Now come on. Let's go again."

Olivier went through it again, at her side this time instead of half a beat behind her. He still wasn't confident. *Putain*, he hadn't been confident two days ago after three weeks of practice. There was no way he was confident after a couple of hours. He managed, though. At that speed, he got all the steps in the right order with something approaching passable technique. Now he just had to do it at about ten times the speed.

It was going to be a *long* week.

JC STOPPED midkick and bent over, resting his hands on his knees. "I am *never* going to get this," he groaned. "The kicks are all wrong." He'd spent years training himself in specific kicks for different strokes, but the kicks and flicks of the jive weren't like any of them, and his legs didn't want to move that way.

"Yes," Chelsea agreed, "but that doesn't mean you can't learn them. How did you learn your kicks for swimming?"

"In the pool. Or by the pool," he added with a shrug. Early on, they'd spent time sitting or lying on the pool chairs, going through the motions of the kicks and pulls required for each stroke. "And lots of practice. More than a week's worth."

"I can't get us more than a week's worth of practice time," Chelsea said, "but there's a pool outside and the weather is perfect for it." She looked down at the leotard she was wearing. "I can go in the water like this, and your exercise shorts are fine to get wet. Let's go. Show me how kicks are done, and let's see if being in *your* natural environment helps you learn how mine are done."

JC looked at Chelsea incredulously. "Do you really think that'll work?" It was probably worth a shot, anyway. If he could get himself into the mindset of learning a new stroke, he might be able to get the kicks and flicks. So far he could easily do them when he mimicked Chelsea slowly, but his legs refused to cooperate with any speed whatsoever. When he tried it as part of the dance, he just wanted to take another step.

"I don't know if it'll help or not, but it's worth trying, isn't it? You're struggling with it on the dance floor, but you're not comfortable here. You're comfortable in the water. What do we have to lose?"

"Nothing, I guess." JC stretched up onto his toes and came down with a grunt. "All right. Let's do this." It might not work, but at least he'd be in his element in the pool, and that alone made it worthwhile. He'd be more confident there, if nothing else, and it was easier to be aware of how his body was moving in the water.

Now if only he could convince the judges to let him perform in the pool too, he'd be golden.

OLIVIER SLUNG his towel around his neck as he walked out of the house they were all staying in and headed toward the pool. He was tired, sweaty, and frustrated, and lounging in the pool sounded pretty much perfect at the moment. He took two steps onto the pool deck and froze. JC was in the water, his face a mask of concentration as he stared past the surface at something on the bottom of the pool.

"Did you lose something?" he asked.

"What?" JC blinked up at Olivier. He'd been so focused on practicing the kicks Chelsea had taught him today he hadn't even heard Olivier come outside. "No. I'm, uh...." He paused and rubbed his hand on the back of his neck as he tried to figure out what to say. He didn't want to give away his trick to a competitor, even though it probably wouldn't work as well for anyone else, and he didn't really want to admit a weakness, either. Most of the stars were friendly with each other and supported each other, but it was a competition, and even the friendliest people wanted to win.

On the other hand, this was Olivier. If anyone had to beat JC, he was JC's choice, and JC really was glad for any excuse to talk to him. "I'm practicing kicks and flicks. I couldn't get them right in the studio because they're *so* different from all my swimming kicks. So Chelsea taught them to me the same way I learned the swimming kicks."

"That is a good idea," Olivier said. "I don't think it would work for me, but it's not the kicks I cannot do. It's the speed. My feet don't move that fast."

"Actually, do you know your steps?" JC asked, grinning. The pool might not be Olivier's element like it was JC's, but it could offer other benefits. "If you do, you should try them in the pool. It'll help with your speed."

"I know them," Olivier said, setting down the towel and sliding into the water, carefully staying turned toward JC so he couldn't see the scars, "but how will it help my speed?" He wasn't unwilling to try, but he didn't see the logic of it either.

"Water resistance." JC took a moment to appreciate the sight of Olivier in his swim trunks. They rode low, exposing his hip bones, and JC was completely distracted until they were covered by the water. "You know how people do physical therapy in pools? That's why. The water resistance keeps their movements slow, so they can't accidentally injure themselves by jerking or something. But if you can get any speed at all in the water, you'll be that much faster out of it."

"That makes sense, I suppose. Now to keep my balance while I do the steps. This is not as easy as you make it look." He managed the first few steps of the dance at about the same rhythm he'd managed when Tricia first taught him, but then his upper body, free of the water, got ahead of his feet, and he lost his balance and splashed into the pool.

JC choked back a laugh as Olivier sputtered. Dripping wet was a good look on him, but JC doubted he'd appreciate the comment at the moment. He went over to make sure Olivier was okay and froze as he saw bumpy scars on Olivier's back and a thick line on his left shoulder. "What happened?"

"A car accident," Olivier said, forcing himself not to hide the scars. "The surgery fixed the damage to my shoulder, but nothing can fix the scars."

"Oh. I'm sorry." It was stupid and inadequate, but JC didn't know what else to say. The scars contrasted with the smooth planes of Olivier's chest, but they weren't as ugly as he seemed to think they were. They added character, and JC liked that. He itched to touch the scars, but that would be too intimate, so he settled for touching Olivier on the forearm. "Maybe move a little deeper," he suggested after making sure Olivier was okay. "Or slow down a little. Work up to it. The water works a little differently than air."

"I see that," Olivier said, relieved JC hadn't made an issue of his scars. He took JC's advice and moved deeper so only his shoulders and head were out of the water. He tried the steps again and managed to keep his balance, although he couldn't complete the arm motions with any grace since he had to move them between the water and air, and the resistance changed when he did. "It will give you a good laugh, even if it does nothing for me."

"Hey, it's not like I look any better." JC moved into the deeper water with Olivier. "It took me all day to learn these kicks, and I'm still not sure I have it right. I don't know how I'm going to do this in six days."

"The same way everyone else does, I suppose," Olivier said. "With much nervousness and as much confidence as we can pretend to feel. Isn't that what we did on Tuesday?"

"Yes. But we had *three* weeks to get ready for Tuesday, and I was still a wreck." JC tried to do his kicks again, but it was harder with Olivier watching him. Or maybe he was just tired. "I didn't struggle with the fox-trot, either. Not like this."

"The cha-cha was hard," Olivier said, "but you are right. This is harder. There is one thing I know, though, and you know it too. When you are tired, you make mistakes and you risk hurting yourself. We should rest now, enjoy the water and the sun, and tomorrow we will start again and see what our bodies have learned, yes?"

Part of JC wanted to keep going until he had the kicks down cold, but he knew Olivier was right. It was hard to do moves he'd managed with ease half an hour ago. It would just get worse if he kept going. "Good point," he said as he kicked his legs up to float in his back. "I keep telling myself I'll get used to this pace eventually, but I swear I get more tired every day."

"Me too," Olivier said, "and you have a commute on top of it. The room that should have been yours is still empty. I know you want to see your family, but don't make the drive there if you're too tired to do so safely."

"I'll be fine tonight." JC already felt better just floating instead of working. The water relaxed and rejuvenated him like nothing else. "I'll keep it in mind, though, if I don't get used to it."

Olivier didn't press more. JC was a grown man, fully aware of his body's capabilities and limits. If Olivier selfishly wanted him around more, that was his problem, not JC's.

THREE DAYS later Olivier was far less sanguine. JC was sitting at the table in the community dining room with his chin resting on his hands, his eyes closed, all but asleep sitting up. "Tonight, you stay here," he said, sitting down next to JC. The way the other man jumped when

Olivier spoke only added to Olivier's determination. "You are in no shape to drive."

JC forced himself to sit up straighter and hoped he could at least look like he wasn't practically falling over with exhaustion. "No. I promised I'd be home for my brothers and sister to call tonight. Mama said they called yesterday and were upset I was still here and couldn't talk to them."

"Then tell them to call here," Olivier said. "You cannot drive like this. You will have an accident, and then your brothers and sister will never be able to talk to you again. Is that what you want?"

"No." JC shook his head, both to emphasize the point and to clear away cobwebs. It worked for the first, but not the second. "I'll be fine, though," he insisted anyway. "I just need to eat something and sit for a few minutes. That's all."

"I think Olivier's right," Chelsea said. "You've been more and more exhausted all week. I had to wake you up when we took a break today. Unless someone can come pick you up, you really need to stay here tonight."

"I can't. I don't have anything to wear." They hadn't gotten in the pool today, so his clothes weren't dripping wet, but he'd sweated enough they were damp. He didn't want to wear them again tomorrow, and he definitely didn't want to sleep in them.

"You can borrow a T-shirt and sweats to sleep in tonight and practice in tomorrow," Olivier insisted, "or I can call your family and have them bring you something. You're being stubborn, and it is not good, JC. Should I tell Abuela you are being reckless?"

"I never should have introduced you," JC muttered as he pulled out his phone. Maybe his cousins could come pick him and his car up so they wouldn't have to drive him back in the morning. "Fine. I'll call. But I'm blaming you two," he added, pointing at Olivier and Chelsea.

"For this? I will take the blame," Olivier said as he waited for JC to make the call. He didn't understand all of the rapid-fire Spanish, but he didn't need to. He just needed to know JC wouldn't get in an accident because he fell asleep at the wheel.

Abuela answered JC's call but quickly dashed his hopes of getting a ride. His cousins were out, and his aunt's car was in the shop, so she'd borrowed Abuela's to run some errands. No one could come get him. "I have to stay here, then," he said, still speaking Spanish. "Olivier and Chelsea won't let me drive home tonight. They say I'm too tired."

"And are you?" Abuela asked in a tone that left no room for anything but a straight answer. She would know if he was lying, and she'd make him pay for it.

"Probably," JC admitted, glad Olivier and Chelsea couldn't understand him. "I can stay awake, though. It's not that far."

"Nonsense. You listen to your friends, Javi. They know best," Abuela insisted. "You thank them for me, and you bring them over for dinner tomorrow so I can thank them properly."

"Yes, Abuela."

"And you tell Chelsea to bring her young man if she has one too. They should enjoy Sunday dinner together."

"Yes, Abuela. I'll see you tomorrow night. Tell Solita and the boys I'll call tomorrow, okay?" He hung up the phone after getting her agreement and turned back to Olivier and Chelsea. "All right, I'll stay," he said in English.

"I'll find something for you to sleep in," Olivier said, getting up from the table immediately. He reached the door out of the kitchen and turned back. "I'm glad you're staying tonight, but you should think about moving in. It is only going to get harder as the weeks go on."

JC had to admit the idea was tempting, but he would make a decision when he wasn't dead on his feet. "We'll see. It might be a moot point after Wednesday anyway. I can make it through Tuesday." He stood to follow Olivier, figuring there was no point in making him come all the way back to the kitchen just to lead JC right back upstairs. "Abuela says you both have to come to dinner tomorrow, though. And she says to bring Joel, Chelsea."

"How does she know about Joel?" Chelsea followed them out of the kitchen. "We're very careful to keep that off camera."

"She didn't say Joel. She said you should bring your young man if you had one." JC felt weird repeating Abuela's phrasing, but he wanted Chelsea to know he hadn't let her secret slip. "That's Joel. But you don't have to if you don't want them to know. Just don't tell them or they'll insist he come next time."

"I'll ask him," Chelsea said. "He might be practicing still." They usually rested on Sunday evenings so they didn't burn out from constant practice, but if Makayla still needed to work on her routine, Joel could very well insist on spending a few more hours in the studio, and no one would blame him.

"As long as none of us are still practicing. I honestly don't think Abuela would forgive me if I don't bring you both. And if I don't show up…." He shuddered dramatically. "You should just let me drive home now if you're going to keep me from dinner. Crashing the car would be preferable to what Abuela would do if I skip out."

"Your grandmother seemed like a lovely woman," Chelsea said. "I'm sure she would understand, but you're doing fantastic, so I'm sure we'll be able to attend, even if Joel decides to stay and practice."

"Thanks." JC kissed Chelsea on the cheek. "I appreciate it."

Chelsea laughed and pushed him after Olivier. "Go change, and get to bed. You're not allowed to nap tomorrow."

"Yeah, yeah," JC muttered. Olivier laughed and led JC the rest of the way down the hall to the room he had claimed as his own. He dug in his drawers, doing his best not to think about the fact that JC was standing in his bedroom, and pulled out a T-shirt and a pair of sweats.

"They'll probably be a little big on you," Olivier said, "but they'll get you through the night. We can put the clothes you're wearing in the wash so they'll be clean for rehearsal tomorrow if you want."

"Thanks." JC took the clothes from Olivier and looked around blankly. He was just alert enough to realize that stripping in front of Olivier probably wouldn't be the best idea. He had no objections to the idea at all, but at the moment, he was too tired to do anything beyond drop his clothes on the floor. "Where, uh, is my room?"

"Two doors down on the left," Olivier said. "There's an en suite bathroom. When you're done, just toss your dirty things out in the hall. I was going to do laundry tonight anyway. I can put your stuff in with mine if you don't mind."

"That would be *fantastic*." JC started toward the room Olivier indicated was his to use but paused in the doorway of Olivier's room. "Thanks. Really. You and Chelsea are—" He yawned, long and wide. "Uh. Probably right. I should get to bed."

"Yes, you should," Olivier said, determined not to envision JC stripping down, showering, and redressing in Olivier's clothes. He'd have enough trouble sleeping without those images in his head. "Go on. *Dors bien.*"

"Thanks." JC didn't completely understand the French, but he got the sentiment, and that was all he was awake enough to process at the moment. "Night." He stumbled into the room Olivier had indicated and changed just inside the door, too tired to explore the room at all. He threw his dirty clothes into the hall and fell into the bed. He was asleep immediately.

Olivier had done his best not to stare at JC as he walked down the hall. Instead he made himself gather his own sweaty workout clothes for the laundry. By the time he'd done that, JC's clothes were waiting for him on the floor in the hall. Olivier grabbed them all and pretended he wasn't imagining JC sleeping in his T-shirt and sweats. If he failed miserably? Well, no one had to be any the wiser.

CHAPTER 9

OLIVIER HAD barely taken three steps from JC's car when the door to the little house opened and JC's grandmother bustled out. She made it down the steps and to his side with remarkable speed. He started to greet her, but before he could say anything, she enveloped him in a huge, motherly hug. "Gracias, niño," she said. "Thank you for making sure JC was safe yesterday."

"It was nothing, Abuela," Olivier said. "He'd just gotten so tired he wasn't thinking straight."

Abuela glared over Olivier's shoulder at JC. "He doesn't think straight," she agreed. "He gets too caught up in his competition and forgets all sense."

"Abuela!" JC flushed. She was right, but that didn't mean she had to tell Olivier, of all people. He wanted Olivier to think highly of him, not that he was an idiot. "Don't tell them that!"

"Why not? It is true." She pointed a finger at JC. "You push yourself when you swim. Now you push yourself when you dance too. It is too much."

"I don't—"

"She's just worried about you, JC." Chelsea patted his arm as she and Joel came up behind them. "It's her job as your grandmother."

"Thank you as well, *pequeña*," Abuela said, giving Chelsea a hug. "And who is this?"

"This is Joel," Chelsea said. "I'm sure you recognize him from the show."

"Of course," Abuela said, "but that is not the same as meeting him. Welcome to my house, Joel."

"Thank you, señora," Joel said. "I appreciate the invitation."

"Bah, I'm only señora to people I don't like. You call me Abuela like all the other hoodlums in my house."

"We are not hoodlums, Abuela!" JC was sure his grandmother was setting out to embarrass him horribly today, probably in retaliation for yesterday. He would never make it through dinner without turning red as a ripe tomato.

"I'd be honored, Abuela," Joel said with a wink, effectively cutting off her return argument. "Do we get to meet the rest of the family?"

"Ah, where are my manners?" Abuela exclaimed. "Come inside. I introduce you to my grandchildren. They are close to your age, JC's cousins. And then we will have dinner. Javi insisted we have it ready when he told you to be here. He says you have to get back early so you can dance tomorrow. Asunción, JC's aunt, made tamales. Better than anything you find in a restaurant because they're fresh, *sí*?"

"I've never had tamales," Olivier said.

"Oh, *pobrecito*," Abuela said, coming to fuss over him. She took his arm and led him inside, pointedly ignoring the way Olivier helped her up the steps to her porch. Olivier wasn't sure she really needed the help, but he wasn't going to let down his own grandmother by taking less than stellar care of JC's.

"She is going to fuss over him all night," JC muttered to Chelsea and Joel as he led the way into the house. "You too, Chelsea, though probably not as much. She's a bit smitten with Olivier."

"Who isn't?" Chelsea asked with a wink. "He's very handsome. And so polite."

"Um. Me?" Joel raised his hand. "I like the guy and all, but I prefer tiny blondes." He pulled Chelsea close with an arm around her waist. "And I hope they prefer me too."

"They do." Chelsea kissed him on the cheek as they stepped into the house. "Olivier is wonderful, but you're the one I love."

JC rolled his eyes. This was the Chelsea and Joel everyone saw backstage, the cutesy couple the public never got to see. "This way."

Olivier was already surrounded by JC's cousins by the time they made it inside. The look he shot JC was such an interesting combination of amused and petrified that JC almost left him there, but Olivier had helped him out the night before. JC couldn't abandon him now.

"How do you keep them all straight?" Olivier asked when JC reached his side through the crowd. "I don't think I remember a single name."

"I didn't have to meet all of them at once, remember?" JC said. "And these are only the ones who live in town. There's a whole contingent back in Texas and another big group down in San Diego. I have a huge family."

Olivier thought about his parents, both only children, and his sister—his only sibling—and how quiet his family gatherings were in comparison. He looked around the room again at the absolute and amazing chaos that was JC's grandmother's house. How boring his family gatherings had been in comparison.

"You get used to it. I promise." JC couldn't imagine anything other than this, though he knew from stories his swim teammates told that such a huge family wasn't a usual thing. He took pity on Olivier and took his arm. "Come, meet my abuelo."

He led Olivier, Chelsea, and Joel over to the corner where his abuelo was seated in a comfortable armchair. Unlike his grandmother, who was a vibrant force despite her years, his grandfather was frail, at least in body. His mind, though, was as sharp as ever, and he grinned when JC approached with his friends.

"Renacuajo, nice of you to finally bring your friends over to meet me."

Olivier's ears perked up at the nickname. He was usually pretty good at guessing what was going on in Spanish since it was so close to French, but that was a word he didn't know and couldn't guess. He'd have to ask JC about it later.

"They've only been here for two minutes, Abuelo. I had to get them away from Abuela." JC leaned in and kissed his grandfather on the cheek. "This is Olivier, Chelsea, and Joel."

Before the old man could start to rise, Chelsea had leaned over and kissed his cheek just as JC had. "It's such a pleasure to meet everyone. JC talks about his family all the time, and now I get to put faces to names."

"He talks about you too," Abuelo said. "He says you are good to him. Firm, but not too firm."

"We're all there to learn and grow as dancers," Chelsea said. "Yelling doesn't help anyone do that, so I try not to do it if I can avoid it."

"Tell that to my rugby coach," Olivier said with a grin. "He thinks the louder he yells, the better we'll understand him."

"I've had swim coaches the same way," JC said. "Though, to be fair, it is sometimes hard to hear when we're in the water. They could have been yelling to make sure we heard them."

"Only if they stopped yelling once they had your attention," Joel said. "Some people like to yell. I had a dance instructor who did once. I didn't stay with him for long."

"We didn't let Javi stay with the coaches who yelled either," Abuelo said as he stood. "If they shout to get his attention when he pretends to be a fish, that is fine. If they keep yelling, that is not."

Olivier reached out to help Abuelo, but JC beat him to it, slipping his arm under his grandfather's to help him toward the dining room, where everyone was gathering. The smell of all the different dishes was wonderful and overwhelming at the same time. "I have no idea what half those dishes are," he admitted to JC after he got his grandfather settled. "You're going to have to help me out here."

"I can do that," JC said, "although you might be better off asking one of my aunts. I just eat whatever they cook because it's always amazing."

"It certainly smells amazing," Olivier agreed. "Maybe I'll just eat and they can tell me what it is later."

"That's probably the way to go." JC turned to make sure Chelsea and Joel were okay and found two of his cousins, Leticia and Alvaro, had taken care of it for him. Alvaro was at Chelsea's side, solicitous but not flirtatious, and Leticia was talking to Joel about school and the internship she hoped to get over the summer.

"I will tell you what we have," Mama said as she put the last plate on the table and took a seat next to Olivier. "You do not need to eat anything you do not like, Olivier."

"If there is anything I don't like, I won't eat it," Olivier promised, "but everything looks and smells wonderful." He paid dutiful attention as Mama went through the dozen different dishes on the table, from the famed tamales to enchiladas and empanadas and everything else. And once she was done, he took a serving of everything because it all sounded fabulous. He pretended not to notice Abuela beaming at him from her seat at the far end of the table. Once everyone started serving themselves, the noise level reached a high enough decibel for him to turn to JC and ask quietly, "Renacuajo? Was that what your grandfather called you?"

JC groaned softly, covering the sound by sticking some tamale in his mouth. "Tadpole," he said after he swallowed. "It's a nickname from when I was a kid. They couldn't keep me out of the water, and everyone was convinced I was going to grow up to be an amphibian."

"You did," Mama said. "Even now, you are in the water more than out of it most of the time."

"Am not," JC said, though it was a weak protest. When he was training, he often spent more waking hours in the pool than out of it. "Anyway, everyone used to call me Renacuajo. It wore off as I got older, but Abuelo still uses it."

Olivier laughed. "I think it's wonderful that you have those memories with your family, and that they are all here to celebrate them with you still. Not everyone is as lucky. Besides, there are worse things they could call you, I'm sure."

THE OPENING notes of "Chantilly Lace" rang through the ballroom, and Olivier was off, his feet flying as Tricia had taught him, kicks and flicks and turns and spins, grabbing her hand, letting her go, only to catch her hands again and pull her between his legs in a move he wouldn't have considered possible for him to do before they started this, but it worked, and she bounced to her feet, turning to beckon to him flirtatiously. He followed her across the floor, giving her a look he usually saved for far more private surroundings and a partner of the opposite gender, but she winked at him, and the crowd roared, so he figured it was worth it as he caught her hand again and spun her into his arms and a back bend for the end of the dance.

JC watched Olivier dance from the waiting area, wishing the whole time those smoldering looks had been directed at him instead of Tricia. He knew the dance required it—there were some in his jive as well—but that didn't make seeing them any easier. He did notice that Olivier had gotten the speed he'd been searching for that day in the pool. It made him doubt his own speed a little, but then every dance he watched made him doubt something about his. He had to stop focusing on that if he wanted to succeed in his own.

Still, Olivier had nailed it, as far as JC was concerned. He clapped wildly along with the crowd and leaned over the railing to listen to the judges' comments. Olivier looked amazing standing there, panting for breath, with a thin sheen of sweat covering his face and the exposed part of his chest, and JC…. JC had to stop thinking these thoughts. Even if there was a chance they were reciprocated, this wasn't the time or the place for them.

Olivier joined Tricia at the edge of the dance floor, where Elizabeth and the judges waited for them. The dance had felt good, as good as any rehearsal they'd done and better than most, so he hoped it would meet with the judges' approval as well. Elizabeth had her real smile on, as opposed to the one she pasted on even when the dance had been awful, and since she'd been a dancer herself, he figured that was a good sign.

"Good job," Tricia said as they joined Elizabeth. "I think they'll like it."

"A great opening to tonight's show," Elizabeth said. "Let's start with our head judge, Henrietta."

"One of the challenges of the jive is how light you have to be on your feet to really keep up with the speed of the dance," Henrietta said. "We've had footballers who could manage it and others who couldn't. Now I know football isn't the same as rugby, but I've seen a lot of similarities in the way you dance, so tonight could have been a challenge for you."

It was, Olivier wanted to say, but he didn't interrupt.

"It was a challenge you met beautifully," Henrietta continued. "Your kicks and flicks were sharp. Your footwork was in sync with Tricia when you did the side-by-side sections, and the choreography wasn't easy. Well done."

Edoardo stood and leaned over the table. "Olivier. You can cast those looks at me all night long. They were so smoldering, I almost forgot you were dancing. But then your feet were just flying around, and you hit all those kicks and flicks so wonderfully. There were a few parts where your shoulders were a little out of line, so watch your frame, but overall, a fantastic performance."

Olivier didn't figure Edoardo would appreciate hearing who Olivier was imagining as he "smoldered" at Tricia. Then again, if Edoardo was as bent as Olivier suspected, maybe he wouldn't mind at all.

Emma Leigh looked Olivier up and down. "Wow," she said, sounding as though she meant it. "I expected you to be good, but I

73

didn't expect *that*. You were fast and flirtatious and everything you should be while dancing a jive. I agree with Edoardo that you need to watch your shoulders some, but other than that, great job."

Tricia all but jumped on him as soon as Elizabeth released them to head to the waiting area above the stage. He twirled her as he hurried across the floor. It would go to a commercial break, but the stagehands needed every second they could get to change the set for the next dance. Olivier and Tricia couldn't be part of slowing that down.

They reached the top of the stairs and were mobbed by everyone except Eugene and Carmen, who had already been collected by Heidi, the stage manager who ran the set with all the precision of a Japanese dojo. Olivier was fine with that, especially when the hug he received from JC was a little tighter and lingered a little longer than necessary.

JC tried to stay as close to Olivier as he possibly could through Olivier's scores—two sevens and an eight from Emma Leigh—and the rest of the dances, until Heidi said he and Chelsea needed to head down to get ready for their dance. When JC headed back, Olivier was tied for first place with Rini, who had nailed her quickstep, but Christine still had to dance, and Freddy had just taken the floor. He tried to catch Olivier's attention before he left, but as Chelsea and Heidi hurried him backstage for last-minute preparations, he focused on his dance instead.

OLIVIER'S HEAD was still spinning with the fact that he'd spent most of the show in first place, and JC's hovering only compounded that. Olivier enjoyed watching his costars dance. They'd all worked their asses off the past week, and he'd grown to enjoy the company of most of them quite a bit as they sat around in the evenings and shared communal meals and the occasional beer, but he'd have gladly wished them all to hell right then if it got him five minutes alone with JC. Everything had been more fraught between them since Sunday dinner at JC's grandparents' house, and Olivier wanted to know what it meant, but he hadn't gotten JC alone for more than a second all day—certainly not long enough to ask.

As the sounds of "Rock this Town" flooded the auditorium, JC whirled Chelsea through the steps they'd practiced for the past week. The time in the pool had paid off, and he found the kicks and flicks feeling right. He wasn't sure if they were—only the judges' comments would tell—but the whole dance felt like it was working. If he thought about Olivier every time he had to cast a smoldering look at Chelsea, well, no one needed to know, and it didn't really matter who he thought about as long as he got the right effect. Chelsea was throwing the same looks at him, and JC knew she had to be thinking about Joel when she managed her sexiest glances.

Almost too soon, the music came to an end, and JC pulled Chelsea close in their ending pose. Regardless of what the judges said, he felt like he had nailed it. He wouldn't get tens—week two was far too early in the season for that—but it felt like he'd at least earned a nine. No matter what he got, he doubted anything could burst the high he was riding on after such an amazing performance.

"JC, my darling," Edoardo gushed when they made their way to the judges' bench, "that was amazing! Last week you danced well, but tonight you danced like a champion. Your kicks and flicks were perfect. Your personality came through with every jaunty glance at Chelsea. You were on beat and in sync and at the top of your game."

JC blushed and looked down long enough to summon a smile. "Thank you. I worked hard on those kicks and flicks." He'd focused on them more than any other part of the dance, and he was glad to see his hard work was paying off.

Emma Leigh squeed. There wasn't any other word for it. "That was brilliant!" she gushed. "I loved everything about your jive, from the costumes to the choreography to the charm. Edoardo is right. You brought your A-game tonight. Well done!"

"I agree." Henrietta graced JC with one of her genuine smiles that were rare in the early weeks of the show. "I was worried about how you'd kick because I know it's so different from what you're used to as a swimmer, but you nailed it, my boy. I don't know how you got that footwork down, but keep doing it, whatever it was."

JC beamed at the high praise and pulled Chelsea into a hug before they headed up the steps. Regardless of what his scores were, the judges' reactions and the feeling he still had from the dance were enough to ensure he'd be on cloud nine for the rest of the night.

Corey met them at the top of the stairs, bumping JC with his hip as he and Chelsea took their places in front of the camera. "If those comments are anything to go by, you'll have quite the set of scores tonight," he said. "How does that feel?"

"Amazing," JC gushed. "Something just really clicked tonight, and I feel like a real dancer instead of someone pretending to be one. It's a pretty incredible feeling."

"Chelsea, how proud are you of JC right now?"

"So proud," Chelsea replied. "It would have been easy to get frustrated or give up when he had to learn a different kind of kick, but he didn't. He stuck with it and nailed it tonight."

"And the judges have their scores."

"Nine!"

"Eight!"

"Eight!"

"For a total of twenty-five," Corey said, "and that puts you in first place for the night. How does that feel?"

JC couldn't believe what he'd heard. He'd hoped for a nine, but he hadn't dared believe he'd actually get one. "That's incredible. I hope the fans liked it as much as the judges, but regardless of what happens tomorrow night, I'm completely overwhelmed. Chelsea and I worked hard on this, but everything I managed was thanks to her. I would never have figured anything out if it weren't for her guidance."

Chelsea leaned into the microphone as well. "JC is a phenomenal student. He worked so hard on this dance, and I'm thrilled it came through in his performance."

Elizabeth began her recap, and Heidi gestured to the cast that the cameras had stopped rolling in their balcony. Pretty much everyone mobbed JC as soon as he was free of Corey, slapping him on the back, hugging him, ruffling his short hair—that was from Freddy. If it had been anyone else, he would have protested.

Olivier hung back a bit, not because he wasn't as excited as everyone else, but because he didn't want to share that moment of congratulations with the others. Finally they started drifting back toward their dressing rooms, and Olivier got his chance.

"You looked marvelous out there tonight," he said. "You and Chelsea did a wonderful job." He pulled JC into a one-armed hug. He wanted more, but he wasn't entirely sure of his welcome.

Still riding high, JC returned Olivier's hug. "Thanks!" he said as he leaned up and kissed Olivier. It was brief and fleeting, something that could be passed off as the heat of the moment between friends if Olivier wanted to interpret it that way, but JC hoped he didn't.

Olivier felt the brush of JC's lips against his own, barely there before JC started to pull back. He should let it go at that—an innocent kiss that didn't mean anything but that JC was excited about his scores—but he couldn't. He'd been watching JC for a month now, wanting him, dreaming of a chance with him, and this was it. He grabbed JC's jaw before he could pull away, steadying both of them, and returned the kiss with enough deliberation that it couldn't be anything but an offer of more. JC would have to accept it before Olivier would take it any farther, but he had to make his interest clear.

JC froze for a second as Olivier deepened the kiss but quickly picked up on what he was doing and returned it with equal deliberation. He'd never dreamed they'd go this far here, where people could see them and a camera might be just around the corner, but he wasn't going to turn Olivier down either. He'd wanted this for too long. With a soft sound, JC slid his tongue over Olivier's lips, not demanding anything, just letting him know the option was available, and tangled one hand in Olivier's hair. Now that he had Olivier where he wanted him, JC wasn't going to let go easily.

Olivier parted his lips and met JC's tongue with his own, just a little taste, before he pulled back, resting their foreheads together. "We shouldn't do this here. The crew will be looking for us to do the postshow interviews, and the last thing we need is for Eugene to see us. Are you staying at the house tonight or going home with Abuela?"

"Going home with Abuela," JC said regretfully. There was no reason to stay at the house tonight, not when Wednesday was the one day of the week they didn't have to practice anything. Sometimes, they'd start choreographing a dance so they could get into it full swing first thing Thursday morning, but they didn't want to put too much energy into something they might not have to do if they were sent home. Last week, JC had appreciated the day off. This week, he wished he had to be at the house early so he'd have an excuse to go with Olivier.

"You really ought to think about moving into the house," Olivier said. He heard Tricia calling his name, so he took a step back. "You wouldn't be as tired from the commute, and we could have a little more time together in the evenings."

It was a tempting idea, especially given how tired he'd gotten last week and the possibility of one-on-one time with Olivier.… "Let me talk to Mama and Abuela. I don't want to upset them. But if I can manage it, I'd like to." He smirked at Olivier. "You know Abuela will still expect me home for Sunday dinner, right? And that I'll probably have to bring you."

"As long as Tricia lets me out of practice, I'll eat dinner with you every Sunday," Olivier promised, too happy at the thought of having JC closer to care how sappy he sounded. "We do have to talk about this at some point," he added as Tricia rounded the corner.

"There you two are. Come on, they're waiting for us to do our postshow interviews. We're the only two couples left."

Olivier let her drag him off with a parting wink for JC.

CHAPTER 10

JC HURRIED down the stairs when he heard the doorbell ring. "I got it!" He opened the door without looking through the peephole, already sure Olivier was in the other side and ridiculously anxious to see him. "Hey."

"Hi," Olivier said, feeling absurdly shy. He wanted to lean in and kiss JC, but he was conscious of the driver behind him and JC's family inside and the fact that they hadn't talked about what the kiss meant or how they wanted to handle things. "How did Abuela take the idea of you moving to the house?"

"I convinced her you and Chelsea would look after me." JC stepped back so Olivier could come in. "I was right, though. I have to come back for dinner at least every Sunday, and I'm required to bring you too. I think Abuela is in love."

Olivier laughed. "It's mutual." He followed JC inside, and true to his word, Abuela waited for him just inside the living room. "Olivier, *niño*, you danced so well last night. The judges, they don't give you enough credit."

"They gave me very good scores for week two," Olivier said. He bent to kiss her lined cheek. "I was pleased with them."

"They don't usually give nines this early in the season," JC said as he also kissed her cheek. He'd already greeted her this morning, but he'd get hell later if he ignored his duty while Olivier was around. "You know that."

"Not the point." Abuela huffed. "Olivier deserved better than he got. He was beautiful." She smiled and patted JC on the shoulder. "You were wonderful too. Now, let me get you boys something to eat."

"We have to pack, Abuela," JC protested. "And then get to practice. We need to start learning our dances for next week."

"And to practice, you need to eat," Abuela retorted. "It is no good to practice on an empty stomach."

"We'll eat after we pack," JC promised. He was anxious to get Olivier upstairs where he could greet him properly. Abuela would approve of… whatever was between them, he knew, but he didn't know how Olivier would feel about her knowing, and he wasn't going to risk making a move until then. Last night he had the excuse of the heat of the moment. That didn't carry over to this morning.

"Go pack," she said with a shake of her head. "I will make lunch."

Olivier thanked her and followed JC up the stairs to the small bedroom at the end of the hallway. From the looks of the room, it had probably belonged to one of JC's aunts before being converted into a guest room-cum-sewing room. "You will be more comfortable at the house," Olivier said. "You won't have to share your space with Abuela's sewing machine."

"The sewing machine doesn't bother me. It's the way my family comes in all the time when I'm not here. I know Abuela and my aunts have stuff in here, but they always end up moving my stuff too." JC was no stranger to sharing rooms when traveling for swimming, but that wasn't the same. He never felt like his roommates or the housekeeping staff were going through his stuff. His family didn't mean anything by it, he knew, but he didn't have to like it. "But I don't have to worry about that anymore, either."

"No, you won't," Olivier agreed. He wanted to bring up the kiss from the night before, to ask if JC had really meant it, but JC was acting like nothing had happened, like nothing had changed, and Olivier didn't want to rock the boat. He would help JC pack, and tonight after the results show, if they were both coming back, he'd test the waters a little more.

"Exactly." JC checked the hall to make sure none of his cousins were lurking and shut the door. "And I'll have more time to spend with you."

That sounded hopeful. "I look forward to it, although we should be careful of the cameras and of our cast mates. I am… not as open about my private life as you have been."

JC nodded. He understood, for the moment at least. If this went somewhere, they'd have to talk about it, but while they were just stealing kisses and perhaps a bit more, there was no need for Olivier to worry about what people would think. "What about my family? I wanted to kiss you downstairs, but I didn't know how comfortable you'd be in front of Abuela."

"I don't know," Olivier replied honestly. "I don't deny that I'm gay. I've just always done my best to make it so no one asks because it's not their business. With your family, if we are together, it is their business. You're their business. But only if this is serious. It's not worth the risk if we're just... what's the phrase? Messing around?"

JC bristled at the implication. "My family isn't a risk. They haven't said anything to anyone about Joel and Chelsea, and they won't say anything about you. If you don't want to tell them yet, that's fine, but they're not gossips. Family business is family business, and no one needs to know about it. And that includes the business of anyone who comes into our home."

Olivier winced. Given JC's reaction, he had explained himself poorly. "I think that did not come out the way I meant it. They are wonderful people, your family, and I am already very comfortable here, but I am a private person by nature. To show that side of myself to anyone, it is not something I do easily. If all we can have is a few secret nights together, I don't want to involve anyone but us. Your abuela, she won't see a kiss as just a kiss. She will see it as leading to more. She will see a kiss and plan a wedding."

He had a point. JC didn't like it, but it was probably a valid one. Abuela did tend to take things to the extreme, particularly when it involved the happiness of any of her children or grandchildren. If JC told her he wanted to marry Olivier, she'd either move the entire family somewhere it was legal, or single-handedly attempt to convince everyone in the United States that they needed to legalize gay marriage immediately. She'd probably come close to succeeding too.

"All right, we won't tell her," he said, smiling at the thought of what Abuela would do. "As long as you kiss me now."

Olivier felt the tension leave his shoulders as he stepped close enough to press a tender kiss to JC's mouth. Sometime soon, when they were assured both time and privacy, he'd kiss JC the way he really wanted to, but he was acutely conscious of JC's family outside the door, and he wasn't at all sure they would knock before they barged in if they decided to come see what JC and Olivier were up to.

JC leaned into the kiss and pulled Olivier back when he tried to step away. "My family won't come in," he murmured against Olivier's lips. "We have rules about closed doors."

Well, in that case….

Olivier angled his whole body toward JC's, bringing the full length of the slim strong body against his. JC smelled fresh, although Olivier couldn't identify the scent exactly, and that only increased his desire. He took his time deepening the kiss, nibbling on JC's lower lip before sucking it into his mouth.

JC let Olivier take the lead at first, setting whatever pace he was comfortable with, but once Olivier started sucking, all bets were off. He wrapped his arms around Olivier's neck and stretched up on his toes, easing the height difference between them. He could feel Olivier's muscles as he pressed against them. He made a mental note to properly admire all of them later as he tilted his head and deepened the kiss further, determined to give as good as he got.

Olivier groaned beneath the sudden onslaught, meeting JC's tongue with his own. JC tasted of coffee and mint, left over from breakfast and toothpaste, probably. The flavor shouldn't have been appealing, but Olivier couldn't get enough of it. He licked and sucked on JC's lips until he had to break away to breathe.

"Oh." JC took a moment to catch his breath and bring his brain back online. His lips still tingled from the kiss, and the rapid pattering of his heart drowned out the ambient sounds of the house. "We should do that again sometime." Preferably very soon. Definitely before they left the room.

"There are no cameras in the bedrooms at the house—only in the common areas, and only during rehearsal hours," Olivier said as he nuzzled JC's jaw. "As long as we are discreet about coming and going, we can do it whenever you want."

JC tipped his head back to give Olivier better access. "Good. Because I don't think I can live with you and never touch you." He guided Olivier's chin up and kissed him again, not as deeply this time. He wanted to keep going and see where this might lead, but he could hear his family moving around downstairs and knew they'd start to get suspicious soon. No one would dare violate the closed-door policy of Abuela's house, but that didn't mean his cousins wouldn't tease them.

Reluctantly, JC stepped back and took Olivier's hands in his so they wouldn't wander. "We should pack and get over to the house or people will start to talk."

"Which people?" Olivier asked, but he let JC end the kiss. "Your family or our costars?"

God, JC hadn't even thought about their costars. He groaned. "Both, probably. Definitely my family. Somehow they'll know what we're doing up here if we don't go down soon."

"Then we should pack," Olivier said. "Abuela promised us lunch." As if on cue, his stomach growled.

OLIVIER HAD no real idea what to expect when they got back to the cast house later that day to prepare for the results show. JC had announced his intention of moving in if he survived elimination, but with everyone pretty much free for the day, Olivier didn't know if anyone would be around to greet them.

It almost looked like they were going to sneak in unnoticed, but as Olivier was leading JC to his room, Amber came out of hers. "JC! You're here!" she exclaimed with a little squeak in her voice.

JC braced himself as she scampered down the hallway toward them. He'd been surprised by Amber so far, but he wasn't sure how much of her attitude was for the cameras and how much was genuine. "Yep." He rocked back on his heels as she stopped in front of them. "I figured I'm either moving in here or headin' back to Texas, so I might as well pack and move out of Abuela's while I had a free day. Tomorrow's going to be busy either way."

Amber beamed, her smile genuine rather than the fake one JC had seen on television. "I'm glad you're here. Now the whole family is together. And I'm sure you'll be sticking around for a few more weeks, at least."

Olivier hoped it would be more than a few weeks, but none of them had any guarantees. Last week, the weakest dancer had gone home, but more than once, he'd seen strong dancers go home too soon because fans assumed their good scores meant they were safe. JC had gotten the first nine of the season, but that didn't guarantee anything. "It will be sad to see anyone go."

Well, maybe not Eugene, but he did not say that aloud. He didn't see any cameras, but that didn't mean they weren't around or that someone wouldn't overhear and ask him about it later. The last thing he wanted was to create ill will in the house or on set.

"True, but I hope you're right, Amber. I'd much rather move in here than head back to Texas tomorrow." He could, of course, stay at Abuela's as long as he wanted provided it didn't interfere with swim practice, but it wouldn't be the same. He wouldn't get to see Olivier every day.

"I am." Amber winked and headed down the hall. "It's nice to have you here, JC."

"Thanks," he said, a little stunned, and then he turned to Olivier. "Is she always that… enthusiastic?"

"Only with people she likes," Olivier said, "but frequently, yes. It is hard not to like her, though. She has… joy within her, and it is contagious." Amber was the most energetic person in the house, but while Olivier frequently got tired just watching her, he always left her with a smile on his face and feeling more at ease with the world. He could not say the same for everyone in the cast.

"Huh." JC shrugged. It wasn't what he'd expected from Amber when he'd first learned she'd be on the show, but then he'd learned through swimming that his expectations didn't always match reality. "Good to know." He went into the room Olivier indicated was his and dropped his bags on the bed. He wasn't going to jinx anything by unpacking, though he was fairly certain he was safe tonight.

"The only one you need to be careful of is Eugene, but you knew that already," Olivier said. "Everyone else is *aimable*, um, amiable? Some are even more friendly. Living together like we do, it is hard not to be friends as we share stories of tired muscles and aching feet."

"Good." JC was familiar with the concept from training with the Olympic swim team. At international events, he'd exchanged friendly banter with teammates and rivals alike. At least here everyone spoke the same language, even if English wasn't always their first language. "Is there anything you guys usually do on Wednesdays?" He wanted to bond with the other cast members while he had the chance. Someone was going home tonight.

"We spend most of the day at the pool," Olivier said. "The pros are busy practicing for their routines tonight. We won't see them until it's time to leave for the studio, so we take today to nurse blisters and drink beer." He winked at JC. "You would be very popular if you wore your suit."

JC laughed and started digging in his bag for his trunks. Out of habit he'd packed them in an outer pocket where they were easily accessible and wouldn't get his other things damp if it was put away wet. "Will everyone be disappointed if I don't wear a Speedo?"

"I will be," Olivier said, pitching his voice to a near whisper so no one else would hear.

"Well, in that case...." JC pushed his swim trunks back into the bag and pulled out the tiny suit most people still thought of when they pictured competitive swimwear. His actual racing suit looked almost like bicycle shorts and covered him from his navel to his knees, but he didn't think that was the one Olivier was referring to, despite the brand name it bore.

He held the tiny suit in one hand as he guided Olivier to the door. "Meet me down at the pool after you've changed?" They'd all seen each other in various states of undress during the competition, but that was different from blatantly changing into a swimsuit in front of Olivier. The first was harmless and hardly noticed in the rush to get ready to go on stage. The second, well, that was a big step up from kissing, and JC wasn't ready to go there just yet.

"I will be waiting," Olivier said with as much promise in his voice as he could muster.

CHAPTER 11

JC PULLED the shorts and a T-shirt he'd been wearing over his suit before he headed down to the courtyard. He had no problem wearing the skimpy Speedo in the pool—either for swimming laps or just horsing around—but he wasn't comfortable enough with the rest of the cast to just show up in it, no matter how much Olivier would enjoy it.

Kevan looked up when JC came out onto the pool deck, still in his shorts and T-shirt. "Not swimming?" he asked. "I thought you loved the water."

"Maybe he just isn't an exhibitionist," Rini teased from where she was seated on the edge of the pool, her bright yellow bikini surprisingly flattering against her golden skin. "Not everyone here has posed for a racy album cover like you, or a nude calendar like Olivier."

"I just didn't want to stun you all when I made my entrance," JC said jokingly as he pulled off his shirt. "Walking out in a Speedo might be too much for some of you."

Deborah looked at JC's chest and shrugged. "I don't know. Why don't you take off the shorts and let us decide?"

"*Bonne idée*," Olivier said with an exaggerated leer. The girls laughed, so he hoped they took it as the joke he wanted it to appear, but JC would know the truth.

"We'll make it a competition," Rini said. "Amber will know how to set it up. Hey, Amber, come over here for a minute."

Amber swam across the pool to join them. "What's up?"

"We're going to have a beauty pageant for Olivier and JC," Deborah said. "We need you to help us set it up."

Amber grinned. "Oh, this is going to be fun. Lose the board shorts, JC. It's Speedos or Olivier wins hands-down, even with the T-shirt on."

"Hey, why's it just those two?" Kevan asked. "I want in."

"Then get over here," Amber ordered.

JC laughed as he pushed his shorts down to his ankles. "I think I know who's going to win this one." He had a swimmer's body, lithe and lean and a little short. It didn't look bad and it served him well in competition, but it was nothing compared to Olivier's rugged frame.

"Don't be too sure," Rini said. "Not every woman likes the same kind of body in a man. You don't know which of you is our type."

"I do." Kevan strutted over and stood next to JC. "It's me, isn't it, ladies? I know everyone's been drooling over my hot bod."

Olivier wouldn't say it out loud because he didn't want to make anyone uncomfortable, but Kevan was undeniably attractive. He had a gym body, but it was a good one, and his mahogany skin certainly caught the eye. Olivier was quite sure he'd be getting a portion of the female vote on looks alone. If Olivier's own preference ran to a slimmer figure, he kept that to himself as well.

"Yes, that's exactly it," Rini said with a wink. "I didn't dance as well as I should have last night because I was thinking about your body."

"I knew it." Kevan jokingly puffed up his chest and strutted forward a few steps. "I almost didn't ask to participate because it really isn't fair to these two, but I didn't want to deprive you ladies."

"And we're oh so grateful," Deborah said smoothly. Kevan was joking—the whole beauty pageant was a joke—but JC appreciated Deborah keeping it at that level so no one's feelings would get hurt. "Amber, do you think you could tell the boys here what to do?"

"Where is Freddy?" Olivier asked. "We should not leave anyone out if they want to participate."

"He's still in rehearsals with the band for his performance tonight," Rini said. "I can't wait to hear him play. My parents love his music, so I grew up hearing how incredible he was, and tonight I get to hear it live."

"Then it is just us, unless you wish to join us, Eugene?" Olivier called. He knew what the answer would be, but it seemed only polite to ask.

Eugene looked disdainfully at the assembled group. "No, thank you," he said, the veneer of his civility growing thin. "I'll pass."

JC had expected the answer and wasn't disappointed by it. "Well, then, what do you want us to do? I usually dive into pools, not walk around them, so you're going to have to give good instructions."

"What do you think, girls?" Amber asked. "We've already watched the talent portion seeing them dance, and we've seen JC and Kevan in their formal attire, so it's just the swimsuit competition that's left. Strut your stuff, boys. We want to see just how big those muscles really are."

JC laughed and motioned to Olivier and Kevan. "After you."

"I would say I should go last so you two would have a chance, but the ladies have already seen me." Kevan strutted clockwise around the pool, flexing his muscles as he passed Amber, Rini, and Deborah.

Olivier had to look away because while the girls tittered and laughed and cooed over Kevan, Olivier couldn't help but admire Kevan's muscles, and staring at another man while standing next to the man he'd just started to get involved with would be the height of stupidity. Of course, staring at JC when it was his turn would be just as bad. He wasn't ready to out himself to the world.

JC watched Kevan until he was on the far side of the pool. The man did have a nice body, but when JC leaned in to say something about it to Olivier, he noticed Olivier's attention was on anything but Kevan. "Hey," he said, looking up at Olivier in concern. "What's wrong? You don't have to do this if you don't want to, you know. It's just for fun. Doesn't mean anything."

"I know," Olivier said. "I was just thinking about…." He stopped, took a deep breath, and pushed away everything except the spirit of fun in which the girls had proposed this "pageant" in the first place. "It does not matter. Who is next? You or me?"

JC was pretty sure it *did* matter, but this wasn't the time or place to push it. Instead, he drew himself up to his full height, thrust out his chest, and flashed a grin at the girls. "I'll go," he said and strutted away before Olivier could say anything else.

As he walked, JC did his best to imitate Kevan, but he could tell after only a few steps that it wasn't working. He didn't have Kevan's build, and instead of looking sexy as he flexed his muscles, he looked like an overgrown kid playing at being a grown man. The others pretended not to notice, but JC could see on the ladies' faces that they did. Thinking fast, he exaggerated his movements for a few steps, holding his arms out farther from his body and puffing his chest out even further. "Look at me, I'm so sexy," he said in the deepest voice he could manage.

Olivier laughed along with everyone else as JC had intended, but he couldn't stop a little thrill at the sight of JC's sharply defined arms and muscled chest. He wasn't bulky like Kevan or like Olivier himself, but Olivier would bet he could swim for hours with those arms.

Deborah, Rini, and Amber all applauded as JC joined Kevan, who slapped him on the back and then draped his arm over JC's shoulder. "Your turn, old man," Kevan goaded. "Show us what you Frenchies got."

Olivier laughed at that. He took a deep breath and pulled off his T-shirt. These were his friends, for the most part. He could let them see his scars. He closed his eyes for a moment, remembering the directions from the photographer during the *Dieux du Stade* photo shoot. Channeling all the smoldering energy that had made that shoot so popular with the calendar's customers, he prowled along the edge of the pool, making sure to look each "judge" in the eye for several long seconds.

"Fuck," JC whispered, wishing there were an unobtrusive way to hide how his body was responding to Olivier. The tiny suit he was wearing left absolutely nothing to the imagination, but putting his hands over his crotch would draw more attention to the area, not less, so he stood still and tried to think about jumping into an almost-freezing pool as he watched Olivier smolder.

"Yeah, we lost," Kevan said pragmatically. "I mean, dayum. How's a man supposed to compete with *that*?"

JC shrugged, relieved that Kevan had misinterpreted him. "Hell if I know. Guess it's a good thing we're in a dancing competition instead of a beauty pageant, huh?"

"If he ever looks at Tricia like that on the dance floor, we'll lose the dancing competition too," Kevan said. "There's not a woman in this country who would vote for anyone else, fan or not, if he looks at the camera that way."

"True." Not that JC could blame them. Olivier did look magnificent. As he got closer, JC leered and wiggled his eyebrows. "Lookin' good!"

Olivier stopped and preened a little under JC's gaze. Kevan roared with laughter, the sound taking the edge off the moment and keeping it from being more revealing than it could have been. Then, starting to feel ridiculous, he dropped the sultry act and joined the other two men. "I passed?" he asked.

"Passed?" Kevan looked at Olivier incredulously. "I think you *won*."

"Really? I was just playing around." Olivier hadn't really meant to steal the show. He'd been trying to find a way to feel a little less self-conscious with his scars there for everyone to see. He turned back to the ladies in the pool. "I didn't win. Did I?"

Deborah, Amber, and Rini conferred quietly for a moment, and then Amber nodded. "I think you took home the grand prize, but JC was the funniest, and Kevan had the best walk."

"I'm going to make up trophies for all of you," Rini promised. "And Deborah is going to make certificates you can hang on your walls."

JC covered his eyes with one hand. "Oh God. Promise me you won't tell Mama or Abuela. Any of you. If you do, they'll tell my aunts and cousins, and I'll never hear the end of it."

"And what do we get in return?" Rini asked with a wicked grin. "Keeping secrets like that comes at a cost."

JC looked at her with wide eyes, dread heavy in the pit of his stomach. "I. Um. *Please?*"

"Just remember you owe us a favor," Amber said, coming to JC's rescue. "We'll decide what it is later, but when we call it in, you have to follow through, or we'll tell Abuela."

"Sure," JC said, willing to promise anything for them to not tell his family. He could easily picture himself in eighty years, with his entire family all gathered around to once again hear the story of how he was voted funniest in an impromptu beauty pageant while on a dance show. By that point it would be embellished beyond recognition, he was sure, and it was that thought that let him push down the dread he felt wondering what the women would ask for... and when.

AFTER THE elimination show that night, JC led Olivier to his new room and sat down on the bed with a sigh. "That gets more painful every week."

"The dancing or the elimination round?" Olivier asked, though he thought he knew. He hadn't known Troy all that well and Makayla only a little better, but of the remaining competitors, he would only be glad to see Eugene go home.

"The elimination." JC slipped off his shoes but left them on the floor, figuring he'd put them away when he unpacked. "I'm not going to miss Makayla, really, but I was afraid someone I like was going to go home." Or that he would go, though that hadn't been likely given his score last night. "We're making friends here, and soon one of our friends will leave."

"That's the way this works, unfortunately," Olivier said, "but you're right. There's only one person remaining I want to see go. Everyone else could just stay and dance all season, and I'd be fine with it. Freddy was amazing tonight. Can you imagine not having him around? Or not having Kevan to join us in being all 'manly' like he did today at the pool? Or the girls to judge us and make it fun?"

"Oh, I think it would be *plenty* of fun without the girls. Or Kevan." JC smirked and looked Olivier up and down. He didn't look quite as good wearing the remnants of his dance costume covered with a tracksuit as he had in his swimsuit, but JC wasn't complaining. "Then I could ogle you the way I wanted to this afternoon."

Olivier laughed even as heat rose in him. He'd had the same desire and wasn't sure he'd hidden it successfully, although no one had called him on it yet. "So I should do a repeat performance?"

JC laughed along with Olivier even as he grew aroused at the idea of seeing Olivier shirtless again. "You'd have to strip if you're going to be accurate," he said huskily. "It won't be the same if you're wearing that."

"Should I be worried about my virtue?" Olivier joked even as he shrugged off the light jacket he'd donned for the trip back to the house. He hoped the answer was *hell yes*. After watching JC at the pool earlier in the day, Olivier was more than ready to get better acquainted with that body.

JC slipped his jacket off as well and started unbuttoning his shirt. If Olivier was going to strip, it was only fair he did so as well. "Maybe a little bit." He wasn't ready to go too far yet, not until he knew how soundproof this house was, but he was willing to challenge Olivier's virtue a little. "If you want."

Olivier couldn't resist the invitation in JC's comment. With a wordless growl, he batted JC's hands away and finished unbuttoning his shirt so he could separate the two sides and reveal the smooth, tanned skin he hadn't been able to admire the way he wanted to with the others around. "Do you have *any* idea how fucking gorgeous you are?"

"Me?" JC squawked, flailing his hands for a moment before he found purchase on Olivier's hips. "I'm gangly! I'm not built like you are. You're gorgeous. I'm just… odd." He wasn't ashamed of his body, but it didn't fit his definition of gorgeous. His muscles were understated rather than defined, and he was short and skinny compared to Olivier.

"You're like… *une loutre*," Olivier said, struggling to remember the word in English. All his blood rushing south at the sight of JC's bare chest did nothing to help him. "An otter. That's the word. You're like an otter—long and slim and sleek and so graceful in the water. I've seen you swim. You're perfect."

JC blushed and looked down. He'd never thought of himself that way before, and though it wasn't his idea of perfect, apparently it was Olivier's. "Thanks," he said softly. He didn't understand how anyone could see him like that.

Olivier knew JC wasn't convinced, so he suited actions to words and ran his hands down JC's chest as he leaned in for a kiss. Maybe that would convince JC of his sincerity.

As Olivier kissed him, JC's doubts started to melt away. He didn't understand, but as he opened his mouth to let Olivier in, he decided it didn't matter why. Olivier clearly saw something in him that he didn't see in himself. As long as that lasted, he would gladly reap the benefits and do everything he could to keep Olivier around.

Olivier deepened the kiss, taking everything JC offered and demanding more. He wasn't a domineering lover normally, but something about JC's self-deprecation made him want to spread JC out beneath him and lavish attention on him until he screamed. Maybe then he'd believe how attractive Olivier found him. He backed them toward the bed, catching JC around the waist and shoulders to lower him to the mattress. Only then did he break the kiss to pepper kisses along JC's jaw. He wanted to nibble and even bite, but he wouldn't risk leaving marks the cameras might pick up tomorrow. He'd save that for another time, when they didn't have to worry about someone asking the wrong questions.

JC gasped and arched up, pressing his body against Olivier's as best he could as Olivier lavished him with attention. "God," he whispered as he grabbed Olivier's shoulders, desperate to touch him. The way Olivier caressed him, with care and tenderness and awe, made JC feel like he really was as gorgeous as Olivier said.

Olivier worked his way down JC's smooth, flawless chest, the muscles sleek and strong beneath his touch, proof of the hours JC spent in the pool. He slid his hands lower, finding the waistband of JC's pants. "If you want me to stop, tell me now. If you don't, I'm going to make you scream."

"No, don't stop." JC barely managed to gasp out the words. Olivier's hands were smooth and warm against JC's sensitive skin. He wanted more, wanted Olivier to keep going until he couldn't take it anymore and then push him past the point where he cared if anyone heard him or not. "I want this."

That was all Olivier needed to hear. He moved so he covered JC completely with the breadth of his body, gasping as he did so at the contact of skin to skin. Even where they still wore clothes, the contact burned through him, making him wonder if he'd last long enough to get the screams he wanted. He wasn't inexperienced by any definition of the word, but he couldn't remember the last time so simple a touch had felt so damn good. He rutted against the juncture of JC's thighs, seeking the friction that would drive them both wild.

JC's breath caught in his throat as Olivier moved. Even clothed, the friction was enough to drive him mad, and he rutted back as best he could pinned against the bed. He needed more contact, more skin, just *more*. "Please," he whispered as he slid his hands down Olivier's back, seeking contact that would let him touch as much as possible without getting in Olivier's way.

"Please what, *bébé*?" Olivier teased before he latched on to a patch of skin below JC's ribs. He nibbled lightly on it for a moment before lifting his head to meet JC's eyes. "What do you want?"

"You," JC said, meeting Olivier's gaze. He could lose himself in it, if given the chance, though at the moment, he had more pressing desires than just staring into Olivier's eyes. "Just. Touch me. Make me scream like you promised."

"*Comme tu veux*," Olivier murmured. He lifted up onto his knees and immediately missed the contact of their bodies, but he had a promise to keep to JC. He traced the line of JC's lips with the tip of one finger, then trailed it down JC's midline until he reached the button of his trousers. He teased beneath the waistband, watching as JC's pupils dilated with lust. He let his hand settle over the bulge in JC's pants and rubbed lightly.

JC let out an incoherent sound that wasn't quite a scream, but it was close. He wasn't going to last long if he reacted like this to just the brush of Olivier's fingers, but he couldn't help himself. Weeks of wanting Olivier paired with the stress of the competition had left him especially sensitive. He wasn't sure he'd have been able to do anything even if he wasn't determined to let Olivier have his way.

As it was he curled his fingers into the sheets beneath him and arched up into Olivier's touch. He cried out again, only belatedly remembering there were people who might hear him if he got too loud. "God, Olivier, don't stop. Please."

"I'm not stopping," Olivier promised as he repeated the caress, more firmly this time. "I won't stop until you've forgotten everything but my name." He popped open the button on JC's pants and worked his hand underneath. JC's underwear still kept him from finding skin, but he didn't want to rush. If one of them was eliminated next week and this was their only chance to be together, he wanted it to be one for the memory books.

"Good." JC willed himself to relax some. It was hard with Olivier hovering over him and the memory of Olivier's touch still burning on his chest, but slowly, JC managed. Olivier's hand was warm against him, even through his underwear, and he focused on that. The gentle brush of Olivier's fingers sent tendrils of pleasure swirling up JC's spine. He moaned as he relaxed into it and gazed up at Olivier with lust. "More."

Olivier grinned down at him and flexed his fingers. He might not have JC's skill in the water, but years of playing rugby had made him very, very good with his hands. JC wriggled beneath his touch, so Olivier did it again. He found the placket at the front of JC's briefs and worked his fingers beneath the fabric. When he found hot, smooth skin, he paused, letting the moment stretch between them.

The feeling of Olivier touching him through his clothes was nothing compared to the feeling of his smooth, warm fingers directly on JC's sensitive skin. The small bit of control he'd managed to hold onto fled, and he curled his fingers around Olivier's hand, holding it in place as he thrust up into it. "Not going to last," he hissed.

"I don't want you to," Olivier replied. He worked his fingers up and down the length of JC's shaft and leaned over to kiss him. Just before their lips touched, he whispered, "Let go for me."

Those words were all it took. As Olivier's lips touched his, JC lost the last bit of control he'd been clinging to. His body shuddered with release as he screamed into Olivier's mouth. If he'd been coherent enough to think of it, he'd have been grateful for the way Olivier muffled his cry, but that wasn't a consideration at the moment. He didn't care if anyone else heard, didn't care what anyone else might say or think. All he was aware of were the waves of pleasure rolling through his body, the press of Olivier above him, and the taste of Olivier on his tongue.

JC's climax was every bit as beautiful as Olivier had known it would be. He rutted against JC's hip, needing release but not willing to break the kiss long enough to ask for JC's help. He sucked JC's tongue deeper into his mouth and gave in to the marvelous friction against his cock. His release rolled through him with all the force of an avalanche, leaving him sweaty and panting into JC's mouth.

JC slid his hands up and tangled them in Olivier's hair, holding him still as he deepened the kiss. Fire raced through him as their tongues touched, but it was a mere candle compared to the raging inferno of a moment ago. The kiss was warm and comforting and just a little bit exciting, the perfect way to pull himself together after letting Olivier take him apart. When he could think again, JC loosened his grip on Olivier and pulled back just enough to take a deep breath without pulling the air from Olivier's lungs. "Wow."

"That is one word for it," Olivier agreed as he nuzzled JC's jaw. They needed to catch their breaths and begin to calm down, but he was loath to lose contact yet. He rubbed their cheeks together and breathed in the heady scent of sex that hung between them. Fuck, he hoped this would be more than a one-time thing. He sure as hell wasn't ready for it to be over.

"Don't think I have the brainpower to come up with anything else at the moment," JC admitted with a chuckle. He slid his hands down Olivier's back, not willing to let go, and tilted his head so Olivier could nuzzle at his neck. "Don't think I have the brainpower to do anything but lie here, really." They needed to clean up and go to bed properly so they would be ready for another grueling day of practice in the morning, but the thought of moving was too much at the moment.

"Ask me tomorrow," Olivier agreed. "Tomorrow I give you all the right words for it." He rolled to one side and pulled JC closer. They needed to get up, but it could wait a few more minutes. He wasn't ready to move yet.

CHAPTER 12

JC JERKED awake as an obnoxiously loud sound echoed through the room, sending his body into hyperawareness even as his brain struggled to keep up. There was too much to process—an unfamiliar noise waking him up, a warm body pressed against his back, and a room bare of the decorations he'd gotten used to. His breath caught in his throat as his muscles tensed, and then he remembered. Moving into the house. Olivier taking him apart last night. And then… nothing.

He realized they must have fallen asleep just as the knock sounded again. "JC?" Chelsea asked, her voice only slightly muffled by the door. "Are you in there?"

Olivier jolted awake at the sound of Chelsea's voice that had no place in his dreams or in his usual morning routine. "*Merde*," he muttered as he realized where he was, what must have happened, and the condition of his pants. "We fell asleep."

"Yeah," JC said softly. His boxers were stuck to his thighs, and he was on top of the covers when he usually burrowed under them. If anyone saw them like this, they'd know immediately what happened. "Sorry!" he called out a little louder, directing his voice toward the door. "Forgot to set an alarm last night."

"If she sees me in here, she will know," Olivier said. He was stating the obvious, but he had to know how JC felt about it. To his surprise the thought didn't make him want to run for the hills or hide under the bed, but that was a huge step to take without giving JC a choice in the matter. He could hide in the closet—oh, the irony—or in the en suite bathroom if JC wasn't ready to take the chance of Chelsea knowing about them.

"They'll probably figure it out anyway. I bet Tricia's looking for you too." The idea of Chelsea knowing didn't bother him at all, but he wasn't the one who was hiding his sexuality from the world at large. He rolled over so he could look Olivier straight in the eyes. "I don't care who knows about us. The whole world knows I'm bi. But if you don't want everyone to know, our best bet might be to let Chelsea and Tricia in on it so they can help us hide instead of inadvertently letting the rest of the house know."

"I'm not ashamed of being gay," Olivier said slowly. "It was never anyone else's business, that's all. It still isn't their business, but I think Chelsea and Tricia need to know, if only so we can ask them to be discreet with that knowledge. On the other hand, I don't really want to tell them while I'm sticky with the proof of what we got up to last night. Maybe we could send her away and tell them each at practice today?"

"I can try," JC said dubiously. "I'll be down in ten minutes, okay, Chelsea?"

"Hey, JC?" The voice didn't belong to Chelsea.

"Yeah?" He looked at Olivier with dread. How had Tricia found them?

"You don't know where Olivier went last night, do you? Didn't you two ride back together?"

"I'm here," Olivier said with a sigh. "I will also need ten minutes before I can be ready for practice."

"We'll leave you to get ready, then," Tricia said. He could hear the smirk in her voice, but there wasn't anything he could do about it now. He'd throw himself on her mercy before they turned the cameras on and hope she was willing to work with him.

JC flopped onto his back and stared unblinking at the ceiling. "Well, that wasn't how I expected to start my first full day in the house."

"It's not how I expected to start any day," Olivier amended, "but it happened. We just have to deal with it." He was surprised at how sanguine he felt about the whole thing, but this felt right, and he wasn't going to question it. "I don't think they'll care, do you?"

"No." JC rolled over and kissed Olivier lightly on the lips. "I didn't say it was bad, just unexpected." He grinned as he climbed off the bed. "Now come on, we're losing rehearsal time."

"SO, THIS week we have the rumba," Tricia said as soon as Olivier walked into the studio where they would be rehearsing. He breathed a sigh of relief that she refrained from commenting on where he had slept last night. "It's a deceptively simply dance because it's slow compared to all the others."

"Deceptively?" he asked.

"The slow rhythm means there's time for the judges to see every mistake in your movement. In a fast dance, they might—only might, of course—miss seeing a small mistake, but in the rumba, there's nowhere to hide. It's also a dance that is all about the emotion between the couple. You have to make the world believe in the emotion we choose to portray." She paused for a moment before giving him a mischievous grin. "You can imagine I'm JC if that makes it easier."

He groaned. "Tease me all you want when we're alone, but not when the cameras are on, please. Our relationship is private, not for the viewers."

"I wouldn't talk about you and JC in front of the cameras any more than I would talk about Chelsea and Joel," Tricia said softly. "No matter what the relationship, it's not my place to tell the whole world about it. I will keep your secret and so will everyone who works here unless you want it aired. This is a dance competition, not a fake romance drama."

"*Merci*," Olivier said. "Thank you. I know that. It's just… habit, I guess. In professional sports, it is hard to be gay. That will change. It is already changing, but it is not easy. I never had anyone to talk about, so it was easy to say I was single and nothing else. Maybe I will say more later, but right now, it is still so new."

"You know," she said slowly, "I think you just gave me an idea for our dance."

"What is that?"

"The newness, the tentative first steps of a relationship, wanting it to be something special, wanting it to be the one that lasts but not yet at the point of knowing. Yes, I think we can work with that, and given that you're in that place in your life, it should make the emotion easier to portray," she mused. "Now to find the music that will work with it."

"Something instrumental," Olivier said. "So that *we* tell the story, not the lyrics."

"Yes. Debussy, I think. *Clair de lune*. It starts out slowly, almost tentatively, and then builds quite dramatically. That should work for us.

And the changes in time signature and rhythm will add a level of difficulty to the routine that the judges will appreciate."

"If we do it right."

"We will," Tricia said. "We'll put in the hours it takes. Now, let's get started."

CHELSEA SMIRKED at JC when he walked into the studio. "Good night last night?"

"Yep." There was no point denying it. She'd heard Olivier in his room, and if he wanted her on their side, he couldn't lie about why Olivier had been there. Instead, he played it up for all he was worth, smiling widely as he sauntered across the room. "The *best*."

Her smirk turned into a real smile. "Good. Just don't let it get in the way of rehearsal time. We have the rumba this week, and with your long arms, we're going to really have to work to make it elegant."

JC bit back a groan. He hated it when his arms got in the way, but there was no point in complaining. They made him a great swimmer, and that was far more important than being a great dancer, though perhaps not right at this particular moment. He shook out the offending limbs and joined Chelsea over by the CD player, where she was sorting through a stack of discs. "That's it? You're not going to give me a hard time about it?"

"Do you want me to?" Chelsea looked at him with a raised eyebrow. "I figure you're here to dance, and whatever you have with Olivier is between the two of you, but if it'll help you focus on the rumba, I can tease you more."

"No. I just thought—" He shrugged and looked away, unsure exactly what he wanted to say. "I didn't know if it would be a problem, that's all."

"Only if you or Olivier make it one. If you don't want the viewers to know, don't tell the other contestants."

JC shuddered at the thought of Eugene finding out about his relationship with Olivier. "What about the crew and the other pros?"

"Don't flaunt it, and they'll keep your secret just like they've kept Joel's and mine." She paused, assessing JC for a moment. "And Luis's."

"Luis's?"

"You and Olivier aren't the only gay men on set," Chelsea said. "Luis's husband comes to all the shows when he's in town. Always sits in the same spot in the audience. The cameramen are careful never to focus on him so the viewers don't start wondering why the same man is in the audience almost every week."

"I didn't know."

"With an idiot like Eugene among the contestants, did you really think Luis would say anything?" Chelsea retorted.

"Fair enough." JC felt something lift off his shoulders, and he stood a little straighter. It was easier to imagine the crew protecting him and Olivier now that he knew they were protecting Luis too. "So, what do I need to know to dance the rumba?"

"It's sensual. You want to look like you're seducing me on the dance floor, drawing me in for a night of long, slow lovemaking." She stepped toward him and brought one hand elegantly up to cup the back of his head and then slid it down over his shoulder. "It needs to be precise and polished but still graceful."

JC swallowed hard as Chelsea stepped back. She could certainly sell the act. If he hadn't known she was head over heels for Joel, he would have thought she was coming on to him. "Precise and polished I can do." That sort of movement was key to propelling himself quickly through the water. "Graceful… I'll try." He did have a certain grace, especially when he was in the pool, but it wasn't the kind Chelsea was talking about.

"Just pretend I'm Olivier," she teased lightly. "Seduce him while you're dancing with me. It'll be a night to remember when the show ends."

"Is that experience talking?" he teased back. Her shit-eating grin was the only answer he needed.

OLIVIER SANK into the hot tub with a groan, relieved to be done with rehearsals and free of the cameras for the day. The bubbling water and the pressure of the jets soothed his aching muscles. He still didn't understand how dancing could be harder than rugby training, but he hadn't gotten to the end of a day without hurting. He smiled absently at

Deborah and Amber, already chin deep in the water, and wondered where JC was and if anybody had actually thought to mention the hot tub to him. He thought about going to look for him, but that would require getting out and drying off. He'd give JC a few more minutes and hope he followed the others in. If not, he'd go looking for him.

It took JC a lot longer than expected to change into his swimsuit. He hadn't hurt much during practice, but the few moments he spent sitting on his bed when he went to change were enough to let his muscles start tightening, and he ached in all new ways. He was tempted to collapse on the bed and not move again until morning, but the thought of warm water and the relief it would bring got him moving.

"God," he moaned as he sank into the tub next to Olivier. At the moment he hurt too much to regret the few inches of space they had to keep between them for appearance's sake. "How am I not used to this exercise yet?"

"I don't know," Olivier said, "but I'm not either. It isn't even a fast dance. The rumba should be easier than the jive."

"Sometimes it's harder to move slowly," Deborah said from the other side of the hot tub. "Everyone watches the ice skaters and comments on the jumps. Yes, those are technically difficult. It's easy to fall. But in terms of strain on your muscles, the long, slow glides are more challenging because you have to hold still or move with perfect control. The rumba is the same way. Controlling the movement takes more effort than just doing it haphazardly."

"Like yoga," Amber added. "You'd think it would be easy to hold poses—at least the easy ones—and move slowly between them, but it's not. At least, not until you build up some stamina."

JC nodded. He'd tried yoga a couple of times with the team, and it was harder than it looked. "Makes sense. It just doesn't feel like it should be so hard to move slowly."

Olivier shifted on the bench as the image of moving slowly over JC flashed through his mind. They hadn't had the patience for slow last night, but Olivier would remedy that the next time they could arrange to be alone together. He sank a little deeper into the water. No one could see his growing erection through the turbulence of the water jets, but that didn't override the instinctive need to hide it.

"Scoot over, Olivier," Tricia said, climbing into the hot tub next to him. "You're hogging half the bench."

Olivier obediently moved to give her room, only to come into contact with JC's leg next to him. He turned back to Tricia, who smiled and said, "Thank you, and you're welcome."

JC could have shifted when Olivier's leg touched his, but it felt too right not to take the convenient excuse Tricia was offering. He put his hands in his lap, covering his growing erection, and pressed his leg back against Olivier's. "Are you both dancing the rumba too?" he asked Amber and Deborah, hoping the conversation would distract him from his thoughts of jerking Olivier off right there.

"No, I have the samba," Amber said. "I'll get the rumba later, I guess. If I last long enough, of course."

"You're a very good dancer," Olivier said. "I'm sure you will be around for many more weeks."

"Maybe," she said, "but my fan base isn't as devoted as some of the others, and we all know that can tip the scales."

"It can," Tricia agreed, "but there are fans of the show rather than of individual stars who will vote based on who dances well. What are you dancing this week, Deborah?"

"The rumba too," she said. Behind her, the timer on her phone beeped. "And that's my cue to get out. I'll see you all at breakfast, probably."

"I should get out too," Amber said. "As good as the hot water feels, I'm pushing the limit of how long it's safe to stay in. Have a good night."

"You too," Olivier said automatically. With Deborah and Amber gone, it left only Tricia and JC in the tub with him. He should move to maintain the illusion of mere friendship with JC, but Tricia knew about them already, and it felt so good to have JC pressed against his side.

Soon after the other two women disappeared into the house, Tricia hauled herself out of the water as well. "Enjoy the tub," she said as she wrapped a towel around her waist. "Just remember other people use it too."

Chapter 13

JC LOOKED down to hide his grin as Tricia left. "What's the fun in remembering that?" he asked as he slid his hand over to Olivier's thigh and up toward his groin. Olivier's board shorts made it hard to tell exactly what was underneath, but he stopped when he thought his hand was just short of anywhere that could be considered inappropriate.

Olivier let his head fall back against the edge of the tub as JC ran a hand up his thigh. The arousal that had simmered from the casual brush of their legs beneath the water spiked at the more deliberate touch. "I don't know." He turned his head, seeking JC's lips for a kiss, but JC hovered just out of easy reach. "Tease."

"Lazy." JC grinned so Olivier would know he was kidding and leaned in to close the distance between them. As their lips touched, he squeezed Olivier's thigh, eliciting a very pleasant sound from him, and then he slid his hand across Olivier's lap. "Not teasing," he whispered when he pulled back for air.

"*Merde*," Olivier cursed as he arched into JC's caress. "You're going to drive me crazy." He reached for JC's hip and tugged until he straddled Olivier's lap. He nipped briefly at JC's lips. "Drive me crazy."

"Gladly." JC looped his arms around Olivier's neck and rocked his hips forward. His cock grew hard as he rubbed against Olivier, and he could feel Olivier's responding in kind. "Like this? Or like this?" he asked, and then he leaned forward and nipped at Olivier's neck. "Or maybe like this?" With a wicked grin, he took a deep breath, slid off Olivier's lap, and submerged himself completely.

It was hard to stay down with the bubbles all around him, but JC braced his feet against the sides of the tub. It wasn't perfect, but it would work for how long he would be able to stay underwater. As soon as he was secure, he grabbed Olivier's board shorts, tugged them down, and slid his mouth around Olivier's cock.

Olivier nearly lost it right then. He reached for JC's head, sure this was a bad idea and he'd end up drowning his new lover, but JC resisted his attempt to tug him to the surface, sucking on him even harder. Olivier gave up trying to control the situation. JC practically lived in the water. Surely he knew his own limits. Instead he let his eyes droop closed and focused on the edgy decadence of JC's mouth around him in the middle of the hot tub where anyone could come out and find them.

JC sucked Olivier's cock all the way into his mouth and pulled back slowly, counting on the dual sensations of the water and his tongue to drive Olivier mad. He swirled his tongue around the tip for a moment and then, lungs burning, he surfaced and grinned wickedly. "That what you had in mind?"

Olivier couldn't even summon the breath to reply. JC had stolen it with his devilish smile and talented tongue. He managed to nod.

"JC?"

Olivier flinched at the interruption, hastily righting his bathing suit beneath the water.

JC momentarily froze at the intruding voice. "Yeah?" he called out as he pushed himself across the hot tub to the nearest bench, hoping it would just look like he'd been changing seats to whoever was interrupting.

"Your mother is on the phone." Amber stepped out onto the deck, holding the cordless phone from the kitchen. "She said she couldn't reach you on your cell phone, so she called the house."

Fuck. JC had promised to call her tonight and had forgotten with everything that had happened today. He winced at Olivier. "I should take this. Sorry."

Olivier nodded again, not trusting his voice while Amber was present. As soon as she handed the phone to JC and went back inside, he pulled himself out of the water. "Come find me when you're done?" he asked as he wrapped a towel around his waist to catch the water and to hide the erection that hadn't flagged in the slightest.

"Of course." JC leaned up and kissed Olivier softly. "I plan to finish what I started."

Olivier was tempted to climb back in the hot tub and wait while JC talked just to make sure he kept his promise, but he didn't feel right listening in on a family conversation. He settled for giving JC one last longing look before heading inside to shower quickly so he'd be in his room when JC was done.

JC sat on the closest pool chair and watched Olivier walk inside before he put the phone to his ear. He didn't need to hear his mother's voice as he took advantage of the only good part of Olivier walking away—the chance to admire the curves of his ass. When the door closed behind Olivier, JC sighed and reminded himself it was his mother on the phone to quickly banish any inappropriate thoughts. "Mama?"

"Hello, *mi hijo*," she said. "I hadn't heard from you since you moved into the house, and I wanted to make sure you were doing well. Do you need anything? Abuela made tamales. I could bring some by the house. And Leticia wants to know when she can come backstage and meet everyone."

"Mama! I just moved in yesterday. I haven't had a chance to call you yet. I've been busy. I'm sorry." He'd intended to call her last night after the show so he could update her on the move and the results, but then Olivier had happened and... well. "I'm good, but I wouldn't say no to tamales. We take turns cooking, and some of us are better at it than others."

"I will bring them by, then. They make good snacks too." They'd clearly been made with the intent to deliver them. "What about your cousin?"

"Leticia can come backstage Tuesday if you bring her to the show. You'll have to get here early, though." He wouldn't be able to introduce her to everyone, but if she came by early enough, he'd introduce her to the people who mattered.

"Good, I will bring the tamales today, and we will be there as early as we need to be on Tuesday. Just tell me what time." JC sighed. He'd hoped to have a little more breathing room living in the house instead of with Abuela and Mama. "Now, tell me all about practice today. What dance do you have next week? Have you decided on a song yet? What about costumes?"

"I'm dancing the rumba to 'Some Enchanted Evening,'" JC said with a laugh. As overbearing as Mama was sometimes, the way she rapidly darted from topic to topic was endearing. "We haven't done anything with costumes yet. And I'm not telling you when we do. You'll have to be surprised on Tuesday."

"Javier Carillo Webster, is that any way to talk to your mother?" JC winced at her use of his full name, but she sounded more amused than annoyed despite the associations from his childhood. They all knew they were in trouble when Mama called them out like that. "I'm going to tell Chelsea to work you extra just for that."

"Mama!" It was a familiar threat—she'd often said the same about his swim instructors—but he didn't want to relax into familiar banter now. He wanted to follow Olivier inside and finish what they'd started. "I have to leave something for you to be surprised by. I'd be terrible at describing it anyway."

She humphed at him, but she didn't press for more details. "It's too late to bring the tamales tonight. I'll bring them tomorrow so I can see what you and Chelsea are planning. That way you don't have to describe it."

"Okay, Mama." There was no point in arguing with her. She'd show up no matter what he said. "I'll let Chelsea know you're coming. I should go now, though. It's been a long day, and I have things to do still." Like eat and finish what he'd started with Olivier, though hopefully not in that order.

"I'll see you tomorrow, *niño*. Te amo." She hung up, and JC leaned back in the chair. Talking to his mother exhausted him on the best of days. When she interrupted him like she had today, it was almost more than he could take. He took a deep breath and stood up. He'd put the handset back on the cradle so anyone else could use it, and then he'd find Olivier. He had a promise to keep.

"SO TELL me what you have in mind," Bruce said as Olivier and Tricia walked into the costume department Friday morning. Olivier liked the man. He was as down-to-earth as anyone Olivier had ever met, something Bruce chalked up to being from Iowa. Salt of the earth, no-nonsense, get the job done. And he'd gotten the job done perfectly that past couple of weeks. Olivier trusted his aesthetic implicitly already.

"Something soft and flowing for me, and something loose and airy but not overly revealing for Olivier," Tricia said immediately.

"*Not* revealing?" Bruce repeated. "That's not typical on rumba night."

"We know," Olivier said. Bruce's concern was almost enough to make him reconsider, but he and Tricia had talked about this, about not making it about their bodies but about their emotions. "We did revealing for the cha-cha. We want to showcase the dancing, the emotional side of it, not my body this week."

"And it's not unheard of," Tricia added. "A hint of chest, maybe down to here." She pointed to Olivier's breastbone about halfway down his chest. "Enough to let a sense of his power come through without focusing on it."

"Mmm, yes, I see what you mean." Bruce walked around Olivier once, tapping his finger on his chin. "If you don't wear something revealing, it'll likely stand out this week. He'll get attention for not taking off his shirt. I can do a V-neck. Something with no collar and loose sleeves. What about the pants? Tight or loose?"

"It depends on the length of the shirt," Tricia said. "If it's long enough to partially cover his ass, then tight. Again, that hint of veiled power. If it's short, then loose as well. Nobody actually needs to see those oak logs he calls legs to know how muscled they are."

Olivier shook off the inclination to protest about being reduced to a collection of body parts, however attractive. The costume was supposed to make the most of his body, whether hidden or revealed. It was so much easier with his rugby uniform, though.

"With something long and untucked over tight pants, we can give the impression that he's just stumbled out of bed and thrown on a shirt without showing anything to the audience. It'll take their minds to the right place without being blatant and let the emotions of your dance do the rest. I like it."

"Maybe something medievalesque?" Olivier suggested. "*Clair de lune* is not truly medieval, but it is more classical than most songs for most dances. Laces instead of buttons on the shirt, like... have you seen *Cyrano de Bergerac*?"

"I'm a costume designer," Bruce replied. "Of course I have. Which version?

"The one with Gérard Depardieu. There's a scene toward the end where Christian isn't wearing his surcoat. A shirt like that one, maybe."

"And the tall boots as well," Bruce proposed. "What do you think, Tricia? Are you up for dancing with a medieval French knight?"

"Oh, I think so." Tricia grinned as she pictured Olivier in the costume. It was a glorious image. "And I'd be happy to wear a dress reminiscent of a medieval lady as long as it's something I can dance in."

"So no corset, obviously, but we could do the stitching to make it look like you have one on anyway," Bruce said. "Or... we're going for the idea that Olivier just rolled out of bed and threw on his shirt. Would you really be fully dressed? What about a gauzy shift of sorts? A little more elegant than an actual night rail would have been back then, but something to suggest you'd left your shared bed for some reason. Olivier mentioned *Clair de lune*. What story are you telling? Lovers reunited? Torn apart by something? Are you coming to him in the night or are you running from him and he's pursuing you?"

"Lovers reunited," Olivier said. "Something has kept them apart, something she has finally escaped, and she comes to him in moonlight."

Bruce's grin widened. "Then what about this? We'll do an overdress with the gauzy shift underneath it, and as you dance, Olivier can work the laces of the overdress. Toward the end, he can slip it off your shoulders, Tricia, and whisk you off to bed in nothing but your shift."

"We can work with that," Tricia said. "The audience will eat it up."

Olivier suspected they would, which would be good for votes. "We will need something to practice with so we get it right the day of the show."

"I can have a muslin mock-up of the dress by this afternoon," Bruce promised. "Now, let's talk colors and fabrics."

"SORRY!" JC called out as he dashed into the costume department and skidded to a halt next to Bruce and Chelsea. "I kept telling Mama I had an appointment I had to be back for, but she kept wanting to talk. I don't know how she manages to come up with so many things I *have* to know in two days."

"She's your mother," Chelsea said with a smile. "Did you enjoy lunch?"

"Yeah, it was nice." Mama had brought the promised tamales by midway through the morning practice session and had stayed to watch so she could take JC out to lunch and catch him up on everything that had happened in the two days since he'd left Abuela's house. "I know *way* too much about what my cousins are up to now."

"Chelsea and I have been busy while we were waiting," Bruce said. He laid out a series of sketches for JC to look at. "Chelsea suggested an open shirt for you, something silky that will cling and reflect the spotlights as you dance."

JC peered at the sketches and nodded. The open shirt didn't bother him at all, and he could easily see how the cling of the material would enhance the moves he and Chelsea had practiced that morning. "Sure. Am I going to keep it on the whole time or take it off?"

"Are you comfortable taking it off?" Chelsea asked. "Because it could add to the intimacy of the dance if it comes off at some point, but we don't have to. I think we can make it plenty powerful even without that. And sometimes it can work against you with the judges, if they think it's only for crowd appeal and not part of the dance."

"I don't want to do it for crowd appeal, but if it works into the dance, I'm okay with it. I'm used to being mostly naked in front of people." JC shrugged. "Swimming does that, even with the high-tech suits that cover more."

"I think I can work something into the dance," Chelsea said. "You're seducing me, so it makes sense that you would start to strip. Maybe I can take it off you when I start to respond? I could have something that comes off too if you want."

"We'll get far more votes with that than we will with my chest," JC said. "I'm not built like Olivier or Kevan to appeal to all the female fans."

Chelsea smirked at him. "I can think of at least one person who would disagree. Let's see how the story plays out as we perfect the dance. With your shirt open and my drape detachable, we have the option of going that route if we want or not going there if we decide we don't need or want it."

"I can make sure the shirt and drape both come off easily," Bruce said. "But remember, seduction doesn't have to mean taking off clothes. My wife can seduce me in a properly suggestive outfit just as easily as she can naked."

Chelsea giggled. "Your wife has to seduce you?"

Bruce grinned, and a hint of color brightened his cheeks. "Well, she could seduce me wearing a burlap sack, I admit, but my point remains. Sometimes a hint of something is more seductive than showing everything."

JC thought back to his first night in the house and how hot Olivier had been fully clothed, and then to how he'd looked last night when JC had found him after his phone call, fresh out of the shower and wearing nothing but a towel. Both images made him think back to lunch with Mama to keep his body from responding in ways he didn't want at the moment, but he had to admit Bruce had a point. The suggestion of muscles under Olivier's shirt had turned him on as much as seeing Olivier's bare chest.

"I kind of like that idea," he said to Chelsea. "Modesty isn't an issue, but I can see the others playing to the other side of the scale. If we go with the open shirt, people will expect it to come off at some point. If it doesn't, it could make the scene more powerful."

"It could work," Chelsea said. "I might want to tweak the choreography a bit if we aren't going that route, but you're right about it being counter to expectations, and that's never a bad thing if we can make it work for us."

"I'll make your costumes so they work either way," Bruce said. "Do what works for the choreography."

"We can try it both ways in practice and see what works best." JC nudged Chelsea's shoulder. "Maybe Joel can give us his opinion, since Makayla went home and he doesn't have anything else to do?"

Chelsea grinned. "He has stuff to do—he's performing with the troupe and other pros! I'm sure he can find some time to help us out, though."

JC winked. "And he won't mind watching you dance either."

CHAPTER 14

A KNOCK on the studio door interrupted rehearsal. JC was pretty sure he'd never been so glad for a break. His entire body hurt, and he couldn't get anything but the simplest moves right. He was beyond frustrated, and even Chelsea's patience was wearing thin.

Joel peeked around the door. "Mind if I come in?"

Mindful of the cameras, Chelsea kept her reaction to a smile. "Of course not."

Joel crossed the room and bumped fists with JC. "How's it going?"

"Not bad," Chelsea said.

"Horrible," JC disagreed. "I feel like a bumbling idiot. I can't get anything right today."

"What are you working on?" Joel asked. "Maybe I can help."

"All of it." JC huffed. Some parts were easier than others, and he knew he was actually getting the choreography, but what he saw in the mirror wasn't anything close to graceful. "I can do most of the steps, but I can't get the feeling right. I look like a marionette, not someone who could seduce Chelsea."

"Well, Chelsea isn't seduced easily, but I think you can pull it off for three minutes." Joel turned so his back was to the camera and winked at Chelsea. "If you show me what you're doing, maybe I can give you a few tips."

"TMI," JC said, but he grinned as he said it. "Okay, so we do this thing—Chelsea can tell you what it's called—where she's in front of me with her arm draped back over my shoulder, and I'm supposed to run my hand down her arm and side as we sway to the music. I get what I'm supposed to do, but it just doesn't look right."

"Show me," Joel said.

"Back up to where we cross and move into that position," Chelsea said. "That way Joel can see what leads up to the moment."

111

JC moved into position on the far side of the studio. He still felt awkward as he raised his arms and waited for Chelsea to count off the beat. He turned and saw her, both of them freezing for a moment before he crossed the floor with large strides, swept her into his arms, and spun her so her back pressed along the length of his front. She lifted her arm to cradle his head, trusting him to support her. He trailed his fingers down her arm and along her side to her waist before spinning her away from him and pulling her back so they faced each other.

"You look like you're thinking about where to put your hands rather than what you want them to do to Chelsea," Joel said after he made JC go through the steps again. "Technically, you're not bad, but the rumba is more about passion than precision. Watch me."

Joel switched places with JC and went through the moves with Chelsea, effortlessly capturing the passion that eluded JC. Physically, he did the same thing JC had done, but it looked so much better, JC despaired of ever getting it right. "How am I supposed to do that?" he asked.

"You pretend," Joel replied. "You think of the person you wish were in your arms instead of Chelsea and make love to her the way you wish you could make love to that other person. How do you think any of us pull it off with our partners? Yes, we get closer as time goes on, and yes, we develop chemistry with them, but a good half of our stars or more aren't single. They aren't in love with us any more than we're in love with them, but you'd never know it for the few minutes of the dance. Try it again, and don't think about Chelsea this time."

JC took a deep breath and assumed the starting pose. He still felt awkward as he raised his arms, but he tried to forget about that and focused instead on imagining Olivier standing in Chelsea's place. As he moved through the now familiar steps, it felt better. Not perfect, because he still had to concentrate too much on counting the beats and remembering what move he did when, but better.

"I'm not going to ask who you're thinking about because it's none of my business," Joel said with a smirk that suggested he knew exactly who was on JC's mind, "but that was much better. You still need to work on your lines, getting the flow all the way to the end of your fingers and stuff, but keep doing what you just did, and you'll get it right on show night."

"Thanks." JC took a deep breath and reminded himself there was always this much to remember and it wasn't much different from being aware of how he moved when swimming. He'd been refining his swimming technique for years now, though. This was like learning a new stroke and refining it within a week, and it had an added performance aspect he didn't have to worry about in the water. Still, there was one advantage to dancing over swimming: he could use the dance to seduce Olivier.

OLIVIER APPLAUDED with everyone else as JC and Chelsea were announced. The lights dimmed so the scenes-from-the-week segment could show on the screens over the audience's heads. The clips of JC and Chelsea flashed by. When Joel came in, the audience cheered, but it was his advice that caught Olivier's attention. Even more than that, he could see the immediate difference in JC's performance after Joel suggested he think not about Chelsea but about someone who meant something to him. His pants suddenly felt one size too small. He considered slipping away to find a place where he could watch the dance without the other contestants and the cameras watching him, but his absence would be too noticeable. He'd just have to suck it up and watch JC seduce Chelsea, knowing all the while that JC was imagining doing those same things to him.

He didn't recognize the music they were dancing to, but that was nothing unusual. It wasn't the music that caught his attention, anyway, as JC and Chelsea appeared in the spotlights on opposite sides of the ballroom.

As they began their dance, JC spied Chelsea across the room, and the look on his face spoke of the immediate interest he took in her, the deep connection he felt. Olivier felt jealousy prod at him. He knew it was just acting, but JC wasn't supposed to look at anyone but him like that.

As the strains of "Some Enchanted Evening" echoed through the ballroom, JC fell into character. He pictured Olivier in his head as he danced, remembering how he'd felt when they'd first met and the way attraction had grown between them. It fit perfectly with the story he and Chelsea were telling—the story of two lovers destined to meet. He seduced Chelsea as he danced, their bodies moving together in a sensual rhythm. They separated and came back together again and again, holding each other for longer each time.

The song built to the climax, and as the singer admonished them, JC pulled Chelsea into his arms and didn't let go. He spun her in his arms, folding her in an embrace from behind, and the look on his face nearly took Olivier to his knees. He looked at her with such utter devotion that Olivier ached to see that expression directed at him. She lifted her arm, and Olivier watched the move from the video clips, the one Joel had helped them perfect. If Olivier had not spent the previous night with JC in his arms, he would have sworn JC meant his seduction of Chelsea, not just for the dance but for real.

He applauded as much as the others when the lights came up, and JC and Chelsea broke their hold to approach the judges' table, but inside he was reeling. Tricia touched his elbow. "Once you have found him, never let him go," she murmured. Olivier nodded. He wasn't going to let JC get away.

He let Tricia lead him away from the viewing area to the backstage area, where they would wait until their dance was announced after the commercial break. His heart pounded in his chest at the thought of the upcoming dance, but he had years of experience with performing through his nerves. He would channel all the churning emotions inspired by JC's dance into his own interactions with Tricia and hope for the best.

JC hurried into the back after the judges gave their scores. He was happy with them—all eights—but what he really wanted was a chance to see Olivier. He found him waiting while Tricia put the finishing touches on her makeup. "I was thinking about you out there," he murmured. Then he smiled. "Good luck."

Olivier ached to kiss JC, but he couldn't while the cameras were around. That clip might not make it on air, but he couldn't take the chance. "Thanks," he said, smiling in return. "I'll be making love to you while I'm dancing with Tricia."

Lust flared in JC's eyes, making Olivier feel a little better about his own state. Now he just had to get through the rest of the show so he could take JC to bed and make love to him for real.

Tricia finished touching up her makeup, and they walked to the wings as the set designers got everything ready for their performance.

With a final hug for luck, Olivier slipped through the darkened studio to take his place on the bed so the dance could begin.

JC's breath hitched as he watched Olivier lie down. He looked exquisite spread out on the bed like that. Even though JC knew it was just for the dance, he couldn't help the surge of jealousy at the thought of the entire viewing audience seeing him like that. He didn't want to share.

The music started, and JC saw Tricia move across the stage out of the corner of his eye, but he kept his gaze fixed on Olivier as Olivier "woke up" and climbed sensuously off the bed. His initial movement toward Tricia was quick, but when they reached each other, they slowed down, not quite touching as they circled around each other. The moment their bodies met, JC desperately wished he could be in Tricia's place and have all that attention and care directed at him.

Olivier focused on Tricia and the movements of the dance, but the emotions he tried to project came entirely from his feelings for JC: Amazement that JC had returned his interest became amazement that Tricia had made her way to him despite everything keeping them apart. Joy at JC's touch channeled into his reaction to Tricia's hand on his face. The passion JC inspired transferred to Olivier's attempts to loosen the laces on Tricia's gown. The music swelled, gaining speed and volume, and Olivier pulled Tricia into his arms, tucking her face against his shoulder as he whisked her across the floor toward the bed.

JC closed his eyes as Olivier guided Tricia down on to the bed and ended the dance in a passionate embrace. Olivier had sold it beautifully, and though JC knew it was all an act for the cameras, he hated watching Olivier do that with anyone else. As the judges gave their remarks, he hurried backstage, practicing his smile so the cameras wouldn't pick up anything but the genuine pride he felt at Olivier's skill.

"You were wonderful," he said when Olivier got backstage and hugged him briefly, as that was the only acceptable thing to do with cameras around. "You really sold the story."

"*Bien*," Olivier said. He glanced around quickly, but the focus had already moved away from Olivier and onto Amber and Tyler, who were preparing to take the floor. He lowered his voice and added, "Then you know how I feel when I'm with you."

JC yearned to lean up and kiss Olivier, but though the focus was on Amber and Tyler, there were far too many cameras around to risk it. It was impossible to tell what would show up in the background of a shot that made it on-air, and since the show was aired live, there was nothing they could do to stop it.

"We have to go back upstairs, or we'll be missed." Olivier hated to pull away, but they couldn't take the chance in public this way. "But when the show is over tonight and the camera crews have gone home, you're all mine."

That was both reassuring and maddening. Going home with Olivier and acting on the passion simmering between them was the best idea JC had heard all day, but they still had the whole rest of the show to get through, plus the ride back to the house… and that was assuming they were able to get away immediately. "I'm going to hold you to that," JC said in a low tone as they entered the viewing area. "The minute we're alone, I'm going to kiss you senseless."

"Just kiss me senseless?" Olivier replied in the same soft voice. "And here I'd hoped you would fuck me senseless. Isn't that what your character was planning to do to Chelsea when the lights went down?" He wouldn't be able to get the image of JC dancing with Chelsea out of his head for a long, long time. He wondered if Joel was feeling the same way. He knew the jealousy was unfounded, but it didn't make him more resistant to its razor-sharp claws.

"I was going to start with a kiss. Then we'll see who fucks who." JC really couldn't decide if he wanted to pin Olivier to the bed or be pinned by him. Both ideas were equally enticing, and as he directed his gaze to the dance floor like a good contestant, he started to get ideas for other things he wanted to do too, like bend Olivier over a table the way Tyler had Amber at the end of their song.

The sambas were hot and fast and fun, and on any other night, Olivier would have loved them, but tonight they served only to make him dream of rubbing up against JC the way the couples on the dance floor shimmied and shook against each other. The rumbas were even worse, all the slow sensuality and prelude to lovemaking. Olivier made sure to lean against the low wall that separated the viewing area from the rest of the studio so no one would catch an inadvertent glimpse of his erection. Between JC's presence at his side, the promise in his words, and the titillation of the other couples, he was hard as a rock and ready for the night to be over.

Hours ago.

When Luis smacked Rini's ass as she shimmied away from him—lightly and in the spirit of fun—Olivier nearly groaned out loud. He needed a handful of ass, but it wasn't Rini's he was lusting after. As soon as their dance was finished, he excused himself and headed for the restroom. He needed a moment away from all the stimulation.

JC cursed under his breath as Olivier left. He needed to do something about the growing bulge in his pants, but he couldn't leave right after Olivier. The cameras might catch it. Hell, Eugene might notice, and God only knew what he would do if he so much as suspected they were together. He already dismissed JC because of the color of his skin. There was no need to give him reason to turn on Olivier too.

When the next song started and Olivier still wasn't back, though, JC slipped out of the viewing area. It was easier to get away unseen in the darkened auditorium, and Olivier had been gone long enough it hopefully wouldn't be obvious JC was following him. He slid through the backstage area silently, trying not to draw any attention to himself—a challenge given the outfit he was wearing—and slipped inside the bathroom.

Olivier splashed cold water on his face. He'd lingered about as long as he dared, using the excuse of needing the restroom, but he wasn't ready to go back out yet. Heat still prickled under his skin like a bad sunburn. He was ruining his stage makeup, but he didn't care. He'd finished with his dance. If he looked a little washed-out under the lights when they went out on the floor for the final credits, no one would notice. They'd all be looking at Tricia anyway. He looked up when the door opened, hoping it wouldn't be Eugene coming in. He could deal with anyone else, even if they teased him about how long he'd been gone, but he couldn't deal with the homophobic bigot right now. When he realized it was JC, he nearly groaned. They couldn't fuck in the restroom on show night. They'd be safe from the cameras, but not from anyone else who might need to use the facilities. The chance of discovery was high, and even if they managed not to be found out directly, the cameras panned the viewing box regularly, and their absence would surely be noticed.

JC crossed to Olivier in three swift steps and pulled him into a deep kiss. For a moment he lost himself in the sensation of Olivier pressed against him and the taste of Olivier on his tongue, but he forced himself to pull back far sooner than he wanted. If they kissed much more, it would be even harder to control himself and nearly impossible to fool anyone into thinking he'd simply come to relieve himself.

"This sucks," he whispered, pressing himself against Olivier. It made the bulge in his pants worse, but it felt so good. "I don't want to wait until we get back to the house."

"You deserve better than a quick fuck in a restroom stall," Olivier protested even as he leaned into JC's heat. "Even if we dared take the chance of getting caught, there's not enough space to do this right. I won't treat you that way."

"No, I know. It's just the worst show ever to perform early." JC kissed Olivier again and stepped back. If they kept this up, he'd come in his pants, and he didn't want to explain that to the costume department. "You should go back. They'll miss you soon."

"In a minute," Olivier said as he pulled JC closer. He kissed him once more, all teeth and tongue and hands wandering the way he'd wanted them to since he'd watched JC dance. He pulled back reluctantly. "That will have to hold us until we get home."

JC smiled. "It'll do." He wanted so much more, but they'd been lucky to remain undisturbed so long. He couldn't risk anything else. "Now go before someone gets suspicious. I'll be back up in a minute." He waited until Olivier had left and then turned to the sink and started splashing his face with water. Tonight could not end soon enough.

OLIVIER TUGGED his T-shirt off and tossed it toward the pile of dirty clothes in the corner. He'd need to find time to do laundry tomorrow while they were waiting for the elimination show, but he'd worry about that later. For now, he'd prefer to focus on relaxing. JC had whispered that he'd join Olivier as soon as he could do so discreetly. Olivier hoped it would be soon.

JC rapped softly against Olivier's door and stepped inside when it swung open at his touch. "You should make sure the door shuts all the way. Anyone could walk in." He meant it to sound teasing and playful, but he was distracted by the sight of Olivier shirtless with his back to the door. The scars he'd only had a few glimpses of before were clearly visible and, unlike the time in the pool, they were something he could touch. At least, he hoped he could. It hadn't come up the first time they'd made love, but they hadn't gotten fully undressed, and after the hot tub he'd been focused on Olivier's cock, not his back.

"And if I left it open so *you* could come in?" Olivier asked. He smiled as he turned to face JC.

"Well, I *suppose* that's acceptable," JC teased as he firmly shut the door and walked toward Olivier. The view from the front was just as enticing as the view from the back, and after the way Olivier had teased him all night, JC was eager to touch wherever he could.

Olivier opened his arms for JC to step into his embrace. The moment JC was close enough, he leaned down and kissed him deeply. Kisses wouldn't be enough, as worked up as he was from the evening, but they were a good place to start.

JC deepened the kiss as he wrapped his arms around Olivier. He slid his fingers over the smooth skin of Olivier's lower back and guided him toward the bed. "God, tonight was torture," he murmured as they broke the kiss to walk.

"And it's only going to get worse each week," Olivier replied as he sat down on the bed. He tugged on JC's hand until he sat down too. "You know they aren't going to let us dial back the heat."

"It won't be that bad. Not all dances are supposed to be as sexy as the rumba is." JC pushed Olivier down on the bed and swung one leg over him. He didn't want to talk about their dances; he wanted to do something about the way they'd made him feel. "And when we get the sexier dances, we'll just have to do this again," he added with a smirk as he ran his hands up Olivier's bare chest. He stopped with his hand just shy of the scar on Olivier's left shoulder and looked down with a more serious expression. He desperately wanted to touch, but not if it would make Olivier uncomfortable. "May I?"

Olivier hesitated. He hadn't had a serious lover since his accident, and the few casual flings he'd had hadn't wanted to touch his scars. JC didn't seem put off by them, though, and they didn't hurt when touched. He didn't have any reason to say no. He nodded slowly.

Just as slowly, JC ran one finger over the line of raised flesh on Olivier's shoulder. It was softer and smoother than the surrounding skin, but not as obvious as Olivier seemed to think it was. He slid off Olivier and lay next to him so he could get a better look. "Why do you hide this?"

"They're ugly," Olivier said. He didn't pull away as JC explored the damaged skin, but only because he didn't want to spoil the moment. JC would lose interest in them soon, and that would be the end of that. "No one wants to see them." If he didn't let anyone see them, he didn't have to listen to comments about them.

"They're not ugly. They're part of you," JC said as he urged Olivier onto his side so he could explore the scar on Olivier's back. This one was bigger and bumpier but it still wasn't a flashing neon sign like Olivier thought. "Besides, most people aren't going to notice them any more than they notice what color your eyes are or what your hair looks like. Not after the first time, anyway. They're just part of the package that makes up you."

"They dictated everything about my life for so long. I guess I still see them as defining who I am," Olivier admitted. He looked back over his shoulder to study JC's face, but JC's expression hadn't changed from the same eagerness he'd shown since he walked in the room. Maybe JC was right, maybe he wasn't, but Olivier could let go of the worry that JC would be repulsed.

"Try to stop worrying about them." JC kissed the scar on Olivier's back and then shuffled around so they were face to face again. "You are fucking gorgeous, and they don't change that."

The way JC said it, Olivier could almost believe him. He pulled JC up into a kiss as he burrowed his hand beneath JC's shirt.

CHAPTER 15

THE SMELL of stir-fried vegetables permeated the kitchen as Olivier came in from his postrehearsal shower, but none of the usual lighthearted chatter filled the air.

"Still no news?" he asked Rini as he sat down next to her at the table.

"No, no one's heard anything since the ambulance left this afternoon," Rini said. "I talked to Preston for a minute before they left, and he said they were practicing like normal when Dawn lost her balance and fell, which wouldn't have been any big deal except they heard a crunch and she couldn't put her weight on her foot."

Olivier winced sympathetically. He'd played in a rough sport for enough years to know that horrible sound. He hoped it wasn't as serious as it appeared.

JC took a seat on Olivier's other side. "Maybe the ER is just crowded. If she's not hurt that badly, she could wait for hours." He remembered when his brother Manuel had fallen off his bike and sprained his ankle by catching his foot on the pedal. They'd rushed to the hospital only to wait for hours while more serious cases were seen and treated.

"She should have gone to a private clinic, then, instead of waiting with the rabble. She has enough money that she can afford it," Eugene said as he came into the kitchen. "Isn't dinner ready yet?"

"Almost. I didn't know what Dawn had planned, so I had to improvise," Amber said from the stove. She'd stepped up when they'd realized tonight was Dawn's night to cook.

"And we appreciate you covering for her," Rini said with a scowl in Eugene's direction. Olivier shared her distaste. Eugene's attitude had gotten progressively worse as the weeks had passed. He'd narrowly escaped elimination last week when Kevan had gone home. Olivier would have preferred the rapper to stay instead of Eugene. Kevan was young and brash and didn't always know when to stop with his teasing, but he didn't have a cruel bone in his body. Olivier couldn't say the same for Eugene.

"Should I set the table?" Olivier offered. "That way everything will be ready as soon as the food is done."

"That's a good idea," Rini said, standing up to help. Eugene, Olivier noticed, flopped down in his seat like he owned the place and the rest of them were nothing more than annoying servants.

JC got up to help as well. When the table was set, he stopped by the stove and peered at the food Amber was cooking. "Anything I can do to help?"

"Can you grab the big serving dish? I'll be ready to bring it over in a minute." Amber beamed as JC handed it to her. "Thanks!"

They'd just started dishing up the stir-fry when the front door opened, and Preston called out, "We're back!"

"How's Dawn?" Freddy stood up as he spoke and headed toward the living room entrance. "Oh, baby."

Olivier's stomach dropped at the exclamation. Freddy was a true Southern gentleman, always standing when a woman walked in the room. The tone of his voice said everything Olivier hadn't wanted to hear. He rose as well and went to the other room, where Preston stood behind Dawn's wheelchair. Her foot was elevated in front of her and covered in a plaster cast.

JC followed, along with everyone else, and his heart sank when he saw the wheelchair and the cast. "How long do you have that for?" he asked once the exclamations of sympathy and dismay had died down. Clearly, she wasn't going to be dancing again anytime soon, but he hoped it wasn't so serious that it would cause long-term issues for her.

"Two weeks with this one, and then they'll reevaluate and see if they can switch to a walking cast." Dawn smiled ruefully. "I'll obviously be withdrawing from the competition. You all get a free pass from elimination this week."

"Oh, Dawn, that's awful," Tricia exclaimed. "You have to stay for this week's show, at least. We want to give you a proper send-off."

"That gives me an idea," Tyler said. "You will stay for the show, won't you, Dawn?"

"Of course," Dawn said. "I only live a couple of hours from here. I'll be back for all the shows, even if I'm sitting in the audience instead of participating."

"Good," Olivier said. "We'll miss having you here with us."

BY THE time practice ended the next day, JC was ready to collapse onto his bed and sleep until he absolutely had to get up again, but he forced his feet to carry him past his door and on to Olivier's. He leaned against the doorframe as he knocked and hoped Olivier was inside. Otherwise, the chances he'd still be awake when Olivier came upstairs were slim.

"*Entrez,*" Olivier called without thinking. Even after two years of living in the US, French still came more naturally than English did. "Come in."

He smiled when JC walked in, looking dead on his feet. "Long day?"

"Yeah." JC flopped onto the bed. "Chelsea decided to change all the choreography. I had to learn twice as much today to stay on track. I'm not sure I'll be able to move in the morning." He rolled his head and looked up at Olivier. "How was your day?"

"Tiring, but not as much as yours. Tricia tweaked a few things like she always does, but not so much that I had to unlearn what we did yesterday." Olivier stretched out next to JC so he wouldn't have to strain his neck. "I thought Chelsea was pleased with what you worked on yesterday. Why did she change everything?"

"She's incorporating some of the choreography Preston was going to use with Dawn. We were both doing the Lindy Hop, and Chelsea thought using Preston's choreography would be a good way to honor her." JC took Olivier's hand. "It's nice, but the man's part in that was choreographed for a pro. So Preston taught it, and then he and Chelsea tweaked it down to what I can do." Preston had planned to swing Dawn in the air far more than JC was physically capable of with Chelsea, for example. He thought the dance was going to be fantastic, but learning the new—and more challenging—choreography had been exhausting.

"Wow, that is asking a lot of you," Olivier agreed. "I love the idea of doing something for Dawn—we are too, although not quite like that—but don't get hurt trying to do more than you're able to. We've already lost one person to injury. I don't want you having to leave early too."

"We're being careful." JC was honored to have been asked, even though he really only beat Eugene out for the part, since no one else was dancing the Lindy Hop. "Chelsea knows what I'm capable of, and she won't let me try anything I can't do." He nudged Olivier with his elbow. "I think she's afraid of what you'd do if she let me get hurt."

"She is not wrong," Olivier grumbled. "It's bad enough worrying one of us will be eliminated. I don't want to rush things along by adding injuries to the process. Although I guess we don't have to worry about that this week, with Dawn withdrawing. I was hoping Eugene would go home. One less person to worry will find out about us and make a scene. I didn't think it would bother me so much, keeping our relationship private."

"Yeah." JC sighed. He didn't particularly care for it either. He'd never hidden a relationship like this before. The few times he'd hidden them at all had been to protect the person he was with, and that wasn't the same. The stakes were completely different when the person he was with was also a public figure. "I don't know what else to do, though. We definitely can't say anything to anyone else until Eugene leaves, and even then I'm not sure we should if you're not ready for people to know you're gay."

"It's none of their business." Olivier struggled to put into words what he was feeling, to explain to JC why he didn't want to go public with their relationship. "I'm not ashamed of being gay or of being with you, but I don't want to be a poster child for the gay-rights movement. That's not who I am. I'm just a rugby player. And now a dancer, I guess, but that's not the point. Whether I'm married or single, straight or gay or somewhere in between, doesn't have any effect on whether I can carry the ball down the field or whether I can dance. But if we tell people, I'm not Olivier Gautier anymore. Suddenly I'm that gay rugby player."

"I know." JC did. He'd been there, back when he'd first broken into national swimming competitions. He'd realized he was bisexual around the same time, and it had been hard to figure out what to tell people, especially since he'd only been a teenager. "I was worried I'd be that bisexual swimmer. Or probably that gay swimmer, since the media doesn't think bisexuality is a real thing," he added in a disgusted tone. He'd seen the headlines calling a celebrity gay when they'd admitted to liking both men and women. "I thought no one would want to get in the pool with me if they knew."

"You have no idea how much I admire you for your openness," Olivier said. "I don't have that courage. Not to mention that if my contract isn't renewed—and there's no clause that says they have to have a reason not to renew it—I'd have to leave the US and go back to France. My visa is only valid if I'm playing for a team. They can't break the contract without cause, but they could choose not to renew it if I came out and it caused problems on the team." He would take the risk if he knew JC was as invested in their relationship as he was, but not for anything less.

JC rolled over on top of Olivier and rested his head on Olivier's chest. "I'm not judging you, I promise. And I'm not going to stop this because you're not ready for the world to know." He wished he could proclaim it everywhere, but he'd keep it a secret as long as possible since it was important to Olivier. If they stayed together the way he wanted them to, their lives would probably reach a point where that wasn't possible anymore, but until then he'd do what he could to keep Olivier safe. "I don't want to deal with Eugene finding out, either. Even if you decide you want to tell the whole world, I'd rather wait until we're not living with him anymore."

Olivier wrapped his arms around JC and held on tight. He could deal with whatever happened as long as JC didn't leave him. "Then let's hope he goes home next week." He kissed the top of JC's head, hoping JC would look up so he could kiss him properly.

JC tipped his head back before Olivier pulled away and kissed him lightly. Then, not satisfied with that, he scooted up farther and deepened the kiss, letting it wash away his tiredness and the anxiety of the day.

OLIVIER STOOD backstage with Tricia as the week's montage screened. He smiled when they played the discussion he and Tricia had had about dedicating the week's performance to Dawn. They couldn't incorporate Preston's choreography the way JC and Chelsea had done, but they had tried to incorporate Dawn's quirky sense of humor and zest for life. Though she had gone on to other things, her entrance routine from her stint on *Captain Kangaroo* was still her most recognizable moment. She had even come into the living room at the house with those jaunty steps a few times. They risked the judges marking them down for something that wasn't part of the Charleston, but they had agreed it would be worth it to use it as their entrance.

The video ended, the lights came up, and Olivier winked at Tricia before linking his arm with hers and beginning their dance.

For once, JC didn't focus on Olivier as he danced. Instead, he focused on Dawn, watching her as she watched Olivier, particularly at the beginning. Olivier had told him what their tribute to Dawn was going to be, and he wanted to see how she reacted before he got out there and danced most of what was supposed to be her routine. She grinned at the jaunty entrance and clapped in delight as they finished off her little routine and moved into the Charleston proper.

JC relaxed a little and then turned his attention to Olivier. As always, he was transfixed by the way his boyfriend moved on the dance floor. The kicks of the Charleston emphasized his ass nicely, especially in his form-fitting pants. It was a pleasure to watch, and JC found his nervousness about Dawn's reaction fade away as he enjoyed the performance.

Despite all the training they had done for the Charleston and his general level of fitness, Olivier was panting hard by the time they finished. He nodded at Elizabeth when she congratulated them on a good job.

"Now let's see what our judges have to say. Henrietta?"

"First, I think it was wonderful of you to include the nod to Dawn, and I think you did a great job of weaving it into the feel of the rest of the dance. Your kicks were sharp and in sync, but you have to work on your hands, Olivier. In the Charleston, especially, the placement of your hands is as important to the character of the dance as the placement of your feet. Still, a very nice job and a lovely tribute to Dawn."

JC hadn't noticed Olivier's hands and wouldn't have known if they were right or not regardless, but it seemed like a fair assessment. Olivier and Tricia evidently agreed, as they both nodded and thanked Henrietta before Elizabeth moved on to Edoardo.

"Oh, Olivier, you looked *fantastic* out there. Those kicks and that costume. I could watch you for hours." He leaned over the table with a comically exaggerated leer. "Absolutely delicious. Henrietta is right, though," he added in a more serious tone. "You do need to work on your hands. Your kicks were excellent, your posture exquisite, but your hands were all over the place in some parts. It was distracting and took away from what was otherwise a fantastic performance. And yes, I agree: it was a lovely tribute to Dawn. You kept it in the intro so we don't have to deduct points and segued it into the actual dance nicely. Good job."

Olivier flushed a little at Edoardo's enthusiasm, as he did almost every week. Edoardo fawned over everyone the same way if they danced well, but it still made Olivier squirm a little. He had honestly expected the comments about his hands. Tricia had gotten on him about them constantly, but it had been one thing too many given the complexity of the choreography and his complete lack of familiarity with the dance.

"The character of the dance was spot-on," Emma Leigh said. "The Charleston is all about the fun and the flirtatiousness. It's over-the-top both in terms of speed and of movement. You came out, you threw yourself into the dance with everything you had, and it showed. Yes, your hands were a bit sloppy at times, but it wasn't because you were holding back or because you didn't care about what you were doing, and that matters. You pulled us in, you made us laugh, you entertained us, and with the Charleston, that's important. Just polish up those hands a little for next week and you'll be on the road to the finals."

Olivier and Tricia thanked them and moved off to get their scores—a nine from Emma Leigh and eights from Edoardo and Henrietta. JC grinned at the scores as he hugged Olivier, careful to keep it just a congratulatory hug between costars, nothing more than he'd do for Deborah or Amber.

They moved into the viewing area together and got comfortable. JC wasn't dancing until last because he had taken Dawn's choreography, so they could sit and watch most of the show together. The other dancers all paid tribute to Dawn as well, their fox-trots and Charlestons all containing something reminiscent of her, even if it was only for a few beats.

Then Eugene danced, and his Lindy Hop didn't contain any tribute at all.

JC focused on keeping his expression carefully neutral, just in case any of the cameras were on them. "I should have known he wouldn't do anything, but I guess I was hoping Carmen would insist."

"There's only so much insisting the pros can do if the stars are set on something," Tricia said softly. "It's supposed to be a team effort, but ultimately, if they can't reach a compromise, the star wins unless it's a safety issue of some kind. He'll pay for it in votes—just you watch. He can't be eliminated this week, but this week's scores and votes will be rolled into next week's."

"He wouldn't be any great loss," Olivier murmured. "Are you ready for your dance, JC?" Several times during the week, JC had worried he wouldn't be able to learn the steps well enough to perform credibly. His tribute to Dawn only worked if he could pull it off.

"I think so. Chelsea and Preston both say I have it down, and I feel like I know it. I'm just worried what Dawn will think." He'd pushed the thought out of his mind while watching the others dance, but it occurred to him now that everyone else had done tributes. JC had taken over her entire dance.

"She'll love it," Chelsea said in the same firm tone she'd been using all week when JC had been plagued by doubts. "Preston wouldn't have suggested it if he thought it would bother her at all."

"I know." JC sighed and remembered just in time not to run his hands through his hair. It was slicked down with more product than he'd used in the entire rest of his life. "It won't stop me from worrying."

There was no more time for that, though. Eugene was standing off to the side, impatiently waiting for Carmen to finish hugging Dawn so they could get their scores, which meant JC had to head back so he'd be ready when Amber left the dance floor.

Olivier watched JC go and wished he could offer more encouragement than the thumbs-up he flashed JC's way as he headed toward the staging area. They were too visible in the viewing box, even if they hadn't been hiding from the cameras and Eugene still, but Olivier chafed at the restrictions nonetheless. Maybe after Eugene went home, they could be a little more open with their costars, at least.

When Amber was done, JC and Chelsea took the stage. Preston's hand was obvious in the opening sequence as JC flipped Chelsea before flipping himself. Olivier held his breath as they successfully navigated that part. If they nailed it, JC's confidence would soar. If they slipped, he'd struggle for the rest of the dance.

He cheered along with the rest of the stars when they hit the mark perfectly. He'd told JC he could do it. Now to watch him do the rest.

Once JC got past the opening flip, the rest of the dance just flowed like it was meant to be perfect. His long arms were actually an advantage in a lot of the Lindy Hop, and the places Preston had tweaked the choreography to accommodate JC and Chelsea's skills took full advantage of that. He danced like mad, reveling in the loose moves of the dance and the way the choreography flowed. It was different from what Chelsea usually did, but Preston was a skilled choreographer, and it worked in a way that JC hadn't seen until it all clicked together.

When the dance was over, he stood next to Chelsea in front of the judges, his chest heaving, and smiled so wide he was sure it would split his face. "Oh my God."

"You nailed it," Chelsea whispered in his ear as she hugged him back.

Elizabeth congratulated them both and then turned the floor over to Edoardo.

"Oh. My. God." Edoardo stood up, leaned over the table, and pointed at JC. "You are *phenomenal*. That was absolutely exquisite. The way you move... your body is perfect for the Lindy Hop, and you embraced it 100 percent and it *worked*. You have never looked so hot on the dance floor. I want to make you go out there and do it again just so I can enjoy the way your body moves. The kicks were spot-on and the way you flipped Chelsea around was perfect. You are on fire, and we're all going to burn watching you."

Olivier agreed completely. He'd be downloading JC's dance from YouTube and watching it every chance he got.

"We've seen some amazing dances tonight," Emma Leigh said when it was her turn. "And we've seen some fantastic Lindy Hops in the history of the show, but I've never seen a star come out in week four and pull off a dance like that. On finals night, maybe, but not in week four. It was brilliant."

"Thank you." JC tried to keep from blushing, but he could feel his cheeks flush. Emma Leigh's praise on top of Edoardo's was almost too much.

"I liked it," Henrietta said when the applause died down. "Edoardo's right that you're built for the Lindy Hop. You've got the upper body strength and range to flip Chelsea and pull off the moves, but it felt a little too frenetic to me, like you tried to put in one move too many. I admire your gumption for stepping into Preston's shoes as a way to pay tribute to Dawn, and I think you did as well as you could be expected to do with very difficult choreography. However, I look forward to seeing *you* dance again next week instead of Preston in disguise."

Olivier thought that was a little unfair, but he wasn't a judge. He didn't always see the elements or even the whole through the same lens they did. He only hoped Henrietta's comments didn't discourage JC, because Olivier thought he'd done an amazing job.

"I'm looking forward to it too," JC agreed with a wry grin. Henrietta's comments stung a little after the effusive praise from Edoardo and Emma Leigh, but she had a point. "It was a fun challenge learning the dance with Preston's choreography, but I'm more comfortable with Chelsea's. I'm glad I got to do this for Preston and Dawn, though."

Elizabeth sent them off to wait for their scores to be tallied and took the opportunity to remind the audience what was going on. "Since Dawn was injured and everyone else is coming back next week, we won't have a results show tomorrow. Instead, votes and scores from this week will be added to next week to determine who goes home next week."

She'd already mentioned it twice, but it was a good reminder and served to pass the time while the judges tallied their scores. Finally, after what felt like forever, the spotlight focused on him, and Elizabeth's voice echoed through the room. "And now, the scores. Emma Leigh?"

"Nine!"

"Henrietta?"

"Eight!" The audience booed, but Henrietta's expression didn't change.

"Edoardo?"

Edoardo grinned at the camera and whipped the paddle out with extra flair. "A ten!"

JC's knees weakened, and he caught himself on Chelsea. "Holy shit." He hadn't expected that, even with Edoardo's effusive praise. It was only week four, and no one else had gotten a ten yet.

130

"The first ten!" Corey exclaimed. "How does that make you feel?"

There weren't words to describe what JC was feeling, but he gave it a shot anyway. "Fantastic. It's an amazing honor, and I hope it means I get to stick around and earn lots of money for the Trevor Project."

"Well, that's up to the viewers now. Vote for JC if you want him to win." Corey grinned at the camera. "We'll be back right after this short break." He shooed JC away as soon as the cameraman nodded he was done. "Go. You don't want to miss saying good-bye to Dawn."

CHAPTER 16

"WE HAVE an extra day of rehearsal this week since we don't have a results show tonight," Tricia said when she dragged Olivier out of his room at the same ungodly hour as every other day. "This is a good thing because this week everything has to come from you—the costumes, the music, even the dance itself, is your choice instead of being assigned. This is your week to show the world through dance why your charity is important to you."

"How are we supposed to do that?" Olivier asked. "I mean, we can hardly recreate a disaster zone and have the doctors coming to the aid of the victims."

"No, we can't," Tricia agreed, "but we can choose a song and emotion that reflect the good they're doing in the world."

"Something like the Bette Midler song about how everyone looks the same from a distance," Olivier said.

"Yes, 'From a Distance,'" Tricia said. "We have to choose a dance we haven't done yet either. If we're going with that kind of emotion, since we've already done rumba, we'll either have to do contemporary or a waltz—either the regular waltz or the Viennese waltz."

"Not contemporary," Olivier said. "I need the structure of a dance with defined steps and rhythm. I'd lose the beat before we made it past the third or fourth step."

"You wouldn't," Tricia insisted, "but we can do a waltz. We won't be able to use 'From a Distance'—the time signature is wrong. It's in a four-beat pattern, not a three-beat pattern—but we'll find something that works. So we want the dance to feel uplifting, to portray the emotions of the people who are helped by Doctors Without Borders. This will be a good challenge."

JC FLOPPED down on the floor next to Chelsea and glared at her halfheartedly. "This is usually my day to sleep in."

"Today it's your day to pick your song and dance," Chelsea retorted. As usual, she was far too perky for the early hour, especially considering how emotional last night had been. "The theme this week is what your charity means to you, so you need to come up with something to show that."

It was far too early for this, but the amount of money the Trevor Project got hinged on his performance, so JC struggled up to a sitting position and tried to turn his brain on. "Well, it saves lives. I don't want kids to think that because they're not straight or whatever that they're not worth it. We need to stop the bullies who make people feel that way, but we also need to let people know it's okay to celebrate who they are."

"Maybe we could go with that last bit," Chelsea mused. "Celebrating life and all its beauty, no matter what form it comes in. You could do a party dance like the cha-cha or the salsa and celebrate who you are."

"I love the Latin party dances," JC said, already liking the idea. "I could celebrate that part of me too. Maybe we could dance to something by Shakira?"

"Probably. I'm not very familiar with her stuff, but if she has songs with the right time signature and beat, we can pick one. Did you have one in mind?"

"No, and I'm not set on her, either. We can look at traditional songs too. Or other artists."

"We have to pick a dance first," Chelsea pointed out. "That affects what we're looking for in a song."

"Well, if I'm going to celebrate, we should do a party dance. So let's salsa."

OLIVIER DRAGGED into the communal living room after practice that evening. They'd finally found a song with the right beat and feel that he liked, and Tricia said they could dance to, and then she'd started in on the choreography. He wanted this dance to be amazing. He wanted to do justice to the work Doctors Without Borders did around the world every day, even when there wasn't a natural disaster to draw attention to their cause. They worked in areas hit by famine or other epidemics and bettered the lives of thousands of people each day. He'd visited their camp in Benin when he was in high school, and the knowledge of the miracles they worked with next to nothing had stayed with him. All the wishing in the world couldn't make his body less sore, though.

Some of the others were already sitting around on couches or at the table, but he didn't see JC. He'd have been careful about where he sat even if JC was already there. He'd overheard Eugene on the phone setting up his next radio show that morning, and he'd been on a rant about gays again. Olivier didn't think he and JC had done anything to exacerbate it, but he didn't want to do so now either. He had no desire to have his name all over Eugene's show.

"Hi, Olivier," Amber said when he took his seat. "How was practice today?"

"Long and tiring," Olivier said. "How about you?"

"I'm very excited about my dance," Amber said. "Amnesty International does such important work. It's a privilege to be able to do something to highlight that, even if it's just a dance and the montage they'll show before that."

"What dance are you doing?" Olivier asked.

"The rumba," Amber said. "Tyler and I talked about it quite a bit and thought it would be particularly appropriate for us, with him being black and all the struggles he's had because of it. What did you choose?"

"We're doing the Viennese waltz. We already did the rumba, and Tricia told me my other logical choice was contemporary. I don't think I could do that, so the waltz it is."

"Oh, but the Viennese waltz is always so lovely and uplifting. It's a gorgeous dance." Amber smiled at Eugene as he walked in. She was always unfailingly polite to him, even though he clearly didn't think much of her. "What about you, Eugene? How was your practice?"

"Tiring, as usual," he said as he sat in the chair he'd claimed the first week. Everyone else just sat where fancy took them, but Eugene had made it clear early on that that chair was best for his back, and he had to have it. "And Carmen got upset with me because I had to stop and record my show! She doesn't seem to understand that some of us have real jobs."

"Everyone here has a real job, Eugene," Deborah interjected. "Just because not everyone works in corporate America doesn't mean the way they earn their living isn't a real job."

134

Eugene made a disgusted face. "If you say so. It's Carmen's job to pick the music and choreograph the dance, then. I'm not sure why she expects me to do it."

"Because the theme is why it's important to you, not to her," Deborah said. "Brody thinks Count Me In is a great charity, but it's not important to him the way it is to me. He can choreograph once I tell him how I feel, but the song and dance have to matter to me. I wanted to tell a story with my body, so I picked contemporary."

"Exactly—that's why I'm doing the yangge. It's a traditional Chinese dance, and the symbol of the World Wildlife Foundation is the panda," Rini said. "Don't you have any connection like that with the MS Society?"

"Sure, but that doesn't mean I want to dance about it. I'm giving them money—that should be enough. My reasons are my own, and I don't need to share them with the world."

"Yeah, well, I'm happy to let the world know why I picked the Trevor Project," JC said. He'd come in just in time to hear Eugene's diatribe and wasn't in the mood for it at all. "My dance is going to be awesome 'cause it's so important to me."

"What are you dancing?" Rini asked.

"Salsa to a Shakira song."

Eugene rolled his eyes. "At least it's a dance the judges have heard of. You picked an obscure dance so they couldn't take technical points off."

"It's not obscure, it's traditional. There's a difference," Rini protested, but Eugene was already shuffling out of the room and didn't respond.

"Well, sorry I missed most of that," JC said as he sat on the couch next to Olivier but not so close they were touching. "What were you talking about?"

"The dances we picked, mostly, and how they relate to our charities," Olivier said. "Then Eugene had to pick a fight. Some days I wonder what he has between his ears because it certainly isn't brains. Why do people listen to his show?"

"Because there's a portion of the American populace that shares his opinion," Christine said. "Then there's a portion of the populace that gets lumped in with him because they vote Republican for different reasons than his. I'm all for smaller government. The last thing I want is the government in anyone's bedroom. Unfortunately I often get painted with the same brush as Eugene by people who see only the party name."

"I didn't mean to imply you were as bigoted as him," Olivier assured her quickly. "You're nothing like him."

"Thank you."

"What dance did you choose for the National Breast Cancer Foundation?" Olivier asked, eager to change the subject.

"The rumba," Christine said. "Mike and I talked about it, and both of us have people close to us who have fought breast cancer. We want to portray that struggle and the courage required to keep going through everything until you come out victorious on the other end."

"I'm sure it will be beautiful," Amber said. "I lost my grandmother to breast cancer last year. It's an incredibly worthy cause."

"Yes, it is," Freddy said as he joined them. "My aunt lost the struggle to breast cancer a few years back. She was the one who got me involved with the Save the Music Foundation."

"I'm sorry she's gone, but it's great you get to earn money for the charity she got you involved in," JC said as he scooted a little closer to Olivier to make room for Freddy on the couch. He still kept a sliver of space between them, but he was close enough now that he could feel the heat emanating from Olivier's body. "What dance are you doing?"

"Swing," Freddy said, puffing up his chest with pride. "We're going for the whole big-band thing. I'm going to start off on the trumpet, and while I'm dancin' a couple of the kids who benefited from Save the Music are going to play with the orchestra."

"Oh, that'll be a dream come true for them," Christine said. "Do you know the kids who will be performing?"

"I'm not sure who it's gonna be yet. I gave the producers a few names, but they gotta find out who's available. I hope they can all come, but even if it's just one of them, it'll be awesome."

"Absolutely," Deborah agreed. "And swing will be fun for you too."

"I think we have a good mix of fun and emotional for the show. It's going to be an exciting week." Amber stood and stretched.

"However, I need my beauty sleep if I'm going to make it until the next show. Good night."

"Night." JC glanced at Olivier, trying to catch his attention without anyone noticing. "I think I'm going to head up myself. I need my beauty sleep too." He winked.

Freddy laughed and patted him on the back hard enough to make him stagger. "Naw, you got plenty of beauty. Save some for the rest of us."

"We're all going to regret not having today off by the time the next show rolls around, though," Christine said, standing as well. "And I'm not as young as I used to be. It's past my bedtime."

A chorus of good nights echoed around the room as they left.

"*MON DIEU*, I'm glad he's gone," Olivier said when he and JC were finally alone after the elimination show for week five. "I will not miss anything about him, but especially not his attitude."

"Me either. I wish he'd gone home the first week." JC sat down on the bed and toed off his shoes. It had been a long night waiting to see who would be eliminated. Even though Eugene had gotten the lowest score total by four points, the hosts still dragged it out, and they'd worried that Rini would end up eliminated instead of Eugene. "At least we don't have to worry about him making life difficult anymore."

"That is true, and with him gone, maybe we won't have to hide quite so completely. I don't think anyone still around would care about us, do you?" Olivier pulled JC closer to him and leaned against the headboard. He pressed a kiss to JC's temple and sighed in contentment.

JC settled against Olivier happily. Sitting like this, fully clothed and on top of the covers, felt more intimate than anything they'd done in days. They'd been working too hard on their dances to have the energy for more than a brief kiss before bed for most of the week. "No, I don't. But there are still cameras everywhere, and if something gets recorded, it could be broadcast."

Olivier knew that, but he found he cared less with each passing day. "They're not usually around in the evenings, during dinner and all, unless we're doing something special. We'd still have to be careful, but I feel like we've reached the point of lying to our friends."

"Yeah, but...." JC trailed off as he tried to explain his feelings without scaring Olivier. He sat up and twisted so he could look Olivier in the eyes. "Are you sure? You're the one who isn't out. I don't think anyone still here would care, but that doesn't mean they won't let something slip, either. The more people you tell a secret, the less of one it is."

Olivier considered that for a moment. JC was right, of course, but each person they didn't tell, each choice to divert or deflect interest, felt like a lie. Even worse, it felt like a renunciation of JC. "Maybe I'm not ready to make a public announcement or take out a full-page ad in *USA Today*, but these are our friends. And who knows? Maybe in a month or two or ten, I'll be ready for more, and our secret won't need to be a secret anymore."

"All right." JC wasn't going to argue if Olivier was sure. Everyone already knew he was bisexual, and he doubted anyone would be surprised he was attracted to Olivier. "We can tell them tomorrow, if you want... though you know we'll have to tell my family if we do."

Olivier wasn't worried about telling JC's family. He'd met some of them, and they'd all been lovely people he'd enjoyed being around and who seemed to like him, plus they'd already accepted JC's sexuality. Telling—or letting the rest of the cast guess—would be harder, but JC was worth it.

CHAPTER 17

OLIVIER WALKED into the common area of the house after practice. Rini was sitting on the couch next to a man Olivier didn't know.

"Olivier, come meet Jon, Luis's husband. Jon, this is Olivier Gautier, one of the other contestants."

"I do watch the show, Rini," Jon teased. "I know who the other stars are."

"It's still polite to introduce you," Rini insisted.

"It's nice to meet you. I wondered if we would get the chance," Olivier said, holding out his hand. Jon shook his hand firmly.

"We decided to wait until after Eugene was eliminated," Jon said. "We try not to let our relationship create drama on the set. The producers know, of course, but we don't want to jeopardize Luis's job if the stars take exception to us."

"It's a shame that's still a problem," Olivier said, "but it's good you're able to come now."

"I'm glad I was able to," Jon said. "I miss having dinner with Luis when he eats here."

"I bet the shows are much more fun to watch from the audience too," JC said, joining them after putting the flatware on the table.

Jon laughed. "I've been in the audience. Luis gets me a seat, but it's off to the side a little so I'm not caught on camera too often, and I don't get in the way of the people Elizabeth wants to talk to."

"Ah." JC shook Jon's hand. "Well, it's nice to actually meet you, then. I'm JC Webster."

"Yes, I know." Jon blushed a little as he pulled his hand back. "I watched you in the Olympics. It meant a lot to me to watch an out athlete compete. Most of the dance world knows Luis is gay, but the whole world knows you're bi. That took courage, man."

"Thanks." JC looked down, trying to hide his blush. "I wasn't trying to be inspirational or anything, though. I was just being myself. My teammates knew, so I couldn't really hide it."

"Still. There were a lot of kids who saw you and realized they could be stars too. Don't downplay that."

"It's definitely one of the things we admire about JC," Rini agreed. Olivier nodded as well. JC didn't even look at him, but Olivier could feel the weight of expectation on him. JC wouldn't make the first move. He'd wait for Olivier to say or do something unequivocal before he did anything to out them.

Amber, Deborah, and Christine came in as they were talking. "Who's this?" Amber asked, coming over to where they were standing. "I thought I knew everyone already."

"This is Jon, Luis's husband," Olivier said.

"I didn't know Luis was married!" Amber exclaimed. "Deborah, Christine, come meet Luis's husband. You know you're married to one of the nicest men on set."

Olivier took a step back to make room for the others, but he wanted to observe as well rather than be the focus of attention. So much depended on their reaction.

"Christine Thompson," Christine said. "It's a pleasure to meet you."

"Congresswoman," Jon said with a nod.

"Oh, please," she said. "First, I'm a former congresswoman and secondly, everyone here is family by now. And if you're worried about my politics, I helped defeat the proposed statute that would have prohibited gay marriage in Iowa in 1998. I'm a fiscal conservative, not a social conservative."

"Then it is wonderful to meet you, Christine," Jon said. "Forgive the hesitation, but Luis and I have learned to be cautious. It's easy to get a persecution complex if you aren't careful."

Christine smiled. "Try being a woman in Congress. I know all about persecution."

"I'm sure you do," Jon agreed with a smile. "Persecution of a slightly different variety, but persecution all the same."

"Yes, well, everyone has battles to fight," Deborah said as she shook Jon's hand. "I had to deal with plenty of misogyny in the restaurant world too. And in figure skating."

"This is Deborah McMillan, former Olympic figure skater and current businesswoman extraordinaire," Rini said by way of introduction.

"I wouldn't say extraordinaire," Deborah protested.

"Nonsense. Arabesque is one of the best restaurants in Los Angeles," Rini protested. "And it's not the first one you've owned. You can't tell me that's not fantastic."

"It is fantastic," Jon agreed. "Maybe we'll get to eat there now that we know the owner."

"Maybe we should all go there one night," Olivier said. "It would be a nice change from always eating here."

"Could we plan that for one night?" JC asked Deborah. "It could be a lot of fun."

"Let me talk to the manager about a good time for us to come in," she said. "With at least fourteen of us, it's already a crowd, and if the producers insist the camera crews come along, it will be even worse. I wouldn't want to spring that on my staff unprepared."

"It would be nice if we could do it without cameras," Olivier said. "Then Jon could come, along with any other significant others." He didn't mention Joel specifically, but he imagined Chelsea would appreciate having her boyfriend there if they went out one evening like that.

"It would be nice. I can try telling the producers we don't allow media in the restaurant for the privacy of our patrons," Deborah said. "How many extras would we have? Jon, of course. Anyone else?"

"Chelsea might like to bring her boyfriend," Olivier said. "Tricia isn't seeing anyone. I don't know about anyone else."

"What about anyone else?" Luis asked as he walked in. He went straight to Jon and kissed him briefly on the lips. "What are you talking about?"

"Visiting Deborah's restaurant." Jon slid his arm around Luis's waist. "We're thinking about planning a trip this week, but we weren't sure if any of the pros other than you and Chelsea had a significant other to bring."

"Not serious ones, anyway," Luis said. "I think Sharon has been on a couple of dates, but it's hard to form a serious relationship while the show is going on."

"You'd have to do it with someone else on the show or you'd never see them." Rini pulled the chicken from the oven and set it on the stove. "Dinner's just about ready. Can someone call for everyone else?"

JC waited a moment to see if Olivier was going to say something about Rini's first comment. He wanted to be around if Olivier decided to take advantage of the opportunity, but when he didn't, JC headed toward the door. "Sure. I'll get them."

Olivier waited to take a seat until JC had come back and found a place at the table. As soon as he had, he sat down next to JC. He wanted to sit there anyway, but that also meant he might get the chance to do something casually to let people know about him and JC without announcing it at random. He was pretty sure the people already in the room wouldn't care, and Freddy hadn't been any more patient with Eugene's rants than the rest of them, but Olivier would wait and see how he reacted to Jon before deciding what he wanted to do. He didn't want to keep hiding, but the part of him that had felt constrained to staying in the closet wasn't as easily overcome as Olivier would have liked.

The other pros greeted Jon familiarly, and Freddy didn't blink at the introduction, so Olivier relaxed a little more. Then Rini set the food in front of them, and he focused on that for the time being. Only after they'd decimated the chicken and were sitting around chatting did Olivier consider his options again. JC leaned forward to make a point— not that Olivier was actually following the conversation; he was too distracted by the swath of skin where JC's T-shirt had ridden up—and Olivier saw his chance. He reached over to tug the T-shirt back into place and then left his hand on JC's back.

JC glanced over at Olivier, but when Olivier remained nonchalant, he scooted a little closer and settled in, waiting for someone to react. No one did, probably because it was hard to see where Olivier's hand was with the table in the way, so when JC got up to put his plate in the sink, he made a point to catch Olivier's hand and squeeze it.

Amber watched carefully as JC returned to his seat. When Olivier slid his hand around JC's back again, she grinned. "Oh my God. *That's* what's been going on between the two of you!"

Olivier shrugged. "Yes?" It wasn't really a question, but he wasn't entirely sure what else to say.

"What do you mean 'yes'? Are you together or aren't you? And if you aren't, why do you have your hand on JC's back?" Amber said, but she was smiling so widely Olivier couldn't help but grin back. He probably looked like a besotted fool, but he could live with that.

"Yes," he said, more firmly this time. "Yes, we're together. We just didn't feel like listening to—"

"Our dearly departed costar," Deborah interrupted. "I don't blame you. I wouldn't have said anything while he was around either."

"It wasn't just what he would have said to us, though." JC didn't deny that their reluctance to say anything had a lot to do with Eugene, but he wasn't the only reason. "Olivier isn't out, so we didn't want to risk anyone saying anything in front of the cameras or to the public."

"Don't worry. None of us will say anything," Christine promised. "We all know how hard it can be to keep something private."

JC nodded his thanks. "We weren't really worried about you guys, or we wouldn't have said anything."

"Thank you," Olivier said. "It feels good not to have to hide anymore." He wasn't entirely sure he was ready for the world to know about him, but all the tension he usually carried around worried someone could ask him if he was single or seeing anyone had disappeared. They all knew he wasn't single now, and nobody seemed to mind.

JC SHOWED up for the first group dance practice early and sat in the corner fidgeting until Deborah walked in. "Morning," he said, trying to sound more enthusiastic than he felt. He liked Deborah and Christine, but he felt like their team was a little unbalanced, as it consisted of the two older women and him. Amber had picked Olivier, Freddy, and Rini when they'd picked teams Wednesday night, while Deborah had picked him and Christine. It felt like Team Cotillion had an advantage over Team Quadrille.

"Good morning," Deborah said happily. "This is so exciting, isn't it? Our first group dance."

"Yeah, I guess." In a way, it was exciting. It meant they'd made it past one of the milestones of the show. "I don't know anything about the quadrille, though."

"I don't think any of us do," Christine said, "but I doubt the other team knows anything about the cotillion either. The one thing I do know about the Regency period was that elegance was the expectation, so we have them at an advantage. As much as I love Freddy and Rini, elegant is not the word I would use to describe them."

"I'm not exactly elegant either," JC said.

"But swimming has taught you control and precision," Deborah said, "and with those, you can learn to be elegant. Right, Brody?"

"Right, what?" Brody asked. "I'm not agreeing to anything until I know what I'm agreeing to."

"Deborah was telling JC he could learn the elegance of the quadrille easily enough since he had to learn control and precision for swimming," Christine explained.

"Sounds right to me. We'll just wait for Chelsea and Mike, and we'll get started. I spent last night refreshing my memory. I haven't done a quadrille since I was a boy going to fancy parties with my mum."

"You danced the quadrille when you were a kid?" JC blinked. The kind of parties he'd gone to as a kid hadn't had fancy dances.

"Oh yeah. My mum loved fancy parties, and she took me to every one she could. It's what started me dancing." Brody grinned. "My mum was never any good, but she had fun, and that's what's most important."

"Absolutely," Christine said. "We're going to have a blast."

"Right." JC pushed all thoughts of looking ridiculous compared to Mike and Brody out of his head. "We're going to have fun." He'd make sure he did, no matter how the dance went.

"Look good doing it," Deborah added.

"Absolutely," Chelsea said as she came in. "I bet we can make Olivier drool watching you, both in this and the waltz."

"Oh *God*," JC moaned as he buried his face in his hands. "I knew there was a reason we shouldn't have told people. Now that everyone knows, you're going to be insufferable, aren't you?"

"Only when you deserve it." Chelsea patted him on the cheek. "Now come on, let's learn the quadrille."

OLIVIER WAS the last to arrive in the studio for the first team rehearsal. His mother had miscalculated the time difference between Carcassonne and Los Angeles, and nothing would do but that he tell her everything before she would let him go. He wasn't technically more than about two minutes late, but he hated the idea that everyone else had to wait on him.

"Sorry I'm late," he said as he rushed into the room. "My mother called."

"Is that what they're calling it these days?" Luis said with a smirk. "We all know now. There's no reason to pretend you weren't making out with your sexy boyfriend."

"I wasn't," Olivier insisted. "My mother.... You know what, never mind. If it makes you happy to think I was making out with JC, you can go right on thinking that."

"It makes me very happy," Luis said. "I hope you had a good chat with your mother."

"She forgets the time difference. She was supposed to call an hour ago instead of now, so I had to cut the call short, but other than that, it was a good chat."

"Good, though I'd almost rather you were making out with your sexy boyfriend," Amber said with a smile. "Then I wouldn't feel as guilty about landing the two of you on different teams."

"No, don't. It's good for them," Tyler said. "They'll both dance their best because they know the other one is watching."

"Besides, if they were on the same team, I'm not sure we'd get anything done," Tricia added. "Chelsea and I have known for a while, and I've seen the two of them together. They can't keep their eyes off each other."

Olivier flushed a little. "Do you blame me?" It was more bravado than anything else, but at the same time, it felt so good not to hide.

"Not a bit," Freddy said. "My wife walks into a room and everything else disappears for a few minutes, and we've been married almost thirty years. When you land a looker, you keep right on lookin' so she—or he—keeps on lookin' back at you. Anybody know anything about this here cotillion we're supposed to be learnin'? I didn't go to no debutante balls when I was that age in New Orleans. I ain't got the foggiest idea what we got to do."

"Don't worry, Freddy," Sharon said, "that's what we're here for."

JC SLIPPED into the wings as Rini took the dance floor during dress rehearsal. She was performing her waltz two dances before his, so he probably wouldn't get the chance to watch it properly tonight as he'd be heading down to get ready for his dance, and he wanted to see her perform. She and Luis looked fantastic dressed as Morticia and Gomez Addams, and he was curious to see if they'd pull off their waltz with the same flair.

They did, though JC knew enough about dancing now to catch a few of the mistakes she made. For all her spirit, Rini probably was the poorest dancer out of the remaining group, and they were reaching the point where personality meant less than dance ability. He complimented her as she walked off stage, though, as it truly had been an amazing thing to watch. "You looked great."

"Thanks." Rini smoothed her hands over her fitted black dress. "I know it's not the standard regency or Victorian look, but Luis and I decided to have fun with it this week. I've had low enough scores that I wouldn't be surprised if I went home."

JC wanted to say she was wrong, but he knew she was likely right. "If you do, you'll go out with a bang."

"I just don't want to drag down my team during the group dance," she admitted. "If I go home, that's my problem. That's different than hurting their scores."

"I'm sure it won't come to that," JC assured her.

She smiled but didn't look convinced as she headed to the dressing room to change into her outfit for the group dance.

"Ready for your waltz?" Olivier asked as he approached JC. "You look fantastic." Olivier couldn't help staring. He'd seen JC in a suit and he'd seen him in nothing at all, but he'd never seen him looking quite like this. His white breeches, waistcoat, and intricately tied cravat provided a stark contrast to his dark hair and skin. The burgundy jacket set off his shoulders and tapered toward his waist, making him look broader than Olivier had expected.

"As ready as I'm going to be," JC said as he took in Olivier's costume. He'd changed into his group dance costume and looked fantastic in his black tailed jacket and emerald green waistcoat. His white pants hugged his legs so tightly it was almost indecent—probably why they were called inexpressibles. The costume department had told JC they'd been worn by real dandies when they'd tried to get JC into them. He'd refused, but damn, was he glad Olivier had agreed.

"You'll do fantastic, I'm sure," Olivier said.

JC had been more sure of it before he'd been distracted by Olivier's costume, but at least he was seeing it now instead of during the live show. He'd missed Olivier's waltz—not to be confused with the Viennese waltz he'd done in week five—as he'd been getting into his own costume and going over things with Chelsea, and he figured that outfit would be distracting enough tonight. "Thanks." He looked around, hoping to squeeze in a kiss, but there were cameras on the dance floor to make sure they had the blocking right for Freddy's dance, and JC could never be sure how much they could see.

Olivier took a step closer, blocking the space between their bodies with his back, and squeezed JC's hand. "Good luck, and I'll see you after the rehearsal. I want a proper kiss before the show tonight."

CHAPTER 18

WHEN THE elimination show was over the next day, Elizabeth rounded up the remaining six contestants. "I know you want to spend more time saying good-bye to Rini, but we need to draw partners for next week first."

JC leaned in closer to Chelsea. "Partners? What for?"

She shrugged. "We'll see. Come on."

He glanced back toward Rini and Luis. It felt wrong leaving them standing alone, but he didn't have a choice. Elizabeth was already motioning for the remaining contestants to hurry up.

Olivier ignored Elizabeth for a moment to give Rini a quick hug. "I don't know what she needs us for, but don't disappear before we can say good-bye properly."

Rini nodded a little tearfully and motioned for him to go with the others. Olivier followed them into the green room and waited to see what Elizabeth would say.

"Next week, in addition to your individual dance, we'll be doing a trio dance, but we're doing it a little differently than last season. Instead of adding an extra pro to the routine, we'll be pairing two stars together, and you'll be dancing with one pro. I'll draw names to see who you're paired with."

Olivier held his breath. He could dance with Deborah or Christine if he had to, and with Amber pretty easily, but he hoped he didn't get Freddy. He liked the man, and his support had been as strong as anyone else's, but from a competition standpoint, he wasn't sure how much longer Freddy would make it.

"And the first name is…." Elizabeth paused for dramatic effect as the cameras panned across the room, catching all the stars' expressions. "Freddy! And Freddy will be dancing with—" She stuck her hand back in the bag. "—Amber!"

Everyone clapped, and Amber came over to give Freddy a big hug. Olivier relaxed. Whoever he ended up with, he had a decent chance of a good dance.

"The second two stars to work together in the trio dance will be Christine and.... Deborah! Good luck, ladies. How are you going to choose between Brody and Mike to have on the dance floor with you?"

Christine and Deborah both shrugged. "I'm sure we'll figure it out when we see what dance and music we have," Deborah said diplomatically.

Olivier had to struggle to keep his expression neutral at the announcement. He got to dance with JC. He wasn't sure that was good for keeping their relationship private, but it was amazing for actually using his newfound skills on the one person in the world he most wanted to dance with.

"And that leaves JC and Olivier to dance together. Any thoughts on which of your lovely ladies you'll take onto the floor with you?"

"I think it's like Deborah said—it depends on the dance and music. Chelsea and Tricia both have their strengths, and we want to dance with whichever one will give us the highest score." JC glanced back at the two pros. "Either way, it's not going to be a hardship to have either of them on the floor with us." He would rather have no one else on the floor with them, but he was confident both Chelsea and Tricia would make sure he and Olivier got to dance the way *they* wanted, at least for part of the performance.

"I think it might be Tricia and me fighting over the position, honestly," Chelsea said with a smirk. "I mean, who wouldn't want to get to dance with *both* these hot men?"

"I wouldn't mind it at all," Tricia added, making a show of looking both Olivier and JC up and down for the cameras.

"Oh, it sounds like this is going to be interesting indeed," Elizabeth said, looking directly at the camera. She paused and waited for the camera to cut off and then nodded at the group. "Thanks. You guys are free to go now. Good luck, and I'll see you next week."

Released from their duties to the show, everyone gathered around Rini, hugging her.

"I knew it was coming," she told them with a watery smile. "You all danced better than I did this week. I'll be in the audience for the rest of the shows. I wouldn't miss seeing what happens now for anything."

"You just want to see what happens when Olivier and I take the floor," JC joked softly when he hugged Rini.

"I can imagine worse things to watch," Rini said. "You'll wow them for sure."

"Yeah." JC felt warm just thinking about it. He hated to see Rini go, but even that wasn't enough to dampen his joy at the idea of dancing with Olivier.

"WELL, BOYS," Tricia drawled when JC and Olivier came into the studio the next morning, "are you ready for this?"

"It depends on what dance we have," Olivier said, "and what you're planning on having us do."

"That's somewhat up to you," Chelsea said. "We drew the Argentine tango, but beyond that, the story we tell is something we can come up with on our own."

"I want to dance *with* JC, not just in opposition to him," Olivier said immediately. "I know it won't be possible the whole time, but at least some."

Tricia grinned. "We can work with that. What do you think, Chelsea? Feel like being fought over by the two handsomest men on set?"

"Like I'd complain about that, but if we're really going for the femme fatale, you do that better than I do. I can do all the steps, but you manage the character better."

"What do you think, boys?"

"Whichever will get us the highest scores," Olivier said. He was comfortable dancing with Tricia, but JC was comfortable with Chelsea, so one of them was going to end up having to get used to a new partner, not to mention getting used to each other on the dance floor.

"It's not Chelsea or me who's going to get you good scores," Tricia said. "It's the way you look at each other that will set the voting lines on fire. When the women who watch the show get a look at you on stage together, it'll be all over."

"Well, neither one of you is going to damage the aesthetics of the dance," JC pointed out. Tricia was more his type—tall, dark, and gorgeous—but Chelsea was a looker in her own right, and if JC hadn't met Olivier he might have been jealous of Joel. "So I guess the real question is: Which one of you wants to sit back and enjoy the show?"

Chelsea laughed. "Whichever one of us isn't dancing will be anxiously waiting in the wings. We'll watch, but we won't be relaxing and enjoying it. How you dance will reflect on both of us, regardless of who's on stage with you."

"What premise do we want, then?" JC asked. "Let's figure that out and then decide which one of you is best."

"Argentine tango is about seduction, but it's also about power, specifically the power negotiation between the man and the woman. Since there are two of you and only one of us, the obvious answer would be to have you two fighting over us. That way, when you come at us to get the pro free from the other one, you'll be able to perform together." Tricia grinned at them.

"Sounds good to me," Olivier said.

"We'll need to figure out which one of them will be in hold if we get them together," Chelsea said.

"Oh, that's easy," Tricia said. "Whichever one had the girl last will lead until they break apart and come back to her."

"So instead of letting Olivier cut in, I'll take him in hold and lead him away from the girl," JC mused. "That could work. It would look natural, and we'd still get to dance with each other."

"Exactly," Chelsea said. "You'll be leading your competition away from the girl."

"Just remember that while you're performing you can't actually be more interested in the competition than the girl," Tricia teased. "Not unless you're ready to share your relationship with the whole world."

"No." Olivier shook his head and vetoed that idea. "I am happy we were able to share with everyone on the show, but I am not ready for the world to know yet."

"And I don't think it's the world's business who I'm in a relationship with," JC added. "Besides, everyone knows I'm bi. I can easily convince everyone I'm lusting after whichever one of you dances with us."

"It might work better if it were Tricia, then," Chelsea suggested. "We've been dancing together all season, and I haven't heard any rumors that the two of us have a thing going on."

"I don't want them to actually think I'm in a relationship with either of you."

"No, but you can really sell the strong character the Argentine tango requires if you seduce a completely new partner," Chelsea pointed out. "Olivier has an advantage there because he's bigger, so putting you with Tricia and letting you seduce her through the dance will even the playing field a bit."

"Even though she's taller than me in heels?"

"Even then," Tricia said. "The moves are at a different angle because of my height, but really it's the same thing. And seducing a taller woman makes you look stronger too."

"All right. We'll dance with Tricia," JC agreed. "So what now?"

"Costumes," Tricia said. "It's all about seduction and power."

"I'd like you both to be shirtless, or at least end up that way," Chelsea added. "Sometimes an open shirt is sexier than no shirt, but the power plays in the Argentine tango really work best if you strip off as much as possible."

An automatic refusal sprang to Olivier's lips, but he caught JC's eye and bit it back. If ever there was a right time to do this, it was now, with JC at his side to boost his confidence. "I'd rather not do the whole dance shirtless," he said, "but if ending up that way works best for the character of the dance, I'll give it a try."

JC smiled at Olivier's comment. He knew how hard that was for Olivier to agree to, and he was proud, though he wouldn't make a big deal of it in front of Tricia and Chelsea. "Maybe vests?" he suggested, knowing that would cover the big scar on Olivier's back and most of the one on his shoulder. "That way they can be open in the front and show off our arms, and we can strip them off at the very end."

"I like that idea," Tricia said. "What do you think, Olivier?"

"That would work," Olivier said with a grateful look for JC.

Chelsea giggled. "I have an even better idea. It's nothing for a man to strip off his own vest or shirt, and not all that big a deal if his partner does, but what if JC and Olivier pulled each other's vests off?"

Tricia grinned. "I like it. Ready to learn some basic moves, boys?" Tricia held her hand out to Olivier. "This afternoon we'll work on our individual dances since we have to do two dances this week.

Chelsea and I will start choreographing this dance tonight, and we'll teach you actual moves in the morning."

JC held his hand out to Chelsea. "Okay. Let's do this."

OLIVIER FOLLOWED JC into JC's room after dinner. They had asked if they needed to work with Chelsea and Tricia while they choreographed the dance, but both pros had shooed them off and told them to get some rest so they'd be ready for practice in the morning. Olivier certainly wasn't going to argue with a chance to spend a quiet evening with JC. They'd have precious few of those as the show got closer and the pressure to rehearse mounted.

As soon as the door closed behind them, shutting out any chance of the cameras seeing something they didn't want to share, Olivier pulled JC into his arms and kissed him thoroughly. He loved the way JC settled into his arms like he belonged there. When he finally lifted his head, JC blinked up at him. Olivier kissed the tip of his nose and shifted so he had JC in the hold Tricia had taught him for the Argentine tango. "Shall we dance?"

JC smiled as he moved into the proper position. He'd been fantasizing about dancing *with* Olivier all afternoon, to the point that he almost hadn't been able to concentrate on his samba. In his fantasies, he'd been the one leading, but he was willing to let Olivier take the lead for now. "God, yes. I've been thinking about this all afternoon."

"Me too," Olivier said. He began the steps, simple though they were. By the time they were done, it wouldn't be simple. He'd figured that much out already, but they didn't have an audience now, no one to impress, no one to care if they missed a step or didn't have the perfect expression on their faces. Given that he couldn't school his expression to anything but adoration, he counted that as lucky.

JC grinned as Olivier led him around the room. It wasn't the full dance they'd be doing on show night, but then he wouldn't get to spend as long in Olivier's arms. Even just learning the basic steps of the Argentine tango had left JC wanting to dance it with no one but Olivier, and he relished the chance to stay pressed against Olivier as long as he could. As Olivier led him around the bed, JC tried one of the moves Tricia had shown them earlier, pressing himself close, and then kicking out one leg and curling it behind Olivier's before straightening it again and returning it to its original position.

It worked the first time, but the second time he tried it, JC lost his balance and stumbled, making Olivier catch him. "Sorry," he gasped, looking up at Olivier with wide eyes. "Messed that bit up."

"That's what practice is for," Olivier said as he bent to kiss JC lightly. "Do you want to try again?"

JC shook his head, so Olivier returned to kissing him, completely ignoring the steps they had learned earlier in the day in favor of swaying with JC in his arms.

CHAPTER 19

OLIVIER DASHED back toward the viewing area from the dressing rooms. He didn't want to miss any of the trio dances if he could help it, both because they were his friends and because he wanted to see how Deborah and Christine handled the Argentine tango. He didn't see them playing up the homoerotic aspect of two women dancing together, so they had to have found some other twist.

He was a little nervous about what Henrietta would say about his and JC's choices, but Tricia and Chelsea had both assured them they hadn't crossed any lines in their choreography. Skated close to a few, but not crossed any.

JC glanced over when Olivier arrived and grinned, glad he'd made it. Deborah and Christine were just taking the floor with Brody, and JC had been worried that since Olivier's salsa was the last individual dance of the night, he wouldn't get to see Deborah and Christine perform. He tried to relax now that Olivier was at his side, but he ended up just shifting his worry to how their dance would compare to the other two trio dances.

The montage was mostly Deborah and Christine talking about how much fun they'd had working together and footage of the two of them dancing with Brody while Mike hovered off to the side and called out instructions, clearly wanting more control than he had. As the lights came up on the floor, JC could see Mike still hovering off to the side, looking more nervous than he had all season long.

"Mike looks like he's about to lose it. Why did they pick Brody? Wouldn't it have been easier to have Mike dance with them?" Olivier asked. Before JC could answer, the music started, and they watched as Christine stalked toward a very innocent, awkward-looking Brody. "Never mind. I understand now. Mike could never look that clueless and slightly scared."

"No. And he could never let them take control like that either," JC said as he watched Deborah grab Brody's tie and spin him toward Christine to pull it from around his neck. They had all the elements of the Argentine tango that Tricia and Chelsea had insisted he and Olivier include in theirs, but they were playing it in a completely different way, with the two women working together to seduce Brody instead of fighting over him. It wasn't something that would ever have occurred to JC, but it worked for Deborah and Christine.

The audience hooted and cheered as Deborah and Christine got Brody down to his shirt and then stripped that off as well. Olivier wondered what they would make of his and JC's open vests. Hopefully they would have as positive a reaction. And if not, well, Olivier's scores from the first round were his best yet, quite a bit better than everyone but JC and Amber, so if they took a bit of a hit from the judges, it would be worth it to dance with JC.

Deborah and Christine finished with a flourish, pushing a half-naked Brody into a chair and perching seductively on either side of his lap. JC clapped along with the audience and whistled in appreciation. "Nice," he commented to Olivier. "Different from ours, too, which is good."

"Yes. I hope ours isn't so different it hurts us, though," Olivier said as he leaned forward to listen to the judges' comments.

The judges were complimentary, praising the way Deborah and Christine made their strengths work for them and the harmony with which they'd disarmed Brody. They even complimented Mike on his choreography, which seemed to calm him some, and all four of them were beaming when they left to meet Corey and get their scores.

Corey fawned over the ladies too, as he tended to do, and made a point of running his hand over Brody's bare chest. "That was lovely to watch, ladies. Think I can help next time you want to undress him?"

Deborah laughed. "I don't know if I'll get another chance, but if I do, absolutely."

Before Corey could tease further, the scores were ready. Deborah and Christine held hands and bounced a little—looking far younger than their years—as the scores were announced. Emma Leigh gave them a ten, which got screams from the audience, and Henrietta and Edoardo both gave them nines. Combined with their earlier scores, Deborah had a fifty-five out of a possible sixty when her cha-cha was included, and Christine had a score of a fifty-one with the paso doble she'd done earlier....

"Nicely done," Olivier said to Deborah and Christine when Corey finally released them. "I hope we do as well."

"I'm sure you will," Christine said. "It was fun, but I'm glad it's done. It was a lot of work."

"Yes, it's two dances a week or more from here on out," Olivier said.

Elizabeth's voice interrupted with the announcement of Freddy and Amber's dance. Olivier hurried to the staging area so he could see what Amber and Freddy had done with the paso doble. Sharon took the stage with them, framing Freddy between the two female dancers as they began their routine. Having watched Tyler do the paso doble two weeks earlier, Olivier thought they'd made a wise choice. Freddy would have looked comical trying to dance next to Tyler, whereas Amber had a decent chance of matching Sharon as long as the choreography wasn't too intense.

The music started, and all three dancers threw themselves into the dance with gusto, but even to Olivier, it was clear how outmatched Freddy was. He trundled along, doing his best, but Olivier winced more than once in sympathy. Their scores weren't going to be pretty, which was a shame, because Amber was doing well and deserved more than they would probably earn.

When the dance finally ended after what felt like a lot longer than two minutes and thirty seconds, JC breathed a sigh of relief. It had been painful to watch Freddy struggling so valiantly to keep up with Amber and Sharon, especially after he'd done so well on his rumba earlier. The judges seemed to agree, as their comments to Freddy were encouraging, but not all that positive. Their comments to Amber, however, were both positive and apologetic, as they had to rate them both together. In the end, they got three eights, giving Freddy a total of fifty and Amber a total of fifty-three when her score was combined with the two tens and a nine from her Argentine tango.

Then it was their turn. JC grinned at Olivier as they took the stage with Tricia and watched the montage. Mostly, it was of them practicing and a little bit of the discussion they'd had around which of the pros they'd dance with, but there were personal comments too. JC cringed as his larger-than-life face filled the screen. It was always a little surreal and embarrassing to watch this part.

"Doing two dances is going to be challenging," he said on the screen, "but I think it'll be fun. The audience will get to see a new side of me. You all know JC Webster, but this week you'll get to meet Javier Carrillo, Latin lover."

JC cringed. That sounded even cheesier now than when he'd said it. He had hoped when it hadn't appeared in his first montage before the samba that the producers had left it out, but of course they'd used it here, right when he was about to dance with Olivier. Fuck. "Sorry," he mouthed across the stage to Olivier, hoping he saw it and knew that JC wasn't trying to out him.

Olivier winced a little at the choice of words, but he could hardly argue the truth of the statement. JC had only done the rumba and salsa from the Latin dances before tonight, so he was showing the audience a new side of himself with both his earlier samba and their shared Argentine tango. He could only hope people wouldn't read more into it than the typical predance boasting they all did as a matter of course. He pushed the thought aside to focus on the dance. They couldn't do anything about the montage now, and they had a dance to perform and hopefully high scores to gain.

When the lights came up, Tricia sat alone on a chaise longue, her red dress outlining her body where it didn't reveal it. On cue, Olivier and JC entered from either side and approached where she sat. Olivier reached her one step ahead of JC, grabbing her hand and pulling her to her feet and into his arms. She recoiled even as she followed his lead, giving JC the opening to grab Olivier's shoulders in the guise of pushing him away from Tricia.

JC pushed Olivier away, but instead of turning to Tricia to take his place, JC stepped closer to Olivier. It was supposed to look like him telling Olivier to back off farther, but as they moved in time with the music, it felt like they were dancing together. After a few beats, JC turned back and pulled Tricia into his arms. They moved together fluidly, kicking their legs around each other and Tricia running her hands over his body. Meanwhile, Olivier circled around them, looking for the opportunity to move in again.

They had debated extensively how much time they had to each spend dancing with Tricia and how much time they could get away with in each other's arms. Olivier didn't have to feign the jealousy on his face as he watched Tricia and JC dance until it was his turn to cut in again, although he hoped anyone seeing him would think he wanted to be in JC's place instead of in Tricia's place. His cue came, and he insinuated himself between them, slipping into JC's arms as he pushed him away from Tricia. JC grabbed him in hold and led him through the next few steps. The audience cheered and shouted, but Olivier kept his focus on JC and on keeping his expression appropriate for the character of the dance.

JC wanted to cling to Olivier like he had back in his bedroom when they first learned the dance, but the choreography called for him to let go after a few steps and let Olivier turn back to Tricia. They were supposed to be fighting each other, not falling into each other's arms. It was easy to stay in character when Olivier and Tricia were dancing together, and even when he was with Tricia, but when he was with Olivier, it was so hard to look angry instead of lust-filled.

They continued circling around each other, each stealing Tricia from the other, and dancing a few steps together whenever the choreography allowed it. Halfway through the dance, when Olivier and Tricia were coming at each other angrily, JC stepped in to push Olivier out of the way. It was supposed to look like he'd intended to shove him and then dance with Tricia, but since Olivier was so primed for Tricia to come to him, they ended up dancing a few bars together, kicks and touches and all, though both Chelsea and Tricia had vetoed JC literally wrapping himself around Olivier.

Olivier grabbed JC's red vest as if to hold on to him so that when JC pulled away to go back to Tricia, the vest stayed behind in Olivier's hand. The crowd went wild, echoing Olivier's pounding heart. He tossed the vest aside and stalked after JC, peeling his own vest off as he went—it just hadn't worked out for JC to strip him as well—so that when he next stole Tricia and ended up in JC's arms for a moment, they danced skin to skin. The contact electrified him, leaving him hard and aching, but they had to finish the dance. Only a few more bars and they'd be done, but they would still have to stand together to listen to the judges' comments and then make it offstage and off camera before he could give in to the emotions assailing him.

He broke away from JC and pulled Tricia back into his arms as the dance ended with him triumphant, but the real triumph was the look on Tricia's face when the audience broke into a standing ovation. She pulled him and JC into an embrace. "You were amazing—both of you."

JC picked up his vest from the floor and held it strategically in front of him as he headed to the judges' table. Just *watching* Olivier dance the Argentine tango would have been enough to turn him on. Actually dancing with him—and with Tricia, who he definitely found attractive—had him half-hard and aching with desire. He wrapped his arm around Chelsea, who had come out to join them, and stood next to Olivier as they waited for the judges' comments.

"Okay, wow. The two of you dancing together? That was *hot!*" Emma Leigh fanned herself with her hand. "It's a little unconventional, but then so is the trio Argentine tango, and you did stick to tango moves. I like the way you fought over Tricia, and I admire the courage it took to take it to the level where you dance with each other, especially in a dance like this one, where it's all about sex. There were a few places where it felt like the third person was extraneous instead of being fully incorporated into the dance, but other than that I really liked it. Good job."

"That, gentlemen, was a marvel," Henrietta said, "one that's a testament to your partners' choreography and your confidence. I don't know many men who would have embraced the moments where you danced together as wholeheartedly as you did. You maintained sharp lines and precise movements even with the constant changing of partners. Well done."

"You two are on *fire*," Edoardo gushed, standing up to start his rave. "When you were dancing with Tricia, you were brilliant and gorgeous and lovely, but the two of you together were just *wow*. I can't even describe it, but I want more. The whole dance was full of passion and sexual tension. I felt like a voyeur watching it, and I love that. Keep it up, both of you."

JC and Olivier thanked the judges and headed back to Corey in the viewing area to wait for their scores. Olivier's pulse still hadn't settled from the dance and having JC in his arms.

"Boys," Corey gushed, "what was that? You've been keeping secrets from us. You didn't tell us you could dance like that."

Olivier tried not to flinch at the comment, all too aware of the secret they were still keeping.

"We couldn't until Tricia and Chelsea taught us," JC said, giving Olivier a moment to recover his composure.

"Now that they have, though, look out, world," Olivier said, hoping his grin didn't seem fake. "We're going to wow everyone with our dancing."

Before Corey could say anything else, Elizabeth's voice rang out in the theater, announcing it was time for their scores. "Emma Leigh."

"Ten!"

"Henrietta."

"Nine."

"Edoardo."

"A *ten*!"

JC hugged Olivier. In his excitement, he almost kissed him but stopped himself at the last moment and turned to hug Chelsea instead. They'd have to celebrate their great scores later, when they could do whatever they wanted without cameras and an audience.

Olivier swung Tricia around and then reached for Chelsea and JC. As long as he hugged all three of them, he could get away with hugging JC on camera. No one would notice if he squeezed JC a little tighter than he embraced the girls. On the dance floor, Elizabeth was making her end-of-show announcements, forcing Olivier to let them go so he and the others could make their way back onstage for the final camera pan across the contestants.

As soon as the On Air light went off, Olivier grabbed Tricia and swung her around again. He thought about pouncing on JC like he would on his rugby teammates, but he wasn't sure JC could support his weight, and he didn't want to injure him. He had plans for tonight.

CHAPTER 20

AS SOON as they were in the house and completely away from anyone who didn't know about him and Olivier, JC pounced, wrapping his arms around Olivier's neck and kissing him soundly. When he pulled back, they were alone in the foyer. He smiled up at Olivier. "Best show ever." There were still three weeks left, but unless one of them won the grand prize, JC doubted any of them could top this one, and maybe not even then. The only thing that would be better would be getting to do a whole dance with only each other.

"It was," Olivier agreed. He switched his grip on JC so he had him in hold for the Argentine tango and danced him down the hall and around the living room, to the catcalls of their friends.

"Get a room," Amber teased.

Olivier thought that sounded like a marvelous idea. Without releasing JC he moved them upstairs and down the hallway toward his room. It wasn't any bigger than JC's, but at least they would be alone together.

JC fell into the steps easily and let Olivier guide him down the hall. They stumbled a little as they pushed the door to Olivier's room open, and then Olivier guided him into it, still keeping him in hold. The bed got in the way, but JC turned as they reached it, and they kept dancing, moving around the furniture as best they could.

It didn't matter that there was barely enough space in Olivier's room. The moment Olivier took the first step, all thoughts of anything other than Olivier fled JC's mind. It wasn't the full Argentine tango—there wasn't enough room to separate and come back together—but it was enough to drive JC mad. The dance was nearly sex itself, and Olivier's firm hand as he guided JC around the room was enough to heighten the comparison in JC's mind. He felt wanted, needed, like Olivier was fighting for *him*, and when he looked up and saw the expression of adoration on Olivier's face, the words just slipped out. "I love you."

Olivier nearly stumbled at the words. He'd come so close to saying them over the past couple of weeks, but one thing or another had held him back each time. He didn't have to hold back anymore. "Je t'aime aussi," he whispered. "I love you too."

He broke hold to slide one hand down to JC's waist, pulling him even closer than the tango required so their bodies touched from chest to thigh. JC stepped into him so Olivier's thigh slotted between his own. Olivier groaned at the feeling of JC's erection against him. He'd had seduction in mind when he started the dance, but he'd planned to do the seducing. Instead JC had seduced him completely. He pressed forward, forcing JC to take a step back. When he began the turn, JC followed him easily, keeping their bodies snugly together. Olivier groaned and came out of the turn with a back step. JC moved right with him into the step and undulated against Olivier.

"That wasn't in the moves Chelsea and Tricia taught us," he said hoarsely.

"We're not on camera now," JC reminded him. "We can try our own moves."

Or no moves at all, as far as Olivier was concerned. The bed was a few feet away. He didn't stop dancing, though. It felt too good to have JC in his arms this way, like all the preparation of the entire season had led up to this moment, just the two of them in each other's arms, dancing for themselves instead of for an audience.

The tango was forgotten completely as they moved together, just doing what came naturally instead of following any choreography or predetermined moves. JC let Olivier continue to lead for a few moments, but when the knowledge that his feelings were returned became too much, he guided Olivier toward the bed. "Want you," he murmured in a voice deepened by arousal. He spun when they reached the bed and sat on it with his legs spread and Olivier standing between them. He leaned back, resting his weight on his elbows so he could better take in the magnificent view in front of him. Even fully clothed, Olivier was gorgeous, a truly magnificent specimen of a man, and he loved JC.

"You have me," Olivier promised as he stared down at JC spread out on the bed. He knelt on the edge of the mattress, one knee between JC's legs, the other on the outside. He leaned over JC so he could kiss him. JC scooted back toward the head of the bed to give Olivier more room, but space wasn't what Olivier wanted. He just wanted JC. Keeping hold of JC's shoulders so JC wouldn't scoot any more, Olivier settled down onto JC's body, chest to chest, groin to groin. They groaned in tandem. "You are so fucking sexy."

Warmth surged through JC at Olivier's words. He struggled to understand how Olivier could think his gangly body was anything other than awkward, but he'd learned over the past few weeks that whatever JC thought of himself, to Olivier, that was the truth. "So are you," he said, wrapping his arms around Olivier and rolling his hips up. He was already half hard from dancing, and the way Olivier pressed against him was quickly taking care of the rest.

Slowly, so he didn't ruin the moment, JC slid his hands under Olivier's shirt. He wanted to touch every inch of Olivier, to worship him and show him just how loved he was, but he also didn't want to move. This moment, right here, was perfect, and JC wanted it to last as long as possible.

"Je t'aime," Olivier whispered against JC's neck. Now that he'd said it, he didn't want to stop. He sucked gently on JC's pulse point, careful not to leave a mark. The others knew about them, but if it showed up on camera, JC could face questions. He arched into JC's touch. Suddenly the impediment of clothing was more than he could stand. He reared up onto his knees and stripped his shirt off over his head. He grabbed the hem of JC's T-shirt and tugged. JC moved obligingly so Olivier could pull it off him as well. When that was gone, Olivier slid JC's shorts and boxers down too, leaving JC naked beneath him. He shucked the rest of his own clothing and then settled atop JC again with a soft moan of delight. JC was all hard muscle and soft skin beneath him. Olivier wanted to rub all over him like a cat in heat.

JC gasped as Olivier settled over him, warm and hard in all the right places. As he slid his hands down Olivier's back to cup his ass, JC laid a trail of kisses along Olivier's shoulder and up his neck to his jaw. Then he captured Olivier's lips with his and kissed him until he couldn't breathe. "Te amo." Olivier had said it in French first, so JC wasn't going to limit himself to English. Spanish was his second language, and while he wasn't nearly as fluent in it as Olivier was in English, he knew enough to say this.

Olivier only knew the Spanish he could figure out from it sounding like French, but that one was easy. He returned the kiss as he rolled to his side. As much as he wanted to stay pressed to the full length of JC's body, he couldn't get his hands on JC the way they were, and he very much wanted to touch as much of JC's honey-tan skin as he could.

JC rolled after Olivier and plastered himself against him. "Te adoro," he whispered, not caring if Olivier understood more than the sentiment. "Eres maravilloso y magnífico y estoy enamorado de ti." He wrapped one hand around Olivier's cock and stroked it a few times, loving the way Olivier squirmed beneath him. He could do this indefinitely, just enjoying the way Olivier moved, but he wanted more. "Bésame," he commanded as he tilted his head up for a kiss.

Olivier didn't understand most of what JC said, but his intent was clear. He met JC's lips with his, kissing him deeply. He reached for JC's cock to return the pleasure JC was bestowing on him, but JC was having none of it. Olivier rolled onto his back, reached for the headboard to steady himself, and let JC have the reins. "J'ai besoin de toi," he murmured against JC's lips. "Prends-moi."

JC kissed his way down Olivier's body, murmuring endearments in Spanish as he moved. He almost ran through the list he knew, and he vowed to have someone teach him more later, when he could think again, but it didn't matter at the moment, because he'd reached Olivier's cock, and talking was unnecessary. He licked the shaft and kissed the tip before taking it between his lips and savoring the flavor. Olivier's cock was hot and heavy in his mouth, and he relished the feel of it as he slid down as far as he could.

Olivier shook with the effort of holding himself still. He wanted to grab JC's head and force him deeper, roll him onto his back and fuck JC's mouth, something, anything to keep the sensations going, but he couldn't do any of those things. All he could do was talk. He whispered endearments and pleas in French, his brain too far gone to summon the words in English. If JC asked later, Olivier would tell him what he'd said—if he could remember—but it didn't matter now. As long as JC continued, nothing else mattered now.

JC lost himself in the taste of Olivier. He wanted to murmur more endearments in whatever language he could remember them in, but that would involve pulling back, and he wasn't willing to do that. Just the feel of Olivier in his mouth was enough to bring him close to orgasm, and as he fingered Olivier's balls, he wondered if he should stop before he came without even being touched. Right now it was the idea that

Olivier loved him and the tone of Olivier's voice that turned him on. The physical act of touching Olivier was just a bonus.

A beautiful, wonderful, *fantastic* bonus.

When he could tell Olivier was almost ready to come, he crawled back up Olivier's body and kissed him thoroughly. "I want you inside me," he whispered when he pulled back.

Olivier cursed softly in French, struggling for the control he would need to prepare JC so they could make love without it keeping JC from being able to dance tomorrow. "Lube and condoms," he ground out, hoping he'd managed to say it in English so JC would understand him. JC was closer to the nightstand, so he grabbed them and practically threw them at Olivier. Olivier set the condom to the side and slicked his fingers. He pulled JC over him until he was straddling Olivier's waist. JC's cock bobbed between them at the movement. Olivier used his clean hand to stroke JC's erection while he slid his lubed fingers between JC's spread cheeks and found his entrance. He probed gently and then stiffened his fingers when JC bore down on them.

JC's gasp at the sensation quickly turned into a moan of delight as Olivier twisted his fingers to hit just the right spot. He almost collapsed forward with need right then, overwhelmed with the sensations shooting through his body. Another wave of ecstasy overwhelmed him when Olivier scissored his fingers, and this time, he leaned forward and caught himself with his hands on either side of Olivier. "¡Joder!"

Olivier had no idea what that meant, but JC wasn't pulling away from him so he took it as encouragement. He stretched his fingers wider and added a third, hoping the pleasure of it would offset any burn from how fast they were going. He didn't have the patience to wait, though, and JC wasn't telling him to stop. He murmured praise and endearments in French against JC's ear as he sought his sweet spot again, determined to make him feel as good as possible.

JC could have come from Olivier's voice alone, especially when he talked like *that* in French, and when it was combined with what he was doing with his fingers, JC found it nearly impossible to maintain any sort of control. He could have come right then, without Olivier touching his cock, except that wasn't what he wanted. He needed Olivier inside him now.

"Please," he whispered, switching back to English so he could be sure Olivier would understand him. "Fuck me now."

Olivier wasn't about to say no to that. He grabbed the condom and rolled it on with trembling hands. Even that touch was almost enough to set him off. He didn't know how long he would last once he got inside JC, but he'd be damned if he came before he ever got there. "Like this?" he asked. "Or do you want to lie down?"

"Like this." JC guided Olivier's hands to his hips for a little extra support, grabbed Olivier's cock, and slowly lowered himself onto it. It felt…. God, he couldn't even think of the words to describe it right now, in English or in Spanish. He sighed softly with bliss and closed his eyes to better enjoy the sensation of Olivier filling him. Then Olivier rolled his hips. His cock hit JC's sweet spot, and JC saw stars behind his eyelids. "Oh."

Olivier wasn't feeling any more coherent than JC seemed. JC's body squeezed around him tightly, making it nearly impossible for Olivier to catch his breath. He thrust up into JC, wanting more of that amazing feeling. His vision blurred as sweat dripped into his eyes, but he ignored it in favor of concentrating on JC's face. He wanted to see JC come apart above him. "Je t'aime," he said again. He would never get tired of saying it.

That was more than JC could take. He came with a wordless cry, his whole body shaking, and then he collapsed forward so his head was resting on Olivier's chest. "Te amo," he whispered as he shifted to kiss the skin above Olivier's pulse point. The taste alone would have been enough to send him over the edge if he hadn't just come, and he couldn't resist licking a stripe along Olivier's collarbone.

The moment Olivier felt JC climax around him, he stopped fighting his own release. His body seized up, every muscle going rigid as he came hard with JC heavy against him and his tongue doing wicked things to Olivier's skin. His vision grayed out, and he fought to catch his breath, a fruitless effort with JC pressing him down into the mattress.

When JC could form a coherent thought again, he moved, pulling off Olivier and discarding the condom before settling down next to him, his head pillowed on Olivier's chest. "It's probably a good thing Chelsea and Tricia didn't let us spend more time in hold tonight. We might have turned the dance into that."

"That wouldn't have gotten us very good scores," Olivier replied. "Besides, I wouldn't have wanted anyone watching us making love."

CHAPTER 21

JC SAT down at the dinner table with a groan and leaned forward to rest his head on the table. "If I don't survive this week, tell Mama and Abuela I love them, and they shouldn't take it out on Chelsea. Freddy got off lucky going home last week."

Deborah patted him on the back. "You're still young. Try learning four dances when you're my age."

"What, twenty-nine?" Olivier asked. "You can't be a day over thirty."

"Save the flattery for your boyfriend," Deborah said with a smile. "It will get you more than it will with me."

"Flattery isn't going to get him anything until I've eaten and soaked in a tub for a while." The hot tub out back had seemed like a luxury before, but now JC could see why it was there. The pace Chelsea was setting so they could learn four dances was brutal, and he desperately needed to relax.

"The food will be ready in a few minutes, and the hot tub is just waiting for you," Olivier said. "You probably won't be the only one heading that way after dinner. I thought the dances we've learned so far were hard, but between the quickstep, the tango, and the samba, I'm completely lost. At least the cha-cha is familiar."

"I'm glad I know one of the dances, at least," Christine said as she joined them in the kitchen. "But it's still new choreography, and three completely new dances to learn. I will definitely be joining you in that hot tub, JC."

"Aww, I think he was hoping to be alone in it with Olivier," Amber teased as she sat down next to JC. "Weren't you?"

The thought had crossed his mind, but he wouldn't dream of asking. Everyone else had to be at least as sore as he was, and Deborah and Christine probably felt worse, jokes about their age aside. Still, he couldn't let a taunt like that go unanswered. "Well, if you all are offering to let us have it...."

"Only if you're willing to wait until after we're done," Christine replied. "Age before beauty and all that."

Olivier thought about telling her she'd have to be last if that was the case, but he'd already been called on his flattery once. He cocked an eyebrow in JC's direction. He didn't really want to wait, but he would if JC was that set on having the hot tub to themselves. Things had certainly gotten interesting the last time.

"No, I think Olivier and I will find other ways to have fun tonight," JC said with a sly grin. "We can get nice and limber in the hot tub after dinner and then, well.... I'll leave the rest up to your imagination."

Honestly, given how tired JC was and the kind of day he anticipated having tomorrow, they'd probably just sleep curled up together. He was happy to play along with the teasing, though. He'd been in situations where people had a problem with him liking men, so it was nice to be able to joke about it.

"Don't use too much energy," Chelsea said as she put plates on the table. "I have plans for you tomorrow, and you're going to need lots of it then."

Olivier flushed at the direction the teasing had taken, but he couldn't help the surge of happiness either. People knew he was gay, knew he was with another man, and didn't care. Or rather, they *did* care, but in the right way. They wouldn't tease if they weren't happy for him and JC.

"I won't leave him unable to dance tomorrow, I promise," Olivier said with a grin.

"Good." Chelsea bumped her hip against Olivier. "I'm sure Tricia will appreciate it if you could dance as well. I know JC still has a lot to learn if we're going to be ready to dance any two of these four dances."

"Don't remind me," JC said with a groan. "I don't remember them doing this any other season. Is it new or did I just miss it?"

"It's new. They always like to throw in challenges," Brody said. "It keeps things interesting for the audience and challenges the pros and the stars."

OLIVIER STOOD with the others backstage, waiting for Elizabeth to show up with the hat they would draw their first dance out of. They had less than an hour until showtime, and they still didn't know which two dances they'd be performing. Olivier hoped he got the quickstep as one of the two. That was his favorite of their choreography, but he had managed to learn all four dances well enough to satisfy Tricia. Now he just hoped he could satisfy the judges.

"Is everyone here?" Elizabeth asked as she joined them all.

"Yes."

"Good, then let's get started. JC, you had the highest score last week, so you'll draw first."

"Great!" JC said with enthusiasm he didn't really feel and flashed a grin at the camera. He was nervous and didn't know which dance to hope he got. The samba was the logical choice, as he'd done well with it last week, but this was all new choreography, and he was a little worried he'd get the two confused.

"Pick something good," Chelsea said as she stepped up to the hat with him.

"I'll do my best." JC stuck his hand in the hat, rummaged around, and pulled out a folded piece of paper. "Quickstep!"

"That's a good one to do first." Elizabeth took the paper back from JC, refolded it, and stuck it back in the hat so the next contestant would have the same four dances to choose from. "All right, Olivier, you're up next."

Olivier stuck his hand in the hat, hoping he'd find the same slip JC had gotten. He pulled one out, opened it up, and felt his stomach drop. "Samba."

"That will be fun to watch," Elizabeth said as she took the paper back. "Nothing like some party music to get the blood pumping."

"Exactly," Olivier said, hoping the cameras would move on to someone else quickly so he could pull Tricia aside and make her go through the samba steps with him a few more times. He'd learned it, but it was his weakest dance of the four.

"And now, Deborah, it's your turn to choose," Elizabeth said. "Do you have a preference to which dance you get?"

Deborah stepped up to Elizabeth, Brody at her side. "I did the cha-cha last week, so I'd like to do something different. I love the tango routine Brody came up with. I think that's the one I'm best at."

"You're good at all of them," Brody said, beaming at her. "No matter what you pick, you're going to be fantastic."

"I hope so." Deborah pulled a piece of paper from the hat and held it up for the cameras. "Tango it is."

"Wonderful! Three different dances so far. There won't be too much repetition this round." Elizabeth took the paper back from Deborah. "Okay, Amber. Your turn."

Amber reached in and pulled out a slip. "Samba," she announced. "I'll have to be at the top of my game or Olivier will make me look bad. Fortunately the samba is Tyler's favorite dance, so I hope we can impress the judges."

Olivier tried not to groan. Despite her kind words, Amber was the best dancer of them all. He'd be the one suffering in comparison tonight, not her.

"Stop worrying," Tricia murmured at his elbow. "With five contestants and four dances, you knew we'd be duplicating at least one of our dances. Yes, she's good, but so are you."

Olivier only hoped he was good enough. They'd come too far to be eliminated now.

Christine stepped up and pulled her dance from the hat. "Cha-cha," she said, holding it so the cameras could catch the word written on the paper. "Let's hope I get better scores than I did the first week."

"Of course you will," Mike told her as he handed the paper back to Elizabeth. "You're a much better dancer now."

"Well, you all have your dances," Elizabeth said, drawing their attention again. "Go get in your costumes and see if you can practice a little before the show starts. You have fifty minutes."

AMBER AND Tyler ran up the stairs to the viewing room where everyone waited to hear their scores on their quickstep. Olivier's stomach was tied in knots. Right now, he and JC were tied with fifty-eight points for the night after his tango and JC's cha-cha. Amber had already had a thirty in round one. If she got a twenty-nine or thirty this time, she would have the high score for the night and be safe from elimination, but the judges hadn't been as overwhelmingly positive about her second dance, giving Olivier hope she might get a nine or two and put him and JC back in the running for the safe slot. Christine and Deborah both did sambas as their second dances, but their scores were low enough to take them out of the running for the top spot. He didn't know how they would settle a tie if that's what happened, but he supposed they'd find out.

Corey chatted with them while the judges prepared their scores. Olivier held his breath. Emma Leigh gave them a ten, but Henrietta and Edoardo both gave nines. Olivier slumped in relief. They still had a chance.

"JC and Chelsea, Olivier and Tricia, Amber and Tyler, please come down to the floor," Elizabeth said.

As Amber approached them, she grabbed Olivier's and JC's hands. "Together," she said softly.

"Okay." JC's heart was threatening to beat its way out of his chest, but he managed to maintain a calm façade as they descended the stairs to the dance floor. Any one of them could be safe from elimination this week, but he didn't know how they'd determine the winner of the night when the three of them had matching scores.

They stopped in front of the judges and kept holding hands. Tyler, Chelsea, and Tricia stood behind them.

"As we said at the beginning of the evening, the dancer with the highest score this week will be safe from elimination," Elizabeth said. "However, we can't grant immunity to all three of you."

The audience laughed, and JC tried to laugh with them, though it ended up sounding hollow to his ears. He desperately wanted to be safe, but he also really wanted Olivier to be safe. He didn't know what he'd do at this point if one of them had to go home. He didn't know what they were going to do at the end of the season if they both made it to the finals.

"In the case of a tie," Elizabeth continued when the laughter had died down, "we grant immunity to the person with the highest cumulative score for the season. Therefore, the winner for tonight and the couple granted immunity from elimination is…. Amber and Tyler!"

Olivier gave Amber a hug to congratulate her because she really had earned it, but that meant he had to face the possibility of elimination tomorrow night. He hadn't really worried about it before because his scores had been relatively strong, but they were about to be in the semifinals. There were no weak dancers left. Whoever went home this week and next would be purely up to chance and the whim of the voters. He looked at JC and felt his heart clench. Tomorrow could be their last night on the show together. Even if they both survived tomorrow night, they were living on borrowed time now. They had, at most, two weeks left.

JC TOOK Olivier's hand as they walked into the house and led him straight up the stairs to his room. He pushed Olivier against the door as he closed it and kissed him like it was the last chance he'd have to do this. That wasn't true—even if one of them went home tomorrow, they'd still have a chance to say good-bye—but the idea that one of them might go home had taken root, and JC wanted to savor every moment he could with Olivier.

Olivier followed JC willingly. As well as his dances had gone, the evening had left him shaken up. Standing there with JC and Amber as they waited to hear which couple was safe from elimination had felt too much like standing at the end of the show waiting to see who was going home. It hadn't happened tonight, but it could happen tomorrow or next week.

He broke the kiss and pulled JC toward the bed. "If I go home tomorrow night—"

"If either one of us, you mean," JC interrupted. "I'm no safer than you are."

Olivier nodded, even if he disagreed. "If either of us goes home tomorrow night, that doesn't mean things are over. I didn't come on *Dance Off* expecting to meet someone and fall in love, but I'm not going to let it end with the show just because it caught me unaware."

"I'm not either, but we need to talk about what we're going to do. Even if neither of us goes home this week or next week, the week after that is the last one, and then we'll go our separate ways." JC ran his hands through his hair and sighed. He would rather spend this time enjoying Olivier, not planning for what-ifs, but if this thing between them was going to last, they had to talk. "You have a rugby contract, and I have swimming to get back to. We're not going to be in the same place like we are now."

"Rugby season doesn't start up until May," Olivier said. "I'll have to be back with the team in time for preseason training, but that's not for several months. I can come visit as often as your training schedule allows until February. I'll have to keep up with my basic conditioning, but I'm sure there's a gym in Houston I can use."

"The long-course season starts in April," JC said, referring to the professional swim competitions that took place in fifty-meter-long pools. "I'll have to be training pretty seriously by February, anyway. And I'll have basic training too. We could go to the gym together if you visit. Of course, if you do, you'll have to put up with my family."

"I can think of worse fates," Olivier said with a smile. "If the rest of your family is like the ones I've met so far, I will be happy to 'put up with them' while I'm visiting." He sobered a little. "I'm not pretending it will be easy. I know long-distance relationships are hard, but I want to keep seeing you. I want this to work between us, so we'll figure out what it takes, and we'll keep doing it because it's worth it."

"You haven't met my siblings. The boys will want you to teach them all about rugby, and my sister is going to *love* you." JC put a hand over his heart dramatically. "You're so *dreamy*. And she's a charmer. I may have to fight her for your affection."

Olivier thought it sounded like heaven. "I'm sure she's adorable, and I will give her all the affection she wants, but you won't have to fight her. You're the one I'm in love with. And I will gladly teach the boys as much about rugby as they want to learn. Mama might not be so happy about that, though. It can be a rough sport."

JC laughed. The idea of his four brothers doing something that wasn't rough was amusing. "They're teenage boys. They live for rough. Mama had it easy with me. I just wanted to swim. My brothers are constantly getting into trouble. You'll meet them if we make the finals. And Solita. The whole family has promised to come up if I get that far."

"I guess it would look a little suspicious if I sat with them, wouldn't it?" Olivier asked. "I look forward to meeting them regardless. I know you think they're a handful, but to someone with only one sibling, a big family like that sounds like heaven."

"The only thing that'll get you out of sitting with my family for the finals is competing in them, so you'd better not get eliminated if you're worried about that." JC grinned as he pictured the epic argument that was sure to happen if Olivier tried to sit anywhere else. "Mama and Abuela will order you to stay with them, Solita will turn on the puppy-dog eyes, and Roberto will physically drag you over and hold on to you the whole time. Even Dad will get in on it. He'll want to ask about your intentions, you know."

Olivier laughed. "Then I guess I'll have to make it to the finals so I can undergo the interrogation in private."

Chapter 22

"Javi! Javi! Javi! Javi! Javi!"

JC froze in the middle of a move when he heard his name screeched from down the hall. "What the…?" He trailed off as the door opened and seventy pounds of ten-year-old hyperactive girl barreled through it and straight into him.

"Javi!"

"Solita!" JC wrapped his arms around his little sister and hugged her tight. She cooperated and stood still for about two seconds before she pulled away and started bouncing up and down in front of him.

"Look, Javi! I got to come up early! Daddy said we were waiting for the finals, but I told him semifinals are a kind of final, and he agreed that we could come up and watch you dance tomorrow! Isn't that great?"

"It is." JC looked toward the door, wondering who else had come to the house with Solita. He assumed his brothers had come up as well, but they weren't likely to want to interrupt him here. They were probably only interested in meeting Amber tomorrow night, since Freddy and Kevan—the only other two the teenaged boys would have wanted to meet—had gone home. Christine had gone home last week, but they wouldn't have cared about meeting a politician. "Who came with you?"

"Mama and Abuela brought me here." Solita spun around and leaned toward the door as if she'd magically be able to see through it if she were just a little closer. "They stopped somewhere else on the way to your room, though."

Somewhere else almost certainly meant they'd gone looking for Olivier. JC wasn't sure he wanted to know the outcome of that conversation, but for now he had Solita to focus on.

Before he could say anything else, Chelsea came over. "Hi, I'm Chelsea, JC's partner."

"I know you," Solita said. "You're the best pro on the show. I started taking dance lessons so I could be just like you. I'm so glad you're Javi's partner."

"Thank you," Chelsea said. "JC told me he had a large family, but he didn't tell me he had an adorable little sister. What's your favorite dance so far?"

Solita pouted a little when Chelsea said she hadn't been mentioned but brightened immediately at the chance to talk dance. "The jive! I'm going to learn how to do it. Mr. Andrew promised. I can kind of already, see?" She started kicking her legs out in a loose approximation of the jive kicks.

"Very good!" Chelsea clapped. "You'll master it in no time!"

"You think?" Solita asked. When Chelsea nodded, she turned to JC. "Javi, why didn't you tell Chelsea about me? Did you tell her about Roberto and Esteban and Carlos and Manuel? You should've told her about me."

"We didn't talk about any of you specifically, honey." JC patted his sister on the shoulder and looked toward the door again, wondering where his mother and grandmother were. They had to be having quite the conversation for it to be taking this long. "I just told her I had a big family, that's all."

"A very big one," Solita agreed. "I have five brothers." She held up one hand with all her fingers splayed. "But I'm the only girl. Most of my cousins are boys too. Mama says it makes me extra special, but I'd rather have a sister."

Before either JC or Chelsea could come up with an answer, the door opened again, and Olivier and Tricia came in, herded by Mama and Abuela.

"Sorry," Tricia said once they were inside. "We were told we had to come meet Solita."

Solita's eyes grew wide as she looked from JC to Olivier and back to JC. "Is that…?"

Mindful of the cameras, JC didn't give Solita the chance to finish her thought. "This is Olivier Gautier, one of the other people on the show. Olivier, this is my sister, Solita."

"Nice to meet you, Solita," Olivier said, offering her his hand to shake.

Solita took it as an invitation, but not the one he'd intended it to be as she threw herself at him and wrapped her arms around his waist. "You danced the Argentine tango with Javi two weeks ago! It was the best dance ever on the show. You were *so dreamy*!"

JC reached toward Solita, intending to pull her off Olivier. "Solita! You can't just launch yourself like that at someone you don't know!"

"Oh, Olivier is fine with it," Abuela said dismissively. She turned a stern look on Olivier. "Aren't you, Olivier?"

"Of course, Abuela," Olivier said obediently. Abuela might not be his grandmother, but Mamie, his own grandmother back in France, would have his hide if she thought he wasn't being properly respectful. He shared an amused look with JC. He had been warned, after all. "How long are you here for, Solita?"

"Until the finals are over." Solita didn't let go of Olivier's waist. "Unless Javi goes home, but he won't. He's too good of a dancer. You are too. Almost as good as Javi. He's the best, even though Manuel says Amber is better. I think he just has a crush on her."

JC refrained from pointing out Solita's clear crush on Olivier. She'd be devastated when she learned he was claimed. "Amber is very good too. So is Deborah. It's going to be a tough show tomorrow night."

"You're not allowed to go home, Javi!" Solita let go of Olivier and wrapped her arms around JC. "If you go home on Wednesday, I have to go back to school on Monday. Maybe even on Friday!" She sagged against JC to illustrate just how devastating that would be.

Olivier refrained from laughing at the tragic expression on her face from force of will alone. "I'm sure JC won't go home tomorrow night. Like you said, he's too good to go home."

AS THE montage of Solita's visit played on the big screen, JC sucked in a deep breath and blew it out slowly. She and Olivier might be convinced that he was too good to go home this week, but he wasn't. Everyone who had made it to the semifinals deserved to be here, and the grand prize was still anyone's to win… or lose.

"Relax," Chelsea whispered by his side. "You're going to be great out there."

"I'd better be," he murmured. "The boys will trounce me if they have to go home tomorrow, and Solita will cry, which is worse."

"Breathe. You can do this. You know these dances."

"Sort of." It was Hollywood week, and they were doing three dances: two individuals—one from the Golden Era and one from modern cinema—and a group dance from the musical *Chicago*. JC had learned the steps, but he'd never compare to Fred Astaire, no matter what Chelsea said, and he was still afraid he'd forget the steps to his contemporary.

"You *know* them." Chelsea tugged on his hand as "Night and Day" started playing.

JC led her onto the dance floor and into the fox-trot. They didn't do the exact same choreography Fred Astaire and Ginger Rogers had done in *The Gay Divorcee,* but they had incorporated a few steps as an homage, and when the first one went flawlessly, JC relaxed into the dance. Maybe he could do this.

Olivier applauded enthusiastically as JC executed the elegant twirls of the fox-trot. He'd thought Chelsea's plan to show off a more debonair side of JC was inspired, but he'd also known JC was nervous about it. As far as Olivier was concerned, he had nothing to be nervous about. He looked every inch the leading man as he guided Chelsea through the dance. Olivier hoped his own stint as Rhett Butler went as well.

By the time the dance ended, JC was riding high. He might not have completely pulled off Fred Astaire, but he'd come as close as it was possible for anyone to get. He was going to get high scores on this—he could feel it as soon as the song ended. As he walked over to the judges' stand, he saw Solita bouncing in her seat and waved at her.

"I see your sister is convinced you're staying this week. What do you think, JC?" Elizabeth asked as he and Chelsea stopped in front of the judges.

JC blushed and smiled. Eight weeks ago, the comment would have had him looking down and stammering, but tonight he kept his head up and looked straight at the camera. "Well, I hope she's right. I think this dance went well, but I still have two more, and I'm sure everyone else will dance well too."

Henrietta smiled at him and Chelsea. "I'm inclined to agree with your sister. You make a very elegant leading man, JC, and you've come a long way since week one and your first fox-trot. Then, you still looked to Chelsea for help. Tonight you led her through the dance with grace, elegance, and flair. Well done."

Edoardo leaned across the table and grinned widely. "Oh, JC, you have come a long way since week one. Henrietta is right, you danced with grace and elegance, but you were also *sexy*. The way you moved was just so… strong and powerful. It touched me deep down. Your dance called up images of Fred Astaire at his best, and I would love to watch more of it."

"JC!" Emma Leigh pumped her fist in the air. "That was everything a good fox-trot should be. Fun and flirty, but also suave and sophisticated, and you pulled off both sides of the dance. As far as I'm concerned, that dance earned you your place in the finals."

Grinning, JC headed over to give Solita a hug and high-five his brothers before heading up to await his scores. They came through quickly.

"Ten!"

"Ten!"

"Ten!"

JC squealed and spun Chelsea around. "Oh my God!"

"A perfect thirty! How does that make you feel?" Corey asked.

"Absolutely amazing. I hope the rest of the night goes as well." There wasn't time to say anything else as Elizabeth interrupted so Deborah's montage could start. Still vibrating with excitement, JC hurried over to the others, hoping to get a hug from Olivier that could be disguised as a congratulatory one.

Olivier waited until Amber and Tyler had hugged JC and then led Tricia over. She winked at him as they hugged JC together and then stepped back so he could tighten the embrace a little. "Great job," he said. "You were brilliant. I knew you would be."

"IT WAS a calculated risk," Tricia said as soon as they left the viewing area to get changed for their second dance. "The Argentine tango is perfect for the tempestuousness of Rhett and Scarlet's relationship, but it's wrong for the time period. A nine and two tens is nothing to complain about. Go get changed. I want my chance to be a Bond girl."

Olivier laughed as she'd intended and hurried to the dressing room to exchange Rhett Butler's suit for James Bond's. The scores weren't bad, but after watching JC and Amber both get perfect scores, he'd wanted to join them. Deborah had also gotten a nine, but that put them tied, and tied for the bottom was not the place to be going into the finals.

JC squeezed Olivier's shoulder as they met in the dressing room. He was on his way out to perform his contemporary to "Concerning Hobbits" from *The Fellowship of the Ring*, but he made sure he caught Olivier for a moment. "Good job."

"Not as good as I would like," Olivier muttered.

"There are two dances left. You'll catch up." JC refused to think otherwise. Solita had to be right about neither of them going home this week, or next week was going to be a disaster.

Olivier hoped JC was right, but he couldn't do anything about it except change clothes and focus on his next dance. If he could get a perfect thirty in his second dance, he'd be in a better position.

He changed from his old-fashioned suit into a tuxedo and headed back out to meet Tricia. With only four dancers left, they didn't have long between numbers, and he didn't want to be late. Plus, he wanted to see as much of JC's dance as he could.

When the judges gave their commentary, Olivier decided Henrietta was simply in a bad mood tonight. She hadn't liked JC's contemporary any more than she'd liked Olivier's Argentine tango. JC's twenty-nine didn't do anything to cheer Olivier up.

"Stop worrying, and focus on the dance," Tricia ordered. Olivier pushed everything else out of his head as they stepped onto the floor and prepared to start their Viennese waltz. Tricia lounged against the bar, looking every bit as elegant as any Bond girl ever had. He approached her, martini glass in hand.

"Bond. James Bond."

Daniel Craig's voice provided the introduction. Olivier set down the martini glass and pulled Tricia into his arms to begin the Viennese waltz. As they twirled around the floor, he focused on keeping the suave sophistication of his Bond persona in place.

JC tried not to let his twenty-nine get him down as he watched Olivier's dance, but it was hard. Yes, they still had a dance left, and yes, the viewer votes could easily make this anyone's game with how close they all were, but Amber had gotten another thirty on her second dance and was now firmly in the lead. It was hard not to think about going home.

"You're going to miss this if you don't stop worrying and pay attention," Chelsea said, nudging him when his gaze wandered. "A twenty-nine is a perfectly good score, and you know the viewers aren't going to want to disappoint Solita. You'll get the votes you need."

If both he and Olivier stayed because his adorable little sister wanted them to, JC would owe her, big-time, and she would never let them forget it. "I hope she's not the only reason they vote for us," he said, wrinkling his nose at the thought. He did return his attention to Olivier, however, so Chelsea's mission was accomplished.

Olivier's Viennese waltz was elegant and glamorous, perfect for James Bond. It wasn't sexy in the same way that the Argentine tango he'd done earlier was, but the elegance of it made JC want to whisk him off the dance floor and take him out to drink champagne and look at the stars. He captured Bond's sophistication perfectly, and if Henrietta didn't give him a ten for this dance, she'd lost her mind. Olivier had earned it.

"Well, hello, Mr. Bond," Elizabeth said when Olivier and Tricia joined her by the judges' stand. "Very nice dancing, Olivier. I'm sure Tricia is very proud of you."

"I couldn't be prouder," Tricia replied.

"Oh, *Olivier*, you are so suave and sexy. Your Bond can break into my bedroom anytime. If Daniel Craig looked as good as you did on that dance floor, the criminals would surrender just for the chance to watch him. The Viennese waltz is a very ethereal dance, and you captured that and brought it down to earth just enough to give it a tiny bit of Bond's gritty realism. You hit all of the elements without too much swishy arm waving"—Edoardo waved his arms in the Viennese waltz manner to demonstrate—"and you made me believe that you were Bond. A fantastic tribute to the movies."

The cameras turned to Emma Leigh as the crowd applauded Edoardo's comments. She squealed Olivier's name so loudly he almost flinched, but that would have looked bad. "You are something else! I've loved the way you move from the beginning, but you've outdone yourself tonight, Olivier. Bond is the dream man of a generation of women and more, and you stepped into his shoes like you were born to be there. Well done!"

Henrietta graced Olivier with a rare smile. "Very well done. Like Edoardo said, you captured all the elements of the Viennese waltz nicely, and though you made it a little grittier than it usually is, you didn't lose the character of the dance. You turned it into a Bond dance but kept it the Viennese waltz. I'm impressed."

Olivier bowed his head in thanks as he and Tricia ran toward the viewing area to get their scores. They chatted nervously with Corey for a minute, but Olivier's mind wasn't on what he was saying. He wanted the scores, and he wanted them now.

"Ten!"

"Ten!"

"Ten!"

Olivier sagged in relief as the others mobbed him. He swore he felt JC pinch his ass, but he couldn't make himself complain. He'd gotten his first perfect score. JC could grope him all he wanted.

"Time to hurry," Tricia said as she pulled away from the group hug. "We have to change for the group dance."

JC pounced on Olivier backstage. "I knew you could do it! Now all you have to do is nail this tango, and Chelsea says Solita will get us the votes we need. Apparently, she's too cute for America to let her down by sending us home."

"She is cute," Olivier agreed. He glanced around and, not seeing any cameras, leaned in for a swift kiss. "Let me get changed, and then we'll go wow them with this tango. Je t'aime."

JC wished the kiss could be longer, but he settled for squeezing Olivier's hand as they parted. "Te amo."

THEY WERE in a commercial break at the moment, and then Elizabeth would have to explain the final dance to the audience, but JC wanted to be in the wings for all of that so he could get into the right mindset before they stepped out onto the dance floor. They were reenacting the "Cell Block Tango" from the movie *Chicago*, and the choreography was challenging. The pros had modified it some to account for the fact that JC and Olivier were going to be two of the prisoners and to cut two of the solos since there were only four contestants left, but they'd kept as much of the movie choreography as possible, and it was challenging.

Plus, four of the troupe members were joining them to fill out the remaining prisoners in the background, making it the biggest group JC had ever danced with.

And it was the final dance of the semifinals. Just in case he wasn't already nervous enough.

Elizabeth was explaining the dance to the audience when Olivier joined him in the wings, and JC flashed a nervous smile. "Ready?"

"Not really, but it's too late to do anything other than go out there and do our best. What about you?"

"As ready as I'm going to be." They got in the queue to head out, and JC followed the others onto the dance floor and took his place behind the "bars" of the prison. As the music started, he fell into the character of a wronged man whose wife had flown into a jealous rage and run into his knife—ten times—when they were arguing. The dance was challenging but fun, and he soon lost himself in the character, first in the background while Deborah danced as the woman whose boyfriend had six wives, and then in the spotlight. He acted out the argument with Chelsea, using the Argentine tango moves to emphasize their fight, and then fell back into the background as Amber took on the persona of the acrobat who had found her husband and sister in the spread eagle.

Olivier hung back a little until it was his turn to explain how he and his wife had artistic differences. He and Tricia played their parts to perfection, and that carried over to the moment when they joined the ensemble. The background group parts for each section had to support the others without drawing attention away from their solos. It was a delicate balance, and one Olivier wasn't sure they could manage, but the spotlights helped, keeping attention focused on the solo couple as they danced. The routine ended, and he grabbed Tricia and swung her around. They'd nailed it. He just knew it.

"THAT WAS really well done, all of you. You were gods and goddesses out there, and it was a joy to watch. I love the minor changes you made and that you were able to mostly stick to the movie choreography. All of you brought something special to the stage." Emma Leigh looked directly at Deborah and Brody. "Deborah, you put forth a valiant effort with those kicks. I wish you'd been able to pull them off a little better, because I could see that you knew what you needed to do, and you were so good in the background stuff that your spotlight faded a little. I love your grace, but you lost it here, and I missed it."

"I wish I'd pulled them off a little better too," Deborah said, already resigned to getting the lowest number of extra points tonight. "I did my best, though, and that's all I can do."

"And you never stopped giving it," Brody added encouragingly. "That counts for something."

"It can," Emma Leigh agreed before turning her gaze to JC and Chelsea. "JC, I could really feel the passion between you and Chelsea. The Argentine tango is perfect for that kind of argument, and the two of you pulled it off wonderfully. It really felt like you were fighting. You shone in your solo and were solid in the ensemble."

"Thank you." JC bounced a little, his high from the dance buoyed by Emma Leigh's words. "The Argentine tango is my favorite dance, and Chelsea made this solo so much fun."

"You made it easy," Chelsea said, hugging him.

"Amber, you made a valiant effort with all those acrobatic moves, but you fell a little short on a few of them. The moves you did hit were fantastic, but that just made the ones you didn't hit stand out more. You have so much talent—embrace what you're good at and push yourself, but not too much."

"I'll keep that in mind, thank you," Amber said, leaning against Tyler.

Emma Leigh nodded at her before turning her attention to Olivier and Tricia. "Olivier, your passion really came through here, and you shone in your solo. It was a joy to watch. You faded a little in the ensemble parts, though, which isn't like you. I think you were trying to make sure attention stayed on the soloists, but I think you pulled that off a little too well."

"Thank you," Olivier said. Emma Leigh was right that he'd tried not to draw attention to himself when it was someone else's solo. Apparently that wasn't the best tack to take. "I'll try to do better if we have another group dance."

"Henrietta, anything you'd like to add?" Elizabeth asked.

"Well, I have to say I've never been a fan of *Chicago*, but after this, I might have changed my mind. You four and your partners put on a spectacle the likes of which we haven't seen on the show before. Emma Leigh was right in her comments about each of your strengths and weaknesses, so I won't repeat those, but I will say that Deborah, you are an inspiration to all of us, keeping up with those young things the way you did. JC, you were born to dance the Argentine tango. Amber, keep believing you can do anything your partner can do because you've proven you can keep up with him. Olivier, don't hide from the spotlight, even when you aren't in it. You deserve to be there."

The four of them nodded, and then Elizabeth turned the floor over to Edoardo.

He stood and directed a sultry gaze toward each couple in turn. "Oh my. All of you are so, so naughty, and it came out so beautifully out there. I'm going to dream about people dancing behind bars tonight. That was the hottest thing I've ever seen." He calmed a little then but remained standing. "I agree with everything Emma Leigh and Henrietta said. You are all fantastic dancers when you're playing your strengths, so what you need to do now is figure out how to harness those strengths when you're doing things you're not as good at. You all have great potential, and I look forward to seeing what you come out with next week."

Olivier winced a little despite the encouraging words. One of them wouldn't be there next week. He just didn't know which one it would be. They all returned to the viewing area and huddled together, waiting for the judges to award the extra points.

Finally, after what felt like forever, the judges were ready.

"We'll start with two extra judges' points. Henrietta, which couple do those points go to?"

"First let me say that this was a hard decision. You saw how long we debated, and we could have kept discussing for another hour. All four stars are incredibly talented and deserve to go to the finals next week. However, the rules only allow us to give the extra eight points to one couple. So we award two extra judges' points to Deborah and Brody."

"That gives Deborah and Brody a total of sixty judges' points for the night. Edoardo, which couple gets the four extra points?"

"Like Henrietta said, this was a difficult decision. We're giving four extra points to Amber and Tyler."

JC relaxed a little. That meant he and Olivier each got either six or eight points, which made it more likely they'd make it to the finals.

"That gives Amber and Tyler a total of sixty-four points for the night," Elizabeth said. "Emma Leigh, who did you award six points to?"

"Six points go to Olivier and Tricia," Emma Leigh declared.

"Which gives them a total score of sixty-five. And that means eight points go to JC and Chelsea for a total of sixty-seven points," Elizabeth announced.

Olivier grabbed Tricia and swung her around. With the six extra judges' points, they were in a strong position going into the elimination round. He knew it wasn't a guarantee, but he hoped it would be enough. He set Tricia down and hugged JC and Chelsea too. "Congratulations!"

CHAPTER 23

"OLIVIER AND Tricia, Deborah and Brody, please come down to the stage."

Olivier grabbed Tricia's hand and walked down to the area in front of the band. He knew what they always said, that being there didn't actually make him one of the bottom two, but JC had the highest score last night, and Amber had done so well all season that he doubted he had gotten ahead of them in the votes. No, he was either third or fourth. If he was third, he'd come back and fight for the win. If he was fourth, it meant going home. Only a week early, but still going home.

"The couple with the lowest combined score and thus going home tonight—after awarding their charity $9,000—is...."

Olivier hated this part. Even when he wasn't up for elimination, he hated the pause that dragged out the moment and made tension build.

"Deborah and Brody."

Olivier buried his face against Tricia's neck as he sagged in relief. They'd dodged the bullet. They might not win, but at least they'd make it to the finals, and he wouldn't have to leave JC early. Another week wouldn't change all that much between them or give them that much more time before their respective careers pulled them in different directions, but it felt like a reprieve. "Thank you," he murmured against her skin. "I couldn't do this without you."

"Oh thank God," JC whispered as he closed his eyes in momentary relief. Olivier was staying, and that was all that mattered, even if it meant he owed Solita thanks for being so adorable. He'd miss Deborah, but it would have been so much worse if Olivier had gone home.

He went first to Olivier and gave him a congratulatory hug while Amber said good-bye to Deborah. "I'm so glad you're staying."

"Me too," Olivier said. He wanted to hold JC tight against him, but the cameras were still rolling. "Come to my room as soon as you can get free of your family?"

"Of course. It could be late, though." It probably would be, with his father and siblings in town, but he'd at least stop in and say good night to Olivier. "Let's go say good-bye to Deborah." They'd lingered together long enough.

Deborah graciously hugged JC tightly. "Good luck next week, but don't forget what's really important." She looked over his shoulder toward Olivier.

JC nodded. There was no way he would let the competition get in the way of his relationship. "I won't. I'll miss you."

She smiled and moved on to Olivier.

Olivier hugged her tightly. "You deserve to go on as much as any of us. You know that, right?"

"Someone had to go home this week," she said as she returned his embrace. "I'm glad it was me because if it had been you, you'd have to say good-bye that much sooner. Next week will be hard enough without making it happen a week sooner."

"We don't deserve you." He kissed her cheek. "We'll make you proud."

"All I need to be proud of you is to see you smiling at each other. That's more important than any dance competition."

She was right. Olivier was glad they'd made it this far in the season without the competition complicating their relationship. They could make it another week.

JC KNOCKED softly on Olivier's door. It was late—even later than he'd anticipated getting back to the house—and it was possible Olivier was already asleep. "Olivier?" he asked when he heard shuffling from inside.

Olivier opened the door and smiled as JC came in. "Did you have fun with your family?" His patience for small talk was limited, but he would refrain from jumping JC before he even got in the door.

"At first. Then I really wanted to get back here, but my brothers kept asking about things. People. You." He shut the door behind him and wrapped his arms around Olivier. "I ended up telling them about us. I hope that's okay."

Olivier leaned into JC's embrace and drew him toward the bed as he considered how he felt about JC's family knowing. "This isn't some fling that's going to end when the show does. I might've liked to be there when you told them, but I'm not upset that they know."

JC kissed Olivier deeply. When he pulled back, he grinned. They were definitely taking that further tonight, but he needed to tell the rest of the story first. "I wanted you there. But Solita started making wedding plans for the two of you—she wants to marry you—and it just slipped out. Now she's making wedding plans for us."

Olivier laughed at the idea of Solita's reaction. "She approves, then?" He grabbed JC's ass and pulled him closer. They had decisions to make and hurdles to overcome before they could start making wedding plans for real, but the thought of being in a position to make that commitment sent heat curling through his body.

"Oh yes. She says that having you as a brother is almost as good as having you as a husband, and I don't have to wait until she's thirty to marry you." JC chuckled a little at the memory. It had been an interesting conversation once his relationship with Olivier slipped out, but fortunately, Solita was still young enough to believe everything she was told about weddings, including that she couldn't get married until she was at least thirty. She also didn't see any issue with the fact that JC could get married before then if he wanted.

"I'll be glad to be her big brother. What did everyone else think?" He wasn't that worried. Mama and Abuela already treated him like part of the family, but better to ask and know for sure than to run into a situation he wasn't expecting.

"I think Mama and Abuela already suspected. My brothers think you're cool enough not to care. Dad wants to meet you, but he's not against the idea." Telling his family had actually gone as well as he could have expected. It might have been better with Olivier by his side, but his family was happy for them, and that was what really mattered.

"Then we should think about when we can meet them for dinner," Olivier said. "Maybe next week, after the show is over. I don't see Tricia and Chelsea letting us take anything more than bathroom breaks between now and then." That made it all the more important not to waste the time they had together tonight. He nuzzled JC's jaw as he ran his hand up and down JC's arm.

JC leaned into Olivier's touch. He was more than happy to stop talking about his family now and focus on Olivier. He was right that they weren't going to have much time to themselves between now and the final, and JC was determined to take advantage of every moment they had left. "Enough about my family. I didn't come here tonight to talk about them."

Olivier rolled JC onto his back and leaned over him to kiss him. JC opened to the caress, so Olivier deepened the kiss. He met JC's tongue with his own and groaned at the way JC responded to every movement of his mouth. He loved how responsive JC was. It made him feel powerful. He propped himself on one elbow and slid his free hand beneath JC's shirt in search of skin. It had been too close a call tonight for him to have any patience with slow. He needed JC and he needed him now.

JC helped Olivier take off his shirt and then tugged at Olivier's. He was happy to let Olivier take the lead tonight, but he wasn't going to lie there passively while Olivier got his way. When they were both shirtless, he slid his hands down Olivier's back, admiring the hard planes of his muscles. He loved how strong Olivier was, how powerful, both physically and emotionally, and yet how gentle he could be at the same time. Tonight, JC didn't want gentle, though, and he urged Olivier to move faster.

JC's urgency was contagious. Olivier ran his hand swiftly over JC's chest and paused to tweak his nipple with a little more force than he'd dared use before now. He had large hands and had learned to temper their strength, but JC didn't seem to want gentle tonight, and Olivier was in the mood to indulge him.

"Oh! Fuck! That...." JC wanted more, and *now*, but he couldn't find the words to say it. Olivier had never been quite that aggressive before, and JC adored it. He thrust his hips up, already wishing there weren't layers of fabric between them, and hoped Olivier got the message. "Please."

It was all the permission Olivier needed. He pinched JC's nipple again, loving the way JC reacted to his touch. When JC met that with another deep, breathless moan, Olivier lowered his head to bite at JC's other side. Need rode him hard, driving him to bite and mark and claim. JC was his, no matter what happened with the show and the finals and the competition. He hoped Chelsea wasn't planning on JC going shirtless, because Olivier wouldn't be able to stop without leaving hickeys all over JC's chest.

JC arched up into the touch, urging Olivier to mark him again. It felt like Olivier was claiming him, trying to leave physical proof that the relationship was strong enough to survive the show ending, and he loved it. He raked his nails down Olivier's back, returning the favor. Then he tugged on Olivier's pants again. He needed the fabric between them gone so he could touch Olivier everywhere. "Off."

Olivier reared up on his knees and stripped off his sweats. He worked open the button of JC's jeans and pulled them down, taking his underwear with them. He certainly wasn't opposed to being naked, but he wasn't going to be the only one. He tossed the fabric aside and fell on JC again, ravenous for the taste and smell of his skin and for the sound of his moans. He'd teased JC their first night together about making him scream, but tonight he wasn't teasing. He needed JC as desperate as he was.

The way Olivier touched him was enough to drive JC mad with desire. He moaned loudly, not caring if anyone else in the house could hear him. He couldn't have been quieter if he'd wanted to, and right now, he didn't. All that mattered was the way Olivier was touching him, stroking him, teasing him to the point that he could think about nothing but how badly he needed this and how desperately he wanted more. Desperate to give as much as he was getting, JC slid his hand between their bodies, wrapped it around Olivier's cock, and started stroking.

"Oh, *putain*," Olivier cursed. JC's hand felt too good on him. If JC kept on like that for long, Olivier wouldn't last long enough to get inside him, and that's where he really wanted to be tonight. He grabbed the lube and smeared some on his fingers. He might have smiled when JC spread his legs, but he needed all his concentration to keep from coming on the spot. JC was hot and tight as always, but he relaxed quickly, letting Olivier stretch him with more haste and less finesse than usual. Olivier hoped he wasn't hurting JC, but he was out of patience for slow and careful.

Olivier's sudden aggression left JC practically incoherent. It felt so fucking good, even with how fast Olivier was moving. This was what he wanted, what he'd wanted ever since he'd seen Olivier standing on that stage next to Deborah, threatened with the very real possibility of going home. They almost hadn't gotten to have this tonight, and that made every touch all the more precious.

Olivier tore open a condom and rolled it on, hissing at the touch of his own hand. The urgency had left him so oversensitive that even his own touch was almost too much. He moved between JC's legs and lined himself up. He wouldn't be able to go slow, so he met JC's gaze. "Ready?"

"God, yes." JC ached for this, needed Olivier so badly that he couldn't put it into words. He pulled his legs up to give Olivier a better angle. JC felt Olivier move against him, and then Olivier pushed in with one smooth motion that left JC gasping. He clenched at the sheets and focused on breathing for a moment as he adjusted to the feeling. Once he caught his breath, he looked at Olivier and tried to convey how amazing this felt with just one word. "Move."

Olivier released his hold on himself at JC's order and pounded into his passage with utter abandon. He tried to aim for JC's prostate, but he wasn't sure he had that much control over his body. He braced his elbows on either side of JC's chest and leaned down for a wild kiss. He needed every point of contact possible to stay grounded and not simply go off immediately.

The sensation of Olivier moving inside him combined with the kiss was enough to make JC lose the small bit of control he had left. He wanted to make this last so he could enjoy it as long as possible, but he wasn't sure he could. He grabbed Olivier's shoulders to hold him in place as they kissed, hoping it would help him last longer, but it didn't work. As Olivier slid his tongue into his mouth, JC lost control and came.

JC clenched around him hard, triggering Olivier's orgasm. His whole body shook as he climaxed, his hips jerking rapidly against JC's ass. He groaned into their kiss and collapsed on top of JC. He had to be crushing him, but he couldn't make himself move.

JC lay still, content for the moment. Olivier was heavy, but not unbearably so, and JC didn't have the energy to make him move. That had been.... God, he couldn't even think how to describe it beyond good, even though it deserved so much more than that. "Wow," he said when he finally regained the ability to form words. It was the only thing that came to mind.

Olivier chuckled. "That bad?" He'd been rough, and it had been faster than he'd intended. JC had come, but that didn't make it good.

"That good," JC corrected. He squirmed a little until Olivier pulled out and took care of the condom. When he collapsed back on the bed, JC rolled over and pillowed his head on Olivier's chest. "It was fantastic. Just what I needed tonight."

"Good." Olivier pressed a kiss to the top of JC's head. "I want to always give you what you need."

CHAPTER 24

OLIVIER HAD barely had time to walk in the door to the practice studio when Henrietta came in. He smiled and greeted her with a kiss on each cheek.

"Are you ready for the finals?" she asked.

Olivier shrugged. "As ready as I can be. I didn't expect to make it this far, honestly."

"Don't sell yourself short," Henrietta scolded. "You're a wonderful dancer. You have grace and agility along with the strength that comes from your rugby background. You need to take advantage of that in your freestyle. It will be fun to see how far you've come when you do your repeat cha-cha, but that will showcase your sexy side, not your strength."

"Tricia and I have been talking about the freestyle," Olivier said. He didn't say they hadn't made any decisions yet. He didn't want that on camera.

"Good. It's often the dance that determines the winner. Now, you have a third dance as well, the judges' pick. We've discussed it, and our favorite dance for you is the Argentine tango. The trio dance and the group dance both showed hints of your potential, but we want to see it with the spotlight on you and only you," Henrietta said. "Take what you did for the group dances and wow us with it when it's just you and Tricia."

"I'll do my best," Olivier promised. "I don't want to let anyone down, Tricia, you and the other judges, the fans." *JC.*

"You won't," Henrietta said. "Go out and give it your all. That's all anyone can ask of you."

EDOARDO WALKED in just as JC tumbled to the floor trying to execute a complicated move Chelsea wanted to put in their freestyle. "That's not what I'm used to seeing from you."

JC scrambled to his feet, embarrassed. "You didn't watch our early practices." He was still far more graceful in water than on land and often fell when learning new moves when his arms or feet got ahead of him.

"He'll get it," Chelsea said, coming to stand next to JC.

"I'm sure it will be *fantastic* by show night," Edoardo agreed. "You always put on such an interesting performance. That's what I'm here to talk to you about. We decided we'd like to see you do the samba again as your final dance. You were so sexy the first time with that Latin flair, and I want to see more of it."

"Oh. Okay." JC had hoped they'd pick one of the other dances he was more comfortable with, like the quickstep or the waltz. He was good at the samba, the judges had loved it, but it required he share a side of himself he didn't show all that often.

"You shared so much of yourself with that dance, JC. Yes, it was sexy and a delight to watch, but it was also you in a way that none of your other dances have been. You want that kind of intimacy in the finals if you're going to win."

"I'll do what I can."

Chelsea slung an arm around his shoulders. "Just be yourself. I have some great ideas for choreographing it."

"Give it your all, and you'll go far, JC," Edoardo said. "You have talent. Don't be afraid to show it off."

OLIVIER COULDN'T believe the difference in how he felt starting the cha-cha now compared to week one when he had no real idea what he was doing. Sometimes he still felt that way, but going back to that original choreography—with a few new moves because, really, week one was so easy in comparison—proved to him how much he'd learned.

"Ready for this?" Tricia asked.

For once Olivier could smile at her and say, "Absolutely."

He led her out onto the floor, and when the music started this time, he *led* the dance instead of hoping he could remember the steps. This... this was what dancing was supposed to feel like.

JC watched from the wings, grinning as Olivier led Tricia through the dance. He remembered that first night, remembered how sexy he'd found the dance then, but that was nothing compared to this. Tonight, Olivier oozed confidence and sex, and JC couldn't tear his gaze away. He wanted nothing more than to take Tricia's place and rip that open shirt off Olivier.

"Down, tiger," Chelsea said, putting her hand on his shoulder as if to hold him in place. "Don't forget what you're supposed to do next."

"Let me enjoy my fantasy," he said without looking at her. "Then I'll let Olivier enjoy his." The fox-trot he'd be doing as his week one repeat dance wasn't sexy in the same way as the cha-cha, but after last week, JC was confident he could be the suave lead it required.

Olivier met Tricia's eyes as they danced and shimmied his hips a little. The crowd went wild, and Tricia grinned, so he did it again. Not enough to make him lose his place in the routine. Just to add an extra punch here and there. They finished the routine and held the pose for a moment as the audience gave them a standing ovation. As soon as they broke the pose, Olivier grabbed Tricia and spun her around. "We did it!"

"Damn straight we did!"

JC applauded along with the rest of the crowd, doing his best not to look too enthusiastic, though he was thrilled at how well Olivier had done. There were plenty of cameras around, and tonight all the other contestants had returned for one last hurrah between the two parts of the show. He bounced on his toes, hoping it would seem like anticipation if anyone noticed, and tried to see where Olivier was standing at the judges' table.

"Great job, you guys," Elizabeth said. "You definitely improved from week one, Olivier. How do you feel about tonight's performance?"

"It felt amazing," Olivier said. "Like how dancing should feel. I only hope the judges and the viewers feel the same."

"I'm sure they will," Elizabeth said. "Let's see what the judges have to say. Henrietta?"

"I'm glad it felt like dancing should feel, because it certainly looked like dancing should look," Henrietta said. "Brilliant job, Olivier, and so much growth from week one. You've proven you have what it takes to be a leading man. I'm looking forward to seeing what you've come up with for your freestyle dance."

"Oh, *Olivier*, I always knew you could move those hips," Edoardo said, making a face that was better kept to the bedroom. "You did not disappoint tonight. That was a glorious cha-cha, with all the right elements. The way you moved your body and led Tricia through the dance was stunning. It was a pleasure to watch on so many levels."

"Olivier!" Emma Leigh squealed. "That's what I want to see! The cha-cha can be a simple dance, which is why we use it in week one, but it's a dance that can, with the right dancers, have depth and complexity as well. You took your week-one choreography and added the depth and complexity you weren't capable of then. You're certainly capable of it now! Well done!"

"Three raves from the judges," Elizabeth said. "Head up to where Corey is waiting for you while they prepare your scores."

Olivier hugged Elizabeth impulsively and then grabbed Tricia's hand and ran with her toward the steps to the viewing area.

"Sounds like you'll have good scores," Corey said when they joined him. "What was it like going back to that early dance?"

"Strange at first," Olivier said, "but good. It showed me how much I've learned. That made it a lot easier to think about the freestyle and the Argentine tango the judges assigned. If I'd come that far since week one, maybe I really could do those dances."

"Well, good luck. I'm sure you'll do wonderfully," Corey said. "Now, let's see what the judges thought."

"Emma Leigh."

"Ten!"

"Henrietta."

"Ten."

"Edoardo."

"A ten!"

Olivier grabbed Tricia and swung her around. Amber and Tyler mobbed him before he could even set her down. They still had two dances to go, but at least Olivier could watch JC and Amber dance without worrying he'd have to play catch-up in round two.

JC wished he could go over and congratulate Olivier, but there was no time before he and Chelsea were sent out to take their places on the stage. As their montage played, he tried to get his mind off Olivier and onto the fox-trot, but it was harder than he anticipated, and with Chelsea across the stage there was no one to calm him down.

Then the music started, and JC's mind cleared. He remembered how nervous he'd been that first night, how certain he'd been he was going to mess something up, but tonight he felt none of that. When the music hit the right count, he started across the stage toward Chelsea, and the whole thing just felt right.

This fox-trot was simpler than the one he'd done last week, even with the additions they'd put in to up the difficulty level, but it felt more personal. As he twirled Chelsea around the stage in the slow-slow-quick-quick steps of the fox-trot, everything came together like magic, and he really understood why the pros loved dancing so much.

Olivier watched JC and Chelsea dance and smiled to see how much fun they were obviously having with their reinterpretation of their first number. He'd noticed JC already by the first week of competition, but only in the way one noticed a beautiful work of art. It had taken longer than that before his attraction had moved into genuine interest. Seeing JC dance now, he wondered why it had taken him so long.

JC spun Chelsea around at the end of the dance, relishing the feeling of leading instead of her urging him around. They ended the dance with the same flourish as they had the first night of competition, but this time JC was certain he'd done well. No, wonderfully. It had felt perfect to him, and he grinned widely as he led Chelsea over to the judges' station.

"Aren't you Mr. Sophisticated tonight?" Elizabeth said as JC and Chelsea joined her near the judges.

As far as Olivier was concerned, JC was far more sophisticated than people—including JC himself—gave him credit for. Yes, he was young, but he was an Olympic athlete. He hadn't gotten there by being crass or naive. He was seriously considering telling off the next person who implied otherwise.

JC chuckled at Elizabeth's comment. "I try."

"I think you did more than try, but let's see what the judges have to say. Edoardo?"

"JC...." Edoardo dragged out his name as he leaned forward over the table toward JC and Chelsea. "You were the picture of sophistication out there, JC. You stepped up and took control of the dance, and it was beautiful. You seduced Chelsea without taking your clothes off at all, and it was glorious to watch. Every move was precise but you didn't lose any of that flair that makes the fox-trot so fun. Marvelously done."

He'd certainly managed to seduce Olivier, but then again, all he had to do was look at Olivier and he was seduced, so Olivier doubted he was a good judge of that matter.

"Emma Leigh?"

"The biggest challenge for our male stars is taking charge of the dance and leading their partners instead of being coaxed through the motions by the pros. You, JC, have become a leading man, and it is a delight to watch. Week one, you were still very much a boy trying to fill a man's shoes. No more. You've proven tonight you can dance with the best of them."

"Thank you." Back in week one, JC probably wouldn't have reacted well to the implication that he was a boy still, but he could see where Emma Leigh was coming from now. He felt like he'd matured, both in dancing and otherwise, and he knew she didn't mean it as an insult, just a comment on his relative age and inexperience compared to most of the other male stars.

"Henrietta?"

Henrietta gave JC a big smile. "Charisma and class. That's what the fox-trot is all about, and you had both in spades, JC. I liked the fun opening and how the mood carried over to the whole dance, but you didn't let the entertainment side distract from the execution of your choreography. Well done!"

JC thanked Henrietta, and he and Chelsea headed over to Corey to wait for their scores. As soon as they got there, Corey patted JC heartily on the shoulder. "Great job! The judges seemed to love it too. How do you feel?"

"Fantastic," JC said. "I did the fox-trot last week too, but this was different, redoing my first dance. It was a different sort of challenge, but I really enjoyed the chance to go back and get it right this time."

"Well, let's see if the judges agree. It's time for your scores."

"Emma Leigh."

"Ten."

"Henrietta."

"Ten."

"Edoardo."

"Ten!"

"That's another perfect score! The evening is off to a great start!" Corey exclaimed. "Great job!"

JC pulled back from hugging Chelsea to grin at the camera. "Thank you!"

Corey waved them off, and JC rushed over to get hugs from Olivier and Tricia. He lingered a little longer on Olivier's than Tricia's, but not so much longer the cameras would notice. After all, they'd both just gotten perfect scores. They'd be expected to congratulate each other.

"You were great," Olivier murmured as he hugged JC. He wanted to say more, to assure JC that he didn't see him as a boy or as lacking sophistication or any of the things some of the comments had seemed to imply, but now wasn't the time. They had to get ready for their freestyle dances, and they wanted to watch Amber as well.

JC LEANED against the railing and watched as Troy and Ella took the floor for a very short routine. Each of the eliminated stars except for Dawn, who was still too injured to dance, had a performance in the intermission while viewer votes and judges' scores were tallied to determine which two performers got to continue on to the final performance of the season. One of them would be eliminated in the next ten minutes, going home with $10,000 for their charity of choice, while the other two would continue on to compete for the $15,000 and $20,000 prizes.

"Watching them makes me feel a little better about my dancing," he said as Makayla took the floor. It wasn't a fair comparison, particularly to the people who had been eliminated first, but at the moment he was clinging to anything that would make him feel like he wasn't the worst of the three of them left. Amber's fox-trot had been even more improved than JC's, in his opinion. Then she'd stunned everyone with her freestyle to "Barbie Girl," throwing in a few gymnastic moves no one had known she could do and making fun of her public persona in the process.

"Yes, it definitely shows how far we've come," Olivier agreed. They'd all agreed not to change into their costumes for the judges' choice dances until after they knew who was eliminated. It had seemed like a small thing, but Olivier understood the value of a show of solidarity. It would be easier for whoever was eliminated not to be left standing there in a costume they'd never perform in. He didn't have any illusions that he'd make it to the final round. Amber's freestyle had been inspired, and JC's had gotten a standing ovation. The fact that he'd gotten a thirty from the judges just like the other two didn't change the reaction of the audience to his dance. He could live with that, though. He and Tricia had done their best and had made it all the way to the finals. If he was eliminated now, he'd have done a great thing for Doctors Without Borders, and he'd walk away with his head high. It came down to the voters' preferences, and he knew he didn't have the same kind of following as JC or Amber.

"It does," Amber agreed as Kevan left the stage. Dawn came out and waved to the crowd, and then Eugene entered for his turn.

JC turned toward Olivier. He tried to make it look like he was just engaged in conversation, not deliberately looking away from the performance, but at this point he didn't really care if anyone thought otherwise. The viewers had five minutes left to vote for tonight's winner, and then the audience opinion didn't matter at all. "We worked for it, though. And no matter what happens, we all earned this."

Rini got a much more enthusiastic response than Eugene had, and her dance was far better. Freddy came out and waved at the audience before joining the band for Christine's big-band swing. The crowd loved it, and Olivier, JC, and Amber all cheered along. When Deborah's turn came, though, they ran down to the floor to hug her before letting her dance. She'd only been gone a week, and it felt like she belonged up there with them.

When she finished, the lights came up again and JC, Olivier, and Amber moved to the stage to wait for the elimination decision to be announced. Tricia, Tyler, and Chelsea stood with them, but it was each other's hands they held as they waited. "No matter who they eliminate, you're both winners as far as I'm concerned," Amber whispered.

"We're all winners," Olivier corrected.

Elizabeth took the card handed to her by one of the people backstage and stood in front of the six of them. "Votes from people in the studio audience as well as people at home have been tallied. Voting is now closed and, unfortunately, one of you will not be continuing on.

The person who is taking third place in this year's *Dance Off* competition and is getting $10,000 for their charity of choice is...."

JC clutched Olivier's hand as she paused dramatically. Ultimately, it only made a difference to their charities who got what place right now, but that didn't make it any less nerve-racking. He hated these pauses, hated these moments when anything could happen. He just wanted Elizabeth to finish and tell them who wasn't going to dance their third dance tonight.

Olivier clutched him back, and on Olivier's other side, Amber bounced anxiously. The band ramped up the speed of the music, adding to the tension.

Elizabeth turned to them as the music stopped. "Olivier. I'm sorry, but you've been eliminated. We will be donating $10,000 to Doctors Without Borders on your behalf."

Olivier hugged Tricia before turning to congratulate JC and Amber. It stung to be eliminated so close to the end, but he wasn't surprised, really. He'd been in the bottom two last week, and with the judges' scores tied for all of them, it had come down to viewer votes. Amber and JC tackled him from opposite sides. He clung to them for a moment before taking a deep breath and stepping back. "Knock 'em dead," he said.

CHAPTER 25

JC WANTED more time with Olivier, but Elizabeth hustled them all off stage before he could do more than return Olivier's hug. They were separated backstage, Olivier sent to wait with the other eliminated contestants and JC and Amber to change into their outfits for their final dances. After he slipped into the tight pants and open shirt he was wearing for the samba, JC smoothed his hands down his legs nervously. The music from the troupe's performance echoed through the backstage area, but when it stopped and Elizabeth started talking about their final performances, the butterflies that had been lodged in his stomach all night started to rebel.

"Shit." He took a deep breath and blew it out slowly. It didn't help settle his nerves. "This is really happening. How'd I get here?"

"By being a good dancer." Chelsea slid out of the chair after the stylist finished with her hair and took JC by the shoulders. "You're here because you deserve to be. Your dancing has improved so much since week one, and the audience loves you."

"Right." That wasn't easy to remember sometimes. He wasn't used to getting audience feedback on his performances. Even at swim meets with an audience, most of the cheering happened while he was in the water and unable to really hear it. "I hope I don't let them down."

"You won't. No matter what happens in this dance, you won't let anyone down." Chelsea kissed his cheek. "Now come on, let's get to the wings so we can watch Amber."

The butterflies were still fluttering in JC's stomach, but this time when he took a deep breath, they calmed a little. By the time he reached the wings to watch Amber dance her paso doble, they were gone, and JC was able to enjoy Amber's performance.

As soon as Olivier had been officially released by the stagehands, he slipped out to sit in the audience. He started to take a seat off to the side, but Solita saw him and waved for him to join them. Unwilling to risk the girl's pout, he squeezed into a seat between Solita and Abuela.

"You should be out there," Solita said loyally.

"Amber and JC have earned their places too," Olivier said. "Now, let's enjoy the last two dances, okay?"

Solita didn't look convinced, but Abuela patted her knee and she subsided and focused on the dance floor again. Amber and Tyler took the stage and performed a commanding paso doble. Olivier hadn't really expected otherwise, but it still stunned him a little to see the power Tyler could bring to bear on a dance when he set out to do it, and Amber met him beat for beat. By the time they were done, Olivier was on his feet with the rest of the audience. He wanted JC to win, but if Amber won instead, she would have earned the title. After this dance, he couldn't argue otherwise.

JC hugged Amber as they passed in the wings. "Good job."

"Thanks. Good luck." She squeezed his hand as she walked backstage.

JC took his place next to Chelsea as they played the video of Edoardo assigning him this dance. He had thought his nerves would come back when he stepped onto the stage, but as the music began to play, the last vestiges of the nervousness he'd felt backstage faded away. This was his last performance on *Dance Off* and, unlike all the other dances this season, he knew it. The audience had voted, the judges had tallied their scores all season, and now, when all that was left was to decide how much money went to the final two charities, the pressure was gone.

When the music hit the right note, JC started to move, rolling his hips as he led Chelsea across the floor. He'd worked to emphasize the Latin lover in himself the last time he'd danced the samba, but this time it came naturally. He felt like he was seducing Chelsea with every move, and the audience didn't matter. He was caught in the swell of the music and the rhythm of the dance, and he forgot about thinking and remembering what he needed to do next, forgot about the judges and the audience and even his charity, and just danced.

Olivier couldn't put his finger on what was different about JC in this dance, but something was. JC danced with a joy and a freedom Olivier envied. JC swiveled and shimmied through the samba with all the Latin flair Edoardo could have hoped for, and Olivier found himself caught up in the mood of the dance. Amber's paso had been all about the power struggle. JC's samba was just as effective without the tension. It was sheer sex, and Olivier felt his body reacting to it. One day soon—very soon—they were going to find a samba club and go dancing, because Olivier wanted to be the focus of JC's attention rather than having it on Chelsea.

When the dance ended, JC stood still for a moment, breathing heavily and basking in the feeling. The audience members came to their feet, and out of the corner of his eye, JC could see his family and Olivier going wild, but the feeling that gave him was nothing compared to the pure rush of pleasure from knowing he'd nailed the samba. Whatever the judges decided, he'd given it his all, and he'd never feel like he let the Trevor Project down.

As Elizabeth and Corey tried to calm the audience so they could continue, Amber and Tyler came out to join JC and Chelsea on the dance floor. They hugged and then stood there for a moment, basking in the applause until Elizabeth came back from talking to the judges.

JC took both Chelsea and Amber's hands as Elizabeth got the audience's attention. He wasn't going to be upset no matter what the result was, but he did want to win, and he did care what the judges thought.

"I look forward to and dread the finals in equal measure," Henrietta said when the audience had finally quieted down enough for her to be heard. "We've had eight amazing performances tonight. Six perfect scores. And if we gave scores for these two dances, it would be two more perfect scores. The quality of dancing on finals night is unsurpassed. You wouldn't still be here if you couldn't dance at that level. That's the part I love. Then comes the end of the night, and we have to pick between you. That's the part I dread. You both delivered stunning performances tonight. Amber, the power of your paso was remarkable. Tyler isn't a small man, and he has a lot of charisma on top of it. In a dance like the paso doble, it's easy for his partner to fade a little in comparison, but you matched him stride for stride and refused to be eclipsed by him. JC, the samba is a party dance, which came through completely in your performance. We were right there with you celebrating. The gusto and vivaciousness you put into the dance were superb, and you took Chelsea right along with you. Know that regardless of the outcome tonight, you're both winners in my book."

"JC, Amber, it is a shame we won't have the privilege of watching the two of you dance anymore. You've both come so far and were so stunning tonight," Edoardo said. "Amber, the raw power you possess is amazing. You were strong and sexy and an absolute joy to watch. The paso doble is all about power and conquering your partner, and after that dance, I think you'd be welcome to conquer anyone here. JC. Oh, JC, that was sexy and hot and a fantastic celebration of everything you accomplished this season. You've really come into yourself, and your samba showed that tonight."

Emma Leigh stood and gestured for Amber and JC to come to the judges' stand. She gave both of them hugs before sending them back to their partners. "What a performance from both of you! Totally different in tone but equally effective in execution. Exactly what we expect on a finals night. Amber, your footwork was exquisite in the paso, not something I say very often about that particular dance. JC, *that's* how you move your hips in a Latin dance. Well done, both of you."

"And now it's time to announce our winner," Elizabeth said. "JC and Chelsea, Amber and Tyler, if you could join me in the middle of the floor, please."

JC took his place beside Chelsea and clutched at her hand, his mind racing with the judges' comments. He was thrilled and flattered that they liked his dance so much, but they'd seemed to like Amber's just as well, and there was nothing in their remarks to indicate who they'd chosen as the winner. He knew they had to make it dramatic for the cameras and make sure the audience understood what was about to happen, but he hated the way Elizabeth was stretching it out, explaining yet again about the prize money that would be awarded to their respective charities.

"Good luck," Amber whispered as she took JC's hand in a show of solidarity. "You were fantastic tonight."

"So were you." JC squeezed Amber's hand but didn't let go. They would stand together until Elizabeth announced the winner.

"And now, the moment you've been waiting for. The winner of this year's *Dance Off* competition is—"

The orchestra played a drumroll, and JC clutched tighter to both Amber and Chelsea.

"—Amber and Tyler!"

Amber's scream of delight was drowned out by the noise of the crowd. She pulled away from JC, jumped into Tyler's arms, and hugged him thoroughly. JC took the moment that gave him to acknowledge his own disappointment. Amber deserved to win, JC had no doubt about that, but it still stung a little to come so close and then not get the grand prize. Still, there were cameras rolling, recording his every move, so as soon as Tyler set her down, JC pulled her into a hug. "Congratulations."

"Thank you," she said a little breathlessly. "You know it could just have easily been you. You were amazing tonight."

In the audience, Olivier cheered for Amber even as he wished JC had won. He squeezed Solita's hand and then edged past her to go down and join everyone in congratulating Amber. He wanted to talk to JC, but he was hyperaware of all the cameras, so he had to talk to Amber first.

It took a few minutes to push through the crowd surrounding her, making him glad for his size and rugby training. When he got to where Amber and Tyler were standing, he hugged her tight and spun her around. He set her down and grinned at Tyler. Tyler's returning smirk was a dare if Olivier had ever seen one, so he grabbed Tyler and spun him around too. The audience would eat it up, and it would make him giving JC a hug less obvious when he was done.

"I didn't think you'd really do it," Tyler said through his laughter when Olivier set him down.

"I never back down from a dare," Olivier replied with a grin.

"Then I dare you to be with JC the way you both deserve," Tyler said. "There's plenty of prejudice in the world, but the best way to combat it is to be happy despite them."

"Thanks," Olivier said. He walked over to JC and gave him a big hug too. "You were amazing, and we're going dancing as soon as we can find a place."

JC immediately felt better when Olivier hugged him. He returned it enthusiastically, holding on perhaps a little too long, and grinned when he stepped back. "I have a few ideas where we can go."

EPILOGUE

OLIVIER PACED the baggage-claim area of Boston's airport. JC's flight had landed a few minutes ago, so now he just had to wait for JC to make his way off the plane and through the airport. It had been a month since they'd seen each other—only for a quick weekend between his matches and JC's training schedule—and six months since the show ended. Olivier was ready for some uninterrupted time together.

JC finally came down the escalator, looking positively delectable as far as Olivier was concerned. Olivier crossed the waiting area to meet JC at the bottom of the escalator and pulled him into a tight hug. "I missed you," he murmured against JC's temple. "How long can you stay for this time?"

"Mmm." JC took a moment to breathe in Olivier's scent. He'd missed it—and him—more and more each time they'd parted, and it felt so good to be wrapped up in it again. "Not sure. At least two weeks. After that, it depends."

Olivier kissed him softly. "Anything I can do to convince you to extend it?"

The kiss helped. Olivier had never kissed him in public before, and it was definitely a step in the right direction. "Well, you can do that again."

Olivier smiled and kissed JC again, a little longer this time. He kept it tame—they were in public, after all—but he wanted JC to know how happy he was to see him.

JC returned the kiss and took Olivier's hand when he pulled back. "Come on. Let's get my luggage."

Luggage was already spilling onto the carousel when they arrived in baggage claim, and it didn't take long for JC to grab his bag. Once they were in the parking lot and out of the crowd, JC took Olivier's hand and glanced over, trying to look far more casual than he felt. "So, I've been thinking about moving."

"Really?" Olivier said, trying to keep the hope out of his voice. He wanted to believe JC was talking about moving to Boston, but he didn't want to assume. "Where to?"

"Here. Or close to here, anyway. I don't know if I can afford to actually live in Boston, but in the area." It would change a lot, but it was time for him to move out of his parents' house and start living on his own. He'd always assumed he'd find a place in Houston, but Boston was closer to a lot of the places he traveled to for endorsements, and it had the added advantage of Olivier. "My coach has grandkids in Connecticut, so he's not opposed to the idea of relocating, but there's still a lot to consider."

Olivier sucked in a breath as hope flooded him. He hadn't wanted to ask JC to move to Boston when his coach and his career were in Texas, but the long-distance thing was getting old fast. "You could always live with me. There's plenty of space for both of us. If you want to, that is."

The idea was tempting. "Maybe." JC leaned up and kissed Olivier as they reached the car. He liked the idea, but he wanted to be sure they were both really ready to live together before they took that step. "We can talk about it… along with about half a million other things."

It wasn't quite the resounding yes Olivier had been hoping for, but it wasn't a no either, so he'd take it. He helped JC stow his luggage in the trunk and got in the car. When JC was settled and Olivier had navigated his way out of the airport, he reached over and squeezed JC's hand. "I had a long talk with my coach yesterday. He wanted me to come in today for some extra conditioning, so I had to explain that I couldn't be there because my boyfriend was flying in from Texas and was expecting me to pick him up at the airport. He said that was only an excuse for today, but that tomorrow I have to go in for a workout. He said you're welcome to come too, if you want to meet the rest of the squad."

JC tried to stay calm. He'd been trying hard not to pressure Olivier to be more open about their relationship, but he wanted Olivier to at least tell the people closest to him so they didn't have to hide quite so much when he came to visit. If Olivier's team knew him, that would make moving up here much easier… assuming they liked him, of course. "I'd love to, if you want to introduce me."

"I wouldn't have mentioned it if I didn't," Olivier said. "I know it's taken longer than you would've liked, but I've told them now. I'm still not interested in making it truly public, but telling my teammates is different."

"Then I'd be thrilled to come." JC lifted Olivier's hand and kissed it. "I don't need us to be truly public. I just don't want to hide from the people you see all the time. And I would like to move in with you—you know that, right? I just want to talk about it and make sure it's really the right time before we decide anything."

Olivier smiled as relief flooded through him. "As long as you keep it in mind for when the time's right." When he stopped at a red light, he leaned over and kissed JC quickly. "I love you, and I'm not ashamed of that fact. The rest will happen as it happens."

"It will," JC said softly. If they hadn't been in the car, JC would have extended the kiss. He settled for squeezing Olivier's hand as Olivier turned back to the road. "So what are we going to do tonight? I thought we could go dance at Rumor, but if you have practice tomorrow...."

"Oh no, we're going dancing. It's just conditioning. A little dancing will be a warm-up for tomorrow," Olivier said. "After all, Tricia and Chelsea would never forgive us if we didn't keep practicing."

"No, they wouldn't." JC had seen Chelsea since he'd last been with Olivier, and she'd helped him with a little surprise for Olivier. If the music was right tonight, JC was going to seduce him, though he wasn't yet sure if he was going to use the samba or the Argentine tango. Either way, he was certain Olivier would love it.

Authors' Note

While the story, show, and characters are fictional, the charities the characters mentioned are real. They do a lot of good work across a wide variety of areas. If any of these causes speak to you, please consider supporting them.

Amnesty International - http://www.amnestyusa.org/
Promotes human rights issues around the world

Boys & Girls Clubs of America - http://www.bgca.org
Provides opportunities for at-risk children that enable them to grow into productive adults

Count Me In - http://www.countmein.org/
Provides support and resources for women entrepreneurs

Doctors Without Borders - http://www.doctorswithoutborders.org
Provides medical care in response to emergencies and lack of health care access worldwide

March of Dimes - http://www.marchofdimes.org/
Works to prevent premature births

National Breast Cancer Foundation -
http://www.nationalbreastcancer.org
Provides support to people affected by breast cancer

National Multiple Sclerosis Society -
http://www.nationalmssociety.org/

Works to find a cure for multiple sclerosis and provides support to those who have it

Reach Out and Read - http://www.reachoutandread.org/
Promotes early literacy by providing books to preschool children and reading advice to their parents through their medical providers

St. Jude Children's Research Hospital - http://www.stjude.org/
Provides treatment for catastrophic pediatric diseases regardless of the family's ability to pay and works toward finding cures

The Trevor Project - http://www.thetrevorproject.org
Provides suicide prevention and crisis intervention services through phone, text, and chat for LGBTQ youth

VH1 Save the Music Foundation - http://www.vh1savethemusic.org/
Works to restore music programs in American schools and raise awareness of the importance of music

World Wildlife Fund - http://www.worldwildlife.org/
Supports nature conservation globally through efforts that have a foundation in science

ARIEL TACHNA lives outside of Houston with her husband, her daughter and son, and their two dogs. Before moving there, she traveled all over the world, having fallen in love with both France, where she found her husband, and India, where she dreams of retiring some day. She's bilingual with snippets of four other languages to her credit, and is as in love with languages as she is with writing.

Visit Ariel:
Website: http://www.arieltachna.com
Facebook: https://www.facebook.com/ArielTachna
E-mail: arieltachna@gmail.com

NESSA L. WARIN lives in a fantasy world that's mostly inside her head, though her physical address is in southwestern Ohio. Her two cats kindly play along with her fantasies and graciously let her pay all the bills, but they do require her to provide pampering on a regular basis. Nessa enjoys exploring the wonders of this world through travel—something her cats strongly disapprove of as it cuts into their pampering time—and can find whimsy in the most mundane places. When the real world becomes too much, Nessa enjoys dressing in costume and going to Renaissance Festivals and fantasy conventions. A short trip to either does wonders for her state of mind, so she makes sure to attend at least one of each every year. These trips help Nessa add to her collection of faerie and dragon art, and she swears she will frame and hang all the prints she's collected some time soon.

When she's not living in a fantasy world, Nessa enjoys tasting and learning about wine, particularly since it's one of the few things she and the rest of her family agree on. She's a regular at the wine tastings held by her local wine shop, and considers it a sin for her wine rack to have more empty spots than full ones. She'd prefer her wine rack to be filled with Pinot Noir, Malbec, and Syrah, but one of her favorite things about wine is the way it can always surprise her. More than once she's been taken aback by which wine she likes best at a tasting, and she loves the way her wine rack illustrates the joys of trying new things.

Contact Nessa:
Twitter:@nessalwarin
Facebook:NessaLWarin
E-mail: nessa.l.warin@gmail.com

http://www.dreamspinnerpress.com

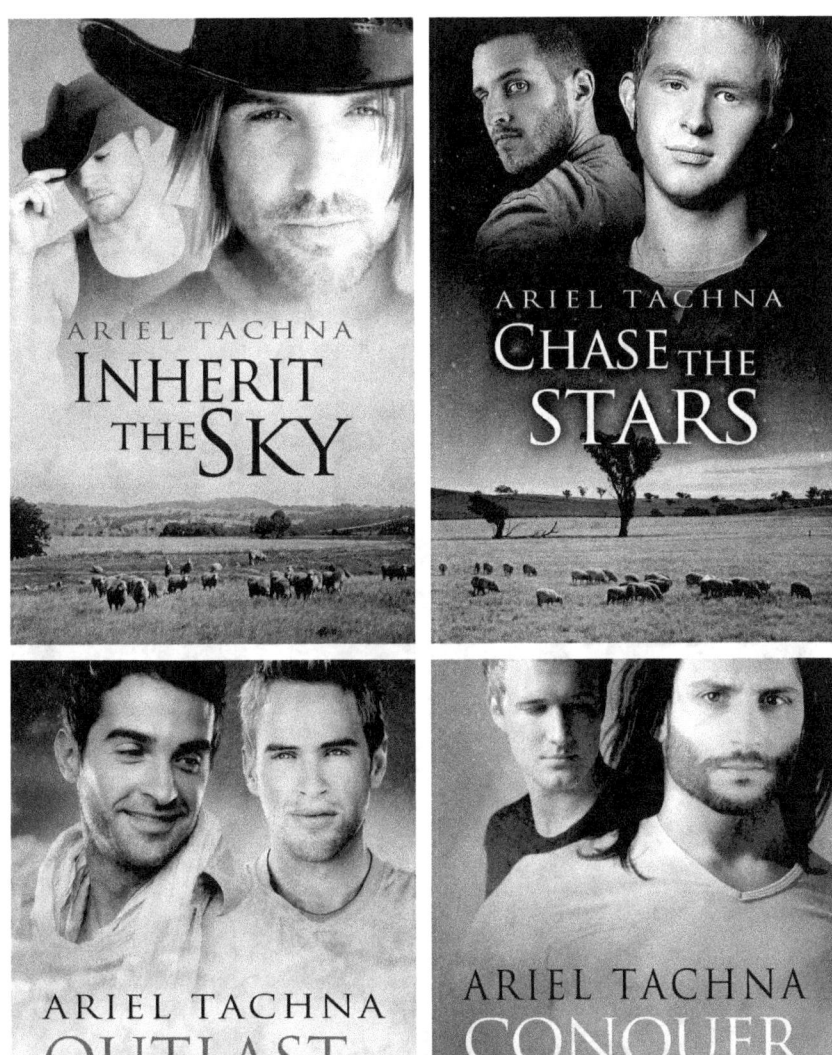

Partnership in Blood

Partnership in Blood

ARIEL TACHNA

CHÂTEAU
D'ETERNITÉ

STAMP
of
FATE
NESSA L. WARIN

the stars are
brightly shining

nessa l. warin

http://www.dreamspinnerpress.com

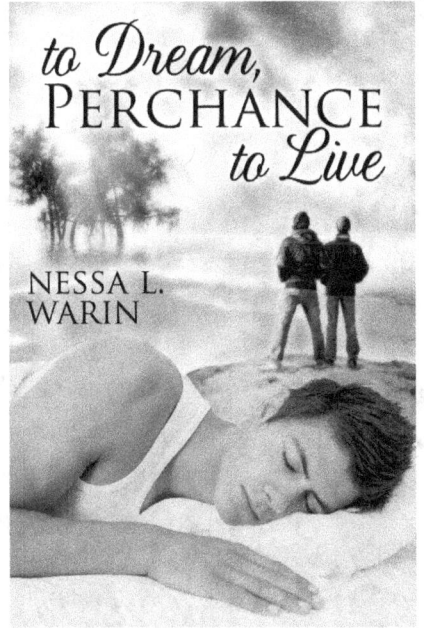

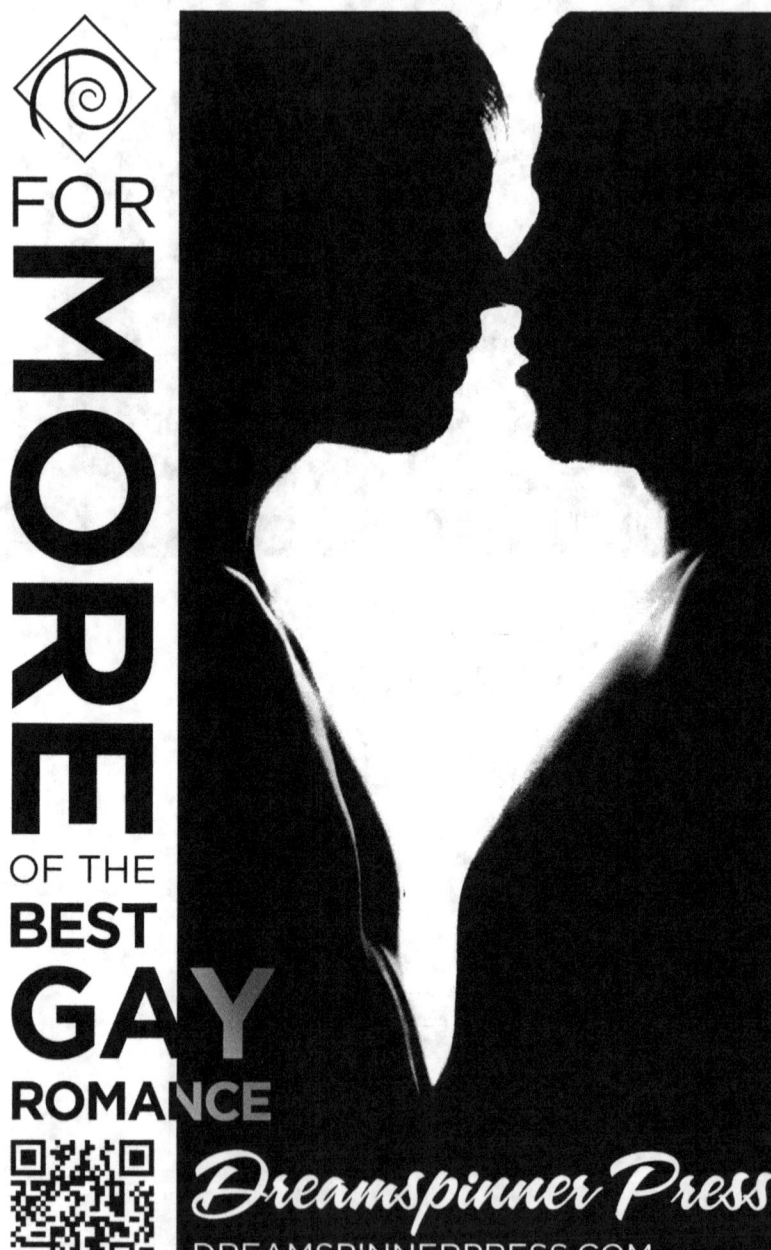

www.ingramcontent.com/pod-product-compliance
Lightning Source LLC
Chambersburg PA
CBHW070107260626
47160CB00004B/1361